"Dialogue that has some snap and a sports setting that's credible. And count on Lupica's fine reputation to create demand."
—*Booklist*

"[Lupica's] got some game." —*Kirkus Reviews*

**Praise for the previous novels of Mike Lupica**

# RED ZONE

"Lupica's funniest. . . . You won't put it down."
—Elmore Leonard

"I'd thought *Bump & Run* was the funniest book on pro football I'd ever read until *Red Zone*."
—Phil Simms, CBS Sports,
Super Bowl–winning quarterback, New York Giants

"Hilarious, gripping, and surprisingly touching."
—Harlan Coben

"Entertaining, funny, off-the-wall . . . Readers . . . are in for a great game." —*Fort Worth Star-Telegram*

*continued . . .*

# WILD PITCH

"Hilarious." — *USA Today*

"Really funny . . . really good." —Robert B. Parker

"Lupica has his best stuff working here . . . the dialogue is right out of the dugout . . . a terrific plot . . . I loved it." —Elmore Leonard

"A terrific comeback story." —Mitch Albom, author of *Tuesdays with Morrie* and *The Five People You Meet in Heaven*

"Big-league humor [from] the master of hilarious sports novels." —*Orlando Sentinel*

"The best sports fiction so far this year, hands down." —*Booklist* (starred review)

# FULL COURT PRESS

"A hilarious satire of the NBA." —*Orlando Sentinel*

"Brutally accurate, unsparingly funny satire—a naughty delight for true basketball fans." —Carl Hiaasen

"Lupica talks the talk, a pro at picking up the rhythms of locker room voices. In other words, it's a howl." —Elmore Leonard

"Lupica skillfully controls a multilayered plot that ridicules the greed and vanity dominating too much of professional sports territory." —*The Washington Post*

"A story with plenty of laughs, but even more heart. This novel must have been as much fun for Lupica to write as it is to read." —*Book Magazine*

# BUMP & RUN

"A big-time touchdown of a book—a hilarious tale of life behind the scenes in the raunchy, rowdy world of pro football."
　　　　　　　　　　　　　　　—Dave Barry

"Truly hip, uproariously funny, and my God, it might even be true. *Bump & Run* places Lupica high up among the funniest guys writing fiction."
　　　　　　　　　　　　　　　—Elmore Leonard

"High-profile sportswriter Lupica goes for the gold with this quip-fueled romp . . . Reminiscent of Peter Gent's *North Dallas Forty* and Dan Jenkins's *Semi-Tough*, this is a deliciously wicked tale of contemporary professional sports and the people who, for better or worse, run the game."
　　　　　　　　　　　　　　　—*Publishers Weekly*

"Captures the beer-and-blood flavor of the NFL."
　　　　　　　　　　　　　　　—*Entertainment Weekly*

"Irreverent, funny . . . and all fiction aside, dead on point."
　　　　　　　　　　—Al Michaels, *ABC Monday Night Football*

"Even if you don't give a rat's *ss for professional football, you should read this savagely hilarious novel."
　　　　　　　　　　　　　　　—Pete Hamill

"*Bump & Run* is outrageous, opinionated, and most important, funny as hell."　　　　　—Phil Simms, CBS Sports

"Sportswriter Mike Lupica tosses a bomb to the end zone with this spirited and funny fictional look at the money monster that the game has become . . . [I]t's certainly a lot of fun to read."　　　　　　　—*The Detroit News*

"Fans of contemporary, irreverent—and decidedly adult—humor will enjoy this novel . . . Everyone is fair game for Lupica's sardonic skewering—players, owners, media, rap stars, organized crime, strippers, politicians, etc."
　　　　　　　　　　　　—*The Cleveland Plain Dealer*

# TOO FAR

## Mike Lupica

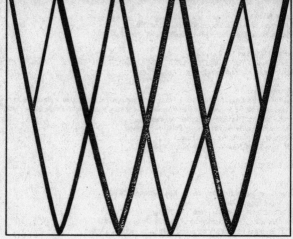

BERKLEY BOOKS, NEW YORK

**THE BERKLEY PUBLISHING GROUP**
**Published by the Penguin Group**
**Penguin Group (USA) Inc.**
**375 Hudson Street, New York, New York 10014, USA**
Penguin Group (Canada), 90 Eglinton Avenue East, Suite 700, Toronto, Ontario M4P 2Y3, Canada
(a division of Pearson Penguin Canada Inc.)
Penguin Books Ltd., 80 Strand, London WC2R 0RL, England
Penguin Group Ireland, 25 St. Stephen's Green, Dublin 2, Ireland
(a division of Penguin Books Ltd.)
Penguin Group (Australia), 250 Camberwell Road, Camberwell, Victoria 3124, Australia
(a division of Pearson Australia Group Pty. Ltd.)
Penguin Books India Pvt. Ltd., 11 Community Centre, Panchsheel Park, New Delhi—110 017, India
Penguin Group (NZ), Cnr. Airborne and Rosedale Roads, Albany, Auckland 1310, New Zealand
(a division of Pearson New Zealand Ltd.)
Penguin Books (South Africa) (Pty.) Ltd., 24 Sturdee Avenue, Rosebank, Johannesburg 2196,
South Africa

Penguin Books Ltd., Registered Offices: 80 Strand, London WC2R 0RL, England

This is a work of fiction. Names, characters, places, and incidents either are the product of the author's
imagination or are used fictitiously, and any resemblance to actual persons, living or dead, business
establishments, events, or locales is entirely coincidental.

TOO FAR

A Berkley Book / published by arrangement with the author

PRINTING HISTORY
G. P. Putnam's Sons hardcover edition / December 2004
Berkley mass-market edition / November 2005

Copyright © 2004 by Mike Lupica.
Cover art: Football Pitch at night, Digital Vision/GettyImages; Hole In Wire Fence, Iconica/GettyImages.
Cover design by Richard Hasselberger.

ISBN: 0-425-20674-2

BERKLEY®
Berkley Books are published by The Berkley Publishing Group,
a division of Penguin Group (USA) Inc.,
375 Hudson Street, New York, New York 10014.
BERKLEY is a registered trademark of Penguin Group (USA) Inc.
The "B" design is a trademark belonging to Penguin Group (USA) Inc.

PRINTED IN THE UNITED STATES OF AMERICA

10  9  8  7  6  5  4  3  2  1

*This book is for the great Neil Nyren,*
*who, thankfully, edits these books by choice.*

*And for Taylor, who does it out of love.*

# *ACKNOWLEDGMENTS*

Lock McKelvy, MSW, who took time out from being a real therapist to help me out with some fictional bad guys.

William Goldman, the best friend and best writing rabbi anybody ever had.

And finally, Christopher Lupica: Peace out.

# 1

Ben Mitchell liked to sit in the same booth at Hiram's every morning, take his time and go through all the newspapers and find out how much dumber the world had gotten in the last twenty-four hours.

He had them all in front of him: *Times, Daily News, Post, USA Today, Newsday, Long Island Press.* Sometimes he would start with the News section, sometimes Sports, once in a while he'd even go to Arts first, just so he could stay up-to-date on which hot movies he wouldn't be seeing and which heartwarming books he wouldn't be reading.

Mostly he liked going through the papers to see how many guys wrote basically the same fucking story, whether they were covering the President or Paris Hilton or the Patriots vs. the Jets.

This was before Mitchell went back home and made his late-morning tour of cable news networks, where there always seemed to be somebody who looked like a Dallas

Cowboys cheerleader telling you about Iraq as though it were some new breakthrough product in hair care.

When he finally got bored with that, he'd just drive around on the back roads of eastern Long Island, through what had once been potato fields and had now turned into cut-out neighborhoods that looked like they'd been airlifted across the Sound from Scarsdale or Greenwich. He'd listen to talk radio, the capital of dumbing-down, and see how long it took him to figure out which of them were the conservative callers and which ones were the conservative hosts.

Mitchell still did all this under the general heading of Paying Attention. Even if reading the papers and watching the news pissed him off as much as it had before he retired.

Even before he wrote a story that ended up killing a guy.

That was the big drama that had sent him out of the business for good, sent him back home. But Mitchell knew it had been coming for a long time, as he watched the whole news business turn to complete shit. It was a business no one had ever loved more than he had, from the time he was a kid staring at his first byline in the school paper like it was prettier than any girl in school, to when he got his first column with the *Chicago Tribune,* six months out of Syracuse.

And over the next twenty years, he'd watched as the whole thing got dumber and meaner, watched as *tabloid* became as dirty a word as *fuck.* Watched guys like Limbaugh try to run the world from their spot on the radio dial. Watched the advent of reality television, where they ate worms for ratings, and would eventually, Mitchell was sure of this, eat each other.

By the time Mitchell got to the *Los Angeles Times,* writing columns in the sports section during the week and Page 1 on Sundays, he'd felt like he was right in the thick of it, even getting himself a regular gig on ESPN and yelling along with everybody else.

He was making more money than he ever thought he could and, at the end, hating just about every minute of it.

Then the guy had died and Mitchell had walked away, from the job and from his marriage to Amy, realizing as he did so that he was going to miss the column a lot more. But wondering at the same time if this was the same kind of phony-ass posturing he'd given in the column at the end, wondering how noble he would have been if he still didn't have enough book and movie money in the bank to keep him going, at least until he figured out what his next move was going to be. . . .

That had been his real job for the last six months, figuring out how close he'd have to be to the money running out to make some kind of move. The newspaper money was already long gone. There was never enough of *that,* even if he'd been making as much as anybody in the business when he'd quit after Robards died. It had always been cash in and cash out with him no matter how much was coming in. Now the money keeping him going was from the big score of Ben Mitchell's career, the best-seller about the dead basketball player from Syracuse and the teammate who'd shot him in the fucking head.

*The Death of Billy Orange* had ended up spending thirteen fast-running weeks on the *Times* list, before it got turned into the movie starring Will Smith and Taye Diggs.

At the time, interviewers would ask him what the best thing was about *The Death of Billy Orange,* and Mitchell would say, "You mean other than finally getting out of the red?" He'd taken a big chunk of the movie money and plunked it down on the house off Jobs Lane, on the other side of South Fork from where he'd grown up. . . .

"Mr. Mitchell?"

He looked up and saw the kid standing where Laurie the waitress usually stood. Tall, good-looking, short dark hair, darker eyes. Wearing a tweed jacket, dark crewneck with white t-shirt showing near the collar, like kids did now, khakis, beat-up Nubuck shoes.

Probably a high school kid, maybe college—Mitchell

knew he was wasting his time even trying to make an edu-
cated guess, everybody who was young was starting to look
the same age to him. The girls more than the boys. Especially the girls. He'd check out the cheerleaders sometimes
when he was watching a college basketball game and feel
older than golf.

"Busted," Mitchell said.

The kid put out his hand. "Sam Perry," he said.

Mitchell shook it.

"I just want you to know," the kid said, jumping right
back in, talking fast, like Mitchell had a timer on him, "that
I don't usually do this. I read somewhere, I forget where,
probably some book, I read a lot of books, you should
never introduce yourself to famous people. Under any circumstances."

"You're safe here, trust me," Mitchell said. "I'm not
famous."

"To me you are."

Mitchell didn't say anything to that, turned a page of the
*Daily News,* as if he'd gone back to his reading.

The kid stood his ground. "I'm a senior at the high
school."

"And you write for the school paper."

"I do, as a matter of fact. And I do some stringing for
the *Press.*"

"Well, good luck with all of that, everybody's got to
start somewhere," Mitchell said, hoping that came out
sounding like, *Have a nice life.*

Sam Perry stayed with him.

"I've seen you here before," he said. "Since you came
back to town, I mean. I just never, like, had the nerve to
come over and introduce myself. Until now, anyway."

"And break your own rule about introducing yourself to
even marginally famous people."

Sam said, "I know you've probably heard this before.
But I always wanted to be you."

Mitchell finished what was left of his coffee. Laurie was at the end of the counter, reading a paper somebody had left there. Mitchell caught her eye, pointed to his cup. "Nobody wants to be me anymore."

"I *meant*," Sam Perry said, "I want to be who you *used* to be."

Mitchell pointed a finger at him, like he was shooting a gun. "Now, *that's* better, I knew you couldn't be a total suck-up," and motioned for him to sit down.

Sam Perry nearly did a racing dive into the booth.

"Why are you really here?" Mitchell said.

"I think I might have a story."

"You've got the wrong guy," Mitchell said. "I'm out of the story business."

"All due respect?" Sam said. "Even I know that's bullshit."

**S**am Perry didn't drink coffee.

Didn't like coffee ice cream. Couldn't speak Starbucks. But when Ben Mitchell asked if he wanted the waitress, Laurie, to bring him a cup, Sam said, sure, absolutely, why not?

Thinking to himself: Great, maybe you can babble even more than you already are.

"I want you to know," he said to Mitchell, "this really is a huge thrill for me, finally getting to meet you."

Jesus, you are *such* a fucking girl.

"Sam?" Mitchell said. "We need to move past that."

"I'm really not as lame as I've been sounding so far."

"Nobody could be," Mitchell said. Laurie poured more coffee for Mitchell, put down a cup and saucer and poured some for Sam. Before she left she said, "Congratulations, you're the first person in here he's ever talked to besides me." And left.

Sam took a better look at him, trying to see him the way

a reporter would. He had looked up Ben Mitchell in the South Fork Alumni Directory, knew what year he had graduated from the high school. So he was either forty or about to turn forty. But there was something about him that made him look older than that. Or more tired, maybe that was it. He had blue eyes, blond-gray hair that was just a little bit longer than a crewcut. He was wearing a faded work shirt with a gray t-shirt showing underneath it, the sleeves rolled up to show a small-faced antique watch. Above the watch, on his left forearm, was a small tattoo that read "B29." Mitchell saw him looking at the tattoo and said, "My old man flew them in Korea. I got crazy one night in college."

"What happened to him after that? Your dad, I mean?"

"He became a New York City cop and then he came out here to be a cop and drank too much and died."

"Sorry."

"Me, too," Mitchell said. "Now, are you going to tell me what your story is, or am I going to have to beat it out of you?"

"I think I might know something related to Bobby Ferraro's death," Sam said.

It had been the big headline for the past few days, the body of Bobby Ferraro, team manager for the South Fork High School basketball team, washing up dead on one of the town beaches.

Sam said, "I didn't know who else to tell. And I figured if anybody could tell me whether I was completely full of shit or not, it was you."

"Was the dead kid a friend?"

"Bobby," Sam said. "His name was Bobby Ferraro."

"Sorry, that was an asshole thing to say, even for me."

"Forget it," Sam said. "How much do you know about the whole deal?"

"I don't write anymore," Mitchell said. "But I can still read. I know that we've got the second coming of LeBron and Carmelo at South Fork High this season."

"Glenn Moore and Show Watkins," Sam said.

"They're as much the reason it's been invasion of the satellite trucks as anything," Mitchell said. "It's like the dead kid . . . Bobby . . . is some kind of sidebar. The story's sexy because it involves what everybody thinks is going to be the best high school team in the country."

Sam said, "Tell me about it."

"Anyway," Mitchell said, "I know Bobby's dad is some kind of money guy. He was away for the weekend. Mommy's long gone. The kid doesn't answer the phone over the weekend, not so unusual. Old man comes back and the kid's not there. Now, that's a *little* unusual. Old man files the Missing Persons on Tuesday. They find the body on Wednesday. Funeral Friday. Did I leave out anything?"

"Nothing that hasn't been in the papers."

"But you've got something that hasn't been in the papers."

Sam looked around, as if somebody could have snuck into the next booth up the wall while they'd been talking.

"Yeah," he said. "I do."

"Something the school doesn't know and the police don't know and his father doesn't know."

"Yeah."

"And you're telling a complete stranger."

Sam said, "I'm telling you because you're you, mostly. Because I don't want to take it to a reporter at the *Press,* even if I do work part-time there. Because I know if I *do* take it to him, I'm smart enough to know it becomes his story and not some high school senior's." Sam shrugged. "Because I came here looking for you today and if you hadn't been here, I would have gotten my balls arranged and come to your house."

Mitchell said, "So tell me."

Sam Perry told him about a girl named Grace Pearson, and the party she'd thrown at her house the weekend Bobby Ferraro disappeared, and what Eric Daneko had told him.

---

**S**am and Eric were both kids from the north side of the highway, the one away from the ocean, everybody over there appreciating that when you grew up on the north side of a town called South Fork, you felt a little bit like you were on the wrong side of the tracks, even though you really weren't.

Eric: Starting small forward with the South Fork Hawks. Not one of the stars on the team, because Glenn Moore and DeShawn (Show) Watkins were the stars, of South Fork and maybe the whole country, two high school basketball players making it seem as if a little town on the water, ninety miles from New York City, had been hit by lightning. But Eric was a nice player, the kind they always called a role player, both ends of the court, six-three but playing bigger. The kind of player you wanted to do the dirty work for a couple of total studs like Glenn and Show.

It seemed like the whole team had shown up late for Grace's party, which was supposed to start at eight. Everybody except Show, who never showed up at all. Eric, looking shitfaced, didn't arrive, in Dave Bender's heap—Dave not getting chauffeured around in Glenn Moore's Mercedes for a change—until about nine-thirty. Sam wondered what Dave's dad, a cop, would have thought about the shape Eric was in. But then he remembered something: This was South Fork and Eric was a basketball player, a *starting* player, and the rules were different for players. Everybody in town knew that. It was just the way things were here and probably, Sam thought, in all towns like this.

Everybody in school knew Grace Pearson had a big crush on Eric Daneko, that she had been giving him the eye since her last boyfriend, captain of the lacrosse team, had gone off to Cornell. So Sam watched as she kept smuggling Eric beers in the backyard, a lot of kids having ended up in the backyard because even in the first week of November, it felt like a summer night in South Fork.

So Eric quietly kept getting drunker. Then the party started to wind down, and Dave Bender was gone along with the other players.

The only player left was Eric.

Sam offered to drive him back to the north side.

It was on the way, the two of them listening to the best station out there, WEHM, when Eric, out of nowhere, started going on about those fucking fuckers and what they'd done at camp.

"Want to know why I got so shitfaced tonight?" he said to Sam. "You want to know? On account of, I started thinking about it all over again. *Camp*, dude."

Sam turned down the radio. "What camp?" he said.

"The woods. The *team*."

"Oh," Sam said, "you mean over in Connecticut."

Every year, before the official start of basketball practice the whole South Fork team would go to a preseason camp—really more like a retreat—over on the other side of the Sound, some little town in Connecticut, Sam couldn't remember the name, just that it was an hour from where you got off the ferry in Bridgeport.

"Said they use the place for Boy Scout shit," Eric said.

Sam watched Eric turn in the front seat, seeming to take up even more than his half, like the Volvo was a couple of sizes too small for him. Saw this fierce look on Eric's face as he grabbed Sam's arm and said, "It was just supposed to be one of those stupid initiation deals, dude, not turn into a scene from fucking *Oz*."

Sam said, "The prison show?"

"Yeah."

Always television. Not something that happened in real prisons. A prison *show*. Where the inmates did enough bad things to each other that Sam stopped watching after about two episodes.

Eric said, "Bad shit like that."

"To *who?*" Sam said.

Eric shook his head from side to side. "Too late to do anything now." He started to mumble, clearly drifting away. "Had my chance and I didn't do *shit*."

Sam wanted to ask, Had your chance to do *what?* But didn't get to ask anything else because Eric Daneko was already snoring away.

**A**t Hiram's now, Mitchell said, "And you never got the chance to ask Bobby about it."

Sam said, "I was going to ask him at school on Monday."

"What about Eric? Have you gone back to him, asked what the hell he meant?"

Sam said he didn't get up the courage until after Bobby's funeral, when he ran into him in the school parking lot. First he said he couldn't remember a thing from the ride home, he was too wasted. When Sam tried to refresh his memory, Eric got hot and told him he must have heard wrong.

"I told him I had a pretty good memory, that sometimes I'd remember a quote exactly without even checking my notes," Sam said.

"He find that information fascinating?"

"That's when he started screaming that I was talking shit and making shit up," Sam said. "That's when he put his hand on my shoulder and squeezed it so hard I thought it had gone numb."

In a quiet voice, Mitchell said, "He put his hands on you?"

Sam nodded. "And asked if I was a friend now, or some weasel reporter? I asked why I couldn't be both, and he squeezed me so hard I could feel my knees buckle."

Then, according to Sam, Eric got into his Explorer and drove away, giving him the finger as he did.

"Sounds like a sweet kid," Mitchell said.

Sam said, "I used to think so."

Mitchell moved a spoon around in his coffee. "Why do

you think whatever happened in Connecticut, that initiation deal Eric was babbling to you about, is somehow tied into Bobby's death?"

"You wrote in your book that only suckers believe in co-incidence," Sam said. "Eric made it pretty clear something shitty happened on the team over in Connecticut a few weeks ago. Four days after he tells me that, the manager of the same team turns up dead. I'm just trying not to act like a sucker here."

"You're saying you think Bobby might have been in-volved in what Eric was talking about?"

"No, I'm not," Sam said. "I just know that if it happened, he knew about it, because he knew just about everything that went on around the team."

"And now you want me to tell you what to do about all that."

"I do," Sam said. "Hey, the biggest story *you* ever had started out with a dead basketball player."

"A player who happened to be a college All-American."

"He still ended up dead. And somebody else on the team killed him."

It was no trick for Sam to quote from *The Death of Billy Orange,* because he knew the book inside and out. Knew it the way other people knew the Harry Potter books, or *The Lord of the Rings.* The player who'd turned up missing was Billy Shaw, an All-American guard out of New York City who hadn't shown up for the last practice before the first game of his junior year. He was missing for a week, and thanks to an anonymous tip, they finally found the body in an onion field in Canastota, about twenty miles east of Syra-cuse. Billy Shaw had been shot once in the head, from close range. It turned out that the shooter had been his teammate, Tayshaun Ferrell. Tayshaun maintained it was self-defense. It turned out to be self-preservation instead. Ferrell had got-ten in with some bad guys, had altered the score of a hand-ful of games and managed to dump one against Boston

College. Billy Shaw, a good kid from a bad neighborhood in the South Bronx, known as Billy Orange because Bill Orange was one of the old-timey nicknames for Syracuse teams, had found out and was going to turn him in.

Tayshaun Ferrell panicked and killed him and drove the body to Canastota one night and buried it, then carried off the role of grieving homeboy until the cops made a second pass at him.

Ben Mitchell, already writing a column in Chicago by then, had graduated from The Newhouse School at Syracuse only a few years before. He'd flown to Syracuse the day it was announced that Shaw was missing.

Sam knew all this because he had Googled up just about every interview Mitchell had ever given about *The Death of Billy Orange.*

"You said that All-American ballplayers don't disappear," Sam said to Mitchell now. "You also said that when you smell a big story, you don't wait, unless you want it to end up being somebody else's big story. Write it or read it, you always said."

Mitchell ended up staying in Syracuse for a month after Billy Shaw's murder. He was riding with the cops when they found Shaw's body in the onion field.

He wrote everything except the last chapter of the book before Tayshaun Ferrell's trial started, and finished it after Ferrell got twenty-five to life. *The Death of Billy Orange* got nominated for a Pulitzer, became a movie, and made Ben Mitchell the most famous columnist in the country for a while.

Now he was sitting across from Sam in the back booth at Hiram's in South Fork, Sam trying to read him well enough to know if he cared one way or the other about what had happened to Bobby Ferraro.

Sam knew what had happened to Mitchell, why he was out of the business and had come back home after the guy died. There'd been a feature about him in the *Press* a few months ago, that's when Sam had found out Mitchell *was* back home. What he didn't know is if Mitchell gave a shit about anything anymore.

Right now all he had going for him was this: Mitchell was still here. And still listening.

Neither one of them said anything now, until Mitchell sighed and said, "It sounds like you might be onto something, kid, it really does. But I can't help you."

"Why not?"

"Because I'm just hanging on," Ben Mitchell said.

# 2

Mitchell didn't live right on the ocean, but close enough that he could sit on the top deck of his house near dusk and smoke one of the few cigarettes a day he still allowed himself, just for old times' sake, and sometimes see ships way out in the water, set his eyes on the place way out there where the water and sky met, like somebody had painted them together.

Sometimes he tried to remember what the view had looked like when he'd still felt like he was going good, when he could sit out here with the sliding door open behind him, listening to jazz, mostly to all his sax guys, Getz and Coltrane and Ben Webster and Joshua Redman and Art Pepper and Charlie Parker and Ornette Coleman. And not just the sax guys. Clark Terry blowing his horn. And Miles, of course. *Kind of Blue* always racked up somewhere, just because Mitchell never got tired of listening to it, only the greatest jazz album of them all.

Different life now. Same soundtrack.

It was six o'clock, about the time when Mitchell fixed himself a Scotch to go with his Winston Light, telling himself one Scotch would be it. Most times it was.

Unless he started thinking about Tom Robards, of course.

**T**om Robards.

He'd kicked around the majors with a half-dozen teams in the '70s and '80s before he decided his future was as a manager. Or at least a coach in the big leagues working his way up to manager. So he'd gone down to the low minors for the Yankees, started out riding buses in Norwich, Connecticut, spent a decade working his way up to Triple A, finally managing the Dodgers' top farm team in Albuquerque. Then, winter before last, the Dodgers had given him the top job.

He was a tough, quiet, hard-looking guy with a Marine tattoo and a mustache. It was always on Robards's résumé that he'd been with the Marines in Vietnam, but he didn't talk about it too much, and finally people stopped asking about it. It wasn't until September, when the Dodgers and the Giants were coming down the stretch together in the National League West, that the players started telling Mitchell about the amazing pregame talks Robards was giving them about Vietnam, about the things he'd seen and done, how he'd even killed a little Vietnamese girl by accident, the girl dying in his arms while he waited for the medic to get there.

Mitchell decided that was a hell of a story, but when he asked Robards where it'd happened, Robards just said, "That wasn't for print."

Mitchell pressed him and Robards said, "I don't talk about Hue anymore. And I wish you wouldn't write about it."

Mitchell was still convinced it would make a hell of a column, but when he tried to research Tom Robards's war record, he ran into a common problem. He found out how hard it is to prove where somebody served and how they served, whether they were in combat or not, or earned medals or not.

It wasn't the only thing he worked on. The season played itself out. The Giants won the division by a game. Mitchell gave up on Robards's war record until right before pitchers and catchers were supposed to report to spring training.

This time he found out that the closest Tom Robards had ever come to Vietnam was playing on the Marine baseball team in Okinawa.

The more he talked to military people, especially ones who had actually been in combat, the more he found out how many guys there were like Tom Robards. Some were just compulsive liars. Others needed to make themselves bigger as actors. Or politicians. Or baseball managers.

Tom Robards had made it up.

All of it.

Mitchell wrote most of his story, and then went to Florida to confront Robards with what he'd found. At first Robards tried to deny it, which the combat guys Mitchell had talked to had said he would, then Mitchell showed him the quotes from the guys he had been playing ball with at the time he was supposed to be liberating Hue.

Robards broke down then, begged Mitchell not to run the story, said that he'd never bring up his war record again.

"All you have to do is say you made a mistake," Mitchell said.

"I can't," Robards said.

Mitchell said that his editors knew about it, that they'd read the three thousand words he'd already written, that there was no turning back now. He told Robards that the only thing to do was to come clean.

People will respect you for telling the truth, Mitchell said to him.

Mitchell didn't know whether he believed it, he just wanted a response from Robards. Then he could get the fuck out of there, go write the rest of his story.

Write it or read it.

"People think I'm that guy now," Robards said in his room at Dodgertown. "I can't tell them I'm somebody else."

"Is that your quote?" Mitchell said.

"I'm begging you not to do this," Robards said.

"Sorry," Mitchell said.

"I never begged anybody for anything in my whole life."

"It doesn't work that way," Mitchell said. "If I can find this out, so can somebody else. And I'm not going to get beat on it."

Robards said, "Then do what you have to do."

"That's your comment?"

"I have no comment."

Then Robards said, "Except for this: What's this going to do for *your* life, Ben? Because it's going to ruin mine."

Mitchell said, "You should have thought about that before you lied to everybody," and walked out the door.

The story ran the next day.

The note Robards left said he'd begged Ben Mitchell not to run the story. And that when he'd read the story on his computer in the morning, he knew he couldn't live with the shame.

They found him dead at Dodgertown later that afternoon, a bullet in his head, a Marine-issue pistol that the police said he had bought at a gun shop in Fort Pierce in his hand.

Mitchell wrote one more column about it the next day, and then resigned.

Let somebody else be first from now on.


Afterward, Mitchell's friends had told him that it wasn't his fault that Robards had lied, and then taken the coward's way out. They'd told him that guys in the newspaper business came back from just about anything. They'd said he had told the *truth*—look at all the guys who came back after making shit up.

They'd told him to write a book, isn't that what everybody did? Write one about himself this time.

Mitchell had gone home to South Fork, without a fucking clue about what he was going to do next. Now it was six months of not knowing what to do next, still enough money in the savings account to last him a while longer, but nobody calling anymore to ask if he wanted to get back in the game.

He had gotten a few calls after the first few months. One from the paper in Spokane. Another from Orlando. The New York *Daily News*.

Mitchell had told them he was retired.

Meaning it every time he said it, but wondering how much he was going to mean it when the money finally did run out.

Now he sat on the deck, feet up, smoking, looking at the water, the sun completely gone behind him. And kept going back to the happy kid from the school paper. Sam Perry. Not happy that a classmate had died. No, the kid was just all on fire with finding out how and why. He had a leg up on everybody else, had information nobody else did. Now *he* wanted to know what to do with it. Mitchell knew exactly what that was like, that it was like shooting the fucking information right into a vein. . . .

He went upstairs with another drink, lit one more cigarette, sat down at the computer, got himself to Google, and saw himself type in "Hazing and school sports." Pretending that Sam Perry's story was his.

Pretending for a few minutes that he was still in the game.


**M**epham High was the first thing that came up, of course. It was the school up-island that had become the capital of hazing a few years ago when it had come out that some football players had brutalized younger kids on their team at a camp like the one Sam Perry was talking about. Pinecones up the ass. Golf balls. Broom handles. One of the victims had finally gone to his parents and the authorities, and the kids who'd done it had gotten prosecuted, even though they'd got away without doing real jail time. One got sent off to military school.

Mitchell remembered writing a few columns about it at the time, even from L.A., going on a few television shows. He remembered now, reading back, how the cops had run into a wall of silence, even from the other victims. No kid, even one who'd had a broomstick shoved up him, wanted to be painted as a squealer.

As if that was worse than what had happened to him.

Mitchell always remembered this: how some Mepham parents had seemed more outraged at the season being canceled than at what had happened to those kids.

All Mitchell himself could remember of hazing was filling the spikes of kids on the JV baseball team with shaving cream when he was on the South Fork varsity. Or some combination of dirt and honey that they all hoped would feel like dogshit when the kids put their baseball shoes on.

Now he read up on Mepham all over again, wanting to refresh his memory, about how hazing traditions that had once been about sticking kids' heads in toilets had evolved into varsity players becoming sexual attackers.

He read this quote from one of the parents: "My son knows one of the boys who was attacked. He tried seriously to treat him like a regular kid, like nothing ever happened. But he knew that boy was never going to be a regular kid ever again."

And this: "I know the family of one of the attackers. They're a beautiful family. My son just thinks it was a bad thing that went too far . . . "

Yeah, Mitchell thought: nearly through the kid's kidneys.

Attackers and attacked. People talking about high school football players like they were kids wilding in Central Park.

Mitchell sat there at the desk on the second floor, wondering if Bobby Ferraro might have been one of the attacked this time, even though he wasn't even a player, just the manager of the team.

And if so, which guys on the team had attacked him?

In South Fork.

He didn't know enough about medical examiners to know whether or not they checked a boy's body for sodomy in a case like this. Or how long the evidence of penetration showed up in an exam.

Mitchell kept reading, shocked at how many more Mephams there were, high schools and colleges all over the country, in football and basketball, hockey, soccer, lacrosse.

Like it was some kind of epidemic.

He read about a frat-house kid at Alfred University in upstate New York who'd died. He read about some girls trying to pledge a sorority at the University of Michigan who were forced to strip naked and stand in a line while other sorority girls wrote in Magic Marker on the parts of the bodies they found unattractive.

About a soccer player in Toms River, New Jersey, who was physically abused and then forced to crawl through mud. The coach had gotten his ass fired for knowing about it and not doing anything to stop it.

Hockey players. Lowell, Massachusetts. Hung from their waists while their teammates punched the shit out of them.

Coach resigned.

Medford, Massachusetts. A sophomore football player was forced to strip and run naked with a Ritz cracker wedged between the cheeks of his ass.

What the *fuck?*

A hockey player at Kent State University, in Ohio, nearly died after upperclassmen on his team made him chug booze and beer through a beer bong.

Lacrosse player at Western Illinois died following a drinking initiation in the woods near the school.

Ontario, Oregon. Six veteran baseball players on the high school baseball team sodomized four younger teammates.

In Lodi, New Jersey, a football player was duct-taped to a table at a camp run by the team's coaches, while other players spread feces and peanut butter all over him. Fourteen boys were in on it. They were going to be suspended from the first game of the upcoming season until the school administrators and coaches realized that game was against one of Lodi's toughest rivals. So they were suspended from a later game, against a team Lodi was sure to beat, with or without the suspended players.

But in Utah, a school superintendent canceled the last game of a season, and a playoff game, after it came out that one of his players had been taped naked to a table while his girlfriend had been brought in to see him like that.

The coach of the team had later kicked the kid off the team. Why? Because the *kid* refused to apologize for reporting the incident to the superintendent.

Thorndale High School. Texas. Four players sodomized a younger player with a Coke bottle.

Rancho Bernardo High School. California. Baseball team. Sodomy. Broom handle.

And always, in all the clips that showed up on Mitchell's screen, there was somebody, a coach, a parent, *somebody,* saying that you had to make allowances, cut the kids some slack, at the end of the day it was just boys being boys.

Mitchell printed it all out as he went, stuffed into the kind of bright-colored folders he used to use when he was really working, when he was actually in the game, not acting like some sort of substitute teacher for Sam Perry.

Then he took his beer and threw on an old sweater and sat on the deck and thought about the South Fork High School basketball team. Supposedly the greatest high school team in the history of the town and probably all of Long Island. The team with Show Watkins on it and Glenn Moore and rough, tough role players, like Eric Daneko.

He wondered if he watched them play a game, or even watched one of their practices, if he'd be able to tell from the faces, or the body language, or the way they hooped it up, if they were the type who could shove wood or a Coke bottle or a golf ball up some kid's ass.

Mitchell knew he was getting ahead of himself here. Bobby Ferraro, a kid he knew nothing about, could have ended up in the middle of some dope deal that had gone wrong. Or picked up the wrong guy at the wrong bar, because even high school boys did that.

Or just been in the wrong place at the wrong time.

Somehow Mitchell didn't think so.

He sat on the deck a long time, and then went to bed, telling himself he was going to sleep in for a change, until his phone rang at one in the morning, Sam Perry telling him that during the night, somebody had come into his driveway and slashed the tires of his car.

"Tell me where you live," Mitchell said, "I'll take a ride over."

The kid said, "There's more."

"They did something else to your car?"

"Somebody threw a brick through the front window of my mom's store."

# 3

There was a South Fork Police black-and-white, blue lights flashing, parked in front of the store belonging to Sam Perry's mom. It was called River Road, and was three doors down from Hiram's and next door to Olde East End, an antique store, and maybe fifty yards from the small town library. There were two uniforms out front, both men, both young, one of them a young black guy, a big guy Mitchell recognized from around town. Carl somebody. The black guy was standing up inside the window, where there were two mannequins, one reminding Mitchell of his ex-wife, modeling what Sam had said were the coolest clothes in town.

The cops looked up as he started to walk through the door to River Road. The black guy said, "Hey." Out of force of habit, Mitchell showed them his press card from the Los Angeles Police Department.

The black guy nodded. BOWDOIN, his badge said.

"Word travels fast," he said.

Mitchell said, "I got a call."

"Don't touch anything."

Mitchell thinking: This is what used to pass for a crime scene in South Fork, Long Island.

The mother—it had to be Sam's mother, he was the spitting image of her—was standing in the middle of her front room, wearing a sleeveless yellow down jacket and a black turtleneck and jeans. She was almost as tall as Sam, short dark hair herself, fashion-model cheekbones, dark eyes.

She had a clipboard in her hands, and must have been taking inventory, seeing if they had grabbed anything, her boots making crunching noises because of the broken glass on the floor. Now she put the clipboard on the shelf of an old wooden bookcase and went back to the middle of the room, hands on hips, and made a slow circle, staring at the mess as if she could glare it away.

Sam came out of what had to be a back room or a storage room, saying, "Everything seems to be in order back there."

He noticed Mitchell standing there. "Hey, Mr. Mitchell, thanks for coming."

The mother looked over at the doorway, noticing him for the first time. If she had been sleeping when it had happened, she came rolling out of bed looking pretty good.

"Is this him?" she said to Sam.

"Yes, m'am," Sam said. "Kate Perry, Ben Mitchell."

Mitchell started over toward her, hand out, then realized both her hands were still on her hips, as if attached.

Mitchell said, "Sorry to meet you under these circumstances."

"Well, Mr. Mitchell, not nearly as sorry as I am."

He said, "Have you ever been robbed before? Or even vandalized?"

"Oh, is that what this is?" she said. "*Vandalism?*"

She turned around now, snapped at Bowdoin, the tall black cop. "Do we still need those flashing lights?"

He went over to the car, shut off his flashers.

Mitchell said, "You don't think it's just some kind of drive-by crap?"

"My alarm goes off at twelve-thirty in the morning," she said. "Not my little wake-to alarm. My Bellringer alarm-company alarm. Which means my store. I wake up my kid, the crusading reporter, and he says, let's take his car. The famous red heap. Only, when we get outside, we can't, because somebody has slashed his tires, in our own goddamn driveway."

She tilted her head and smiled in a way that Mitchell knew whatever came next was going to be snippy.

"So, Mr. Mitchell, what do you think the odds are of my kid's tires getting slashed and his mother's store getting a brick thrown through it on the same night in our sleepy little town?"

"It seems like you got singled out."

Kate Perry said, "Ya *think?*"

Mitchell could see she needed to vent at somebody, and he was handy.

"My kid says you were one of the world's great reporters. So you would have to say this looks like more than one of those crazy coincidences you get in life sometimes. *Right?*"

Mitchell started to answer her, say something about how he was only here because Sam had called him, but before he could, she put a finger to her lips.

"It was a rhetorical question," she said. "My real question for you is, what have you gotten my son into?"

Sam said, "Mom, Mr. Mitchell . . ."

"Ben," he said.

" . . . Ben didn't get me into anything. I'm the one who's been trying to get him to help me look into Bobby's death."

"That's what the police do," she said.

"Not just them," Mitchell said in a quiet voice, not wanting to set her off all over again. "You've got a great kid here."

Sam looked at him. Mitchell shrugged.

Kate Perry said, "Well, you have known him for *such* a long time."

"Mom . . . "

"Zip it, young man."

Pow, as Mitchell's own mom used to say, right in the kisser.

"I would like to know, right now, Mr. Mitchell . . . "

"Ben."

" . . . if whatever it is he's working on for the paper, whatever it is that he can't share with me but can share with strangers who he only knows from books and the damn Internet, resulted in what happened to both of us tonight?"

Mitchell couldn't help himself, he felt himself smiling at her.

"What's so damn funny?" she said.

"I actually followed that," he said.

She waited. "Well, do you think there's some kind of connection between all this"—she made a gesture that took in the broken window and the broken glass—"and some little questions he says he's been asking?"

Mitchell said, "Could you do me a favor?"

"What?"

"Lower your voice."

"Ex*cuse* me?"

He took a couple of steps so that he was right up on her, thinking briefly that this was as close as he'd gotten to someone this good-looking in a long time.

Even if she was somebody's mother.

Mitchell said, "I think that what Sam's been working on, and asking questions about, has a whole shitload to do with what happened here tonight, and to his car. And might very well have something to do with whatever caused Bobby Ferraro to end up dead on the beach. And if it's all the same to you, I'd rather the police didn't find out about that just yet."

"That's the way big-time reporters look at things?" she

said. "Like they're in some sort of competition with the police?"

"Occasionally."

It was as if all the air in her came out at once, even making her voice crack a little.

"My son is still a boy," she said.

"Mom," he said. "I'm eighteen."

Mitchell said, "And this scared both of you."

"Yes," Kate Perry said.

"Me, too," Mitchell said. "And I'm not a big-time reporter anymore."

He nodded to Sam. "But your boy might be."

Kate Perry said, "Is that a good thing?"

"Occasionally," Mitchell said.

**W**ith Kate Perry calmed down, they had all gone back to the Perrys' house, a good-sized saltbox set back from the road on a street called Bridge Lane, directly across from the Montessori school. Sam told her everything, including what had happened with Eric Daneko.

Kate Perry said, "*Eric* did this?"

Mitchell said, "Not necessarily. All he had to do was say something to somebody about Sam asking questions. It could be anybody on the team. Or even friends of guys on the team." Sitting at the Perrys' kitchen table in the night, their voices sounding louder than they should have, Mitchell said to Sam, "How many guys were on that trip?"

The twelve players on the team, Sam said, Coach Glass, Bobby Ferraro. The assistant coach, a young guy named John Koutsos, had left South Fork right before the school year started when his wife got a job in San Francisco, and Glass had decided it was too close to the season to replace him.

"Well, a *coach* wouldn't do something like this," said Kate.

Mitchell said, "Yeah, because all the coaches I've ever known are so well adjusted."

They went all around the block for a while, Kate telling Sam she wanted him to drop this, Sam saying he couldn't: If this was what he was going to be, then she had to *let* him be it. Then Kate saying they should go to the police.

Mitchell said he would handle that.

Now he was walking down Main Street at seven-thirty in the morning, taking a right on School, going around the South Fork Town Hall to the police station.

He remembered doing a feature piece on the station for the South Fork *Star* when he was Sam Perry's age. If they hadn't changed everything too much, the way so many other things had changed in South Fork, the squad room and the chief's office were on the first floor, the town's two jail cells on the second.

Mitchell remembered the cells from the night he'd spent in one of them after his junior prom.

He saw one satellite truck, from Channel 12, set up in the back parking lot, but no action around it. Maybe they were getting coffee. Mitchell knew they had one of those round-the-block news cycles going, so maybe the reporter had already done some kind of standup.

He came up on a metal detector first, took out his car keys, put them in the tray. The uniformed cop at the metal detector said, "Cell phone?" Mitchell shook his head no, said, "The vibrator was getting me more excited than Viagra." The uniform, a ham-faced kid, nodded, waved him through, told him to check in at the security desk right in front of him.

"It doesn't look too crazy here right now," Mitchell said.

The ham-faced kid said, "Wait. This town has turned into spring break in Lauderdale all of a sudden, just without the wet t-shirt contest."

When Mitchell got to the security desk, he pulled out the press card again and asked if Detective Hank Bender was in.

The cop was wearing a name tag that said her name was

Halsey. She had long black hair and wore big black eye-glasses, square, too much for her face, but somehow giving off a cool, retro look. Almost sexy.

Maybe I'm cool and sexy in a retro way, Mitchell thought, and just haven't gotten the memo on that yet.

Officer Halsey said, "Can I tell him what this is in reference to?"

"You can tell him it's about Bobby Ferraro."

"I think he doesn't have his formal press conference until later in the day."

"Actually, we're old friends," Mitchell said. "Went to the high school together. Even played a little ball."

"That's wonderful news, if irrelevant to our conversation," she said. "Your card says you're with the *Los Angeles Times.* You've come a long way to cover Bobby Ferraro."

"I'm actually not with the *Times* any longer," Mitchell said.

She closed her eyes, exhaled dramatically. "Then exactly who are you with, Mr. Mitchell?"

"No one."

"Detective Commander Bender isn't doing any one-on-one interviews."

"It's not an interview, it's a visit."

"But you said you're here about Bobby Ferraro and showed me a press card. Like it was official business. I'm just trying to be clear about this."

Mitchell smiled. "Well, I was here about Bobby when I came in. But that was before I apparently got picked off first base."

"Is that sarcasm?" she said.

"Is this ball-busting for no good reason?" Mitchell said.

"Probably," Officer Halsey said, and punched a button on what looked like a retro intercom and said, "A Ben Mitchell here to see you. Says you know him from your glory days."

Mitchell had known it was Hank Bender as soon as his

face filled the screen on the early-evening news shows the day before, even though he hadn't seen him in at least twenty years. Mitchell had played only baseball at South Fork High, even though most good athletes in those days played all three major sports. Hank Bender, the best all-around athlete in school, had been a total three-sport star: linebacker in football, power forward in basketball, base-ball pitcher. If he could have found the time to play lacrosse, he would have kicked ass there.

Even back in the day, he'd kept his hair straight-arrow short, and he was one of the first guys Mitchell knew to really spend time in the weight room. He was ripped then and, Mitchell had seen on television, still looked pretty ripped now, as if he were about to come out of his blue blazer like the Incredible Hulk. And when they interviewed him near the cut where Fogg Pond met the ocean, or tried to interview him, Mitchell could see that Hank Bender still didn't take much shit from anybody.

One news bunny, from Channel 2, said to Bender on camera, "When will we know more?"

Bender said, "When I want you to, would be my guess."

Now he came around the reception desk, checking him out, saying, "I heard you were back."

"You know what they say," Mitchell said. "Home is the place that when you go there, they can't send you to a Holiday Inn." Mitchell grinned. "Having fun the last couple of days dealing with my people?"

"Fucking riot," he said.

"I'll bet."

"I'm sorry about what happened there in L.A. Poor bastard."

"Me," Mitchell said, "or him?"

"C'mon," Bender said, "we'll talk at my desk," and walked him through a door that opened into a room that looked as if it were the set for some kind of small-town cop TV show.

Everything reminded him of something on television these days.

Hank Bender's desk was in the corner, the bay window next to him facing out on the Little League ballfield on Corwith, on the other side of the back parking lot. There was a coffee machine and coffee setup on a metal table in front of the window. Bender asked if he wanted a cup, but Mitchell said he'd been mainlining it at Hiram's since seven in the morning and would pass, it made him feel old when he had to take a piss about every fifteen minutes. Bender said he didn't even need coffee to do that.

Then, without being asked, he took Mitchell through the procedures involved with a death like Bobby Ferraro's, even with a small force like the one in South Fork. It was like he was showing off for some reason, or still the captain of the high school baseball team: the patrol supervisor arriving first at the scene, followed by a detective. The detective being yours truly, Hank Bender said. The beginning of the crime-scene log. The arrival of the chief medical examiner, who worked out of Arrowhead, about forty-five minutes away. The official cause of death, for now, even with the obvious injuries Bobby Ferraro had sustained, was "drowning by suspicious circumstances." So it was and wasn't an official homicide investigation at the same time. By now, the body had been sent to a state forensic branch laboratory, farther up-island at Port Madison, and they had begun a chain of custody with evidence, including the clothes Bobby had been wearing, his cell phone records, the family phone records, any activity on the American Express card his father had given him for his eighteenth birthday, his laptop computer.

"The beginning of trying to fit together a jigsaw puzzle," Bender said, "even though you know going in that you don't have all the pieces."

"You'll figure it out," Mitchell said, having no way of knowing whether Hank Bender would or not.

"Change the subject," Bender said, while he poured

himself more coffee. "I heard you were at River Road last night after somebody pitched the brick."

"I've gotten to know the kid a little bit," Mitchell said. "I think he wanted me to help calm his mother down."

Bender smiled. "Kate always seems pretty calm to me."

Mitchell said, "You get a lot of shit like that?"

Bender sat down, put his feet up on his desk. "Only when the bars are open."

Mitchell thought about asking him how often tires got slashed, but asking him about Sam's car would only bring a lot of other questions from Hank Bender that he didn't want to answer, at least not yet.

On Bender's desk was a color photograph that had been taken at the beach: Bender in a gray South Fork sweatshirt with the sleeves cut off so he could show off his arms, a tall pretty blond woman, and a boy who was already a head taller than his old man, but who looked just like him.

"Anna and Dave," he said. "I don't know if you remember Anna Parsons, she was two years behind us. My boy is eighteen now, if you can believe that shit. Six-two. The doc says he might grow a couple inches more, even though he's a senior. One of those late-growth-spurt deals."

"I'm still waiting for mine."

"Six-two and not even as tall as the point guard on his team. You heard of him? DeShawn Watkins. They call him Show."

"Been reading all about him, and about your other star hooper. Sportswriters act like they're Bird and Magic."

"The other kid's name is Glenn Moore," Bender said. "You wouldn't believe it was possible that you'd come up with two like that on the same team. Well, maybe on some team in the city. Just not our team. Glenn grew up here, of course. Parents are big-shot lawyers, in the city as often as they're here. DeShawn grew up in the South Bronx." Bender tilted his head. "You have to know some of this, right?"

Mitchell said, "Some."

Bender said, "Old man got shot a long time ago. His mother, who wasn't so nice from what I'm told, died last spring in some hotel near Times Square. The kid had some beefs after that, got into a couple of bad fights outside clubs, so they decided he should come out here and live with his grandma." Bender grinned. "Nearly, by the way, over the dead body of the head basketball coach at DeWitt Clinton High School."

He nodded at the family picture. "Now I'm figuring that if they'll just pass the ball to my kid once in a while, we can get a scholarship out of the deal."

We, Mitchell noticed. First person jock plural.

Spoken by sports moms and dads everywhere.

"Maybe when the season starts," Mitchell said, "we can take in a game."

Bender said, "Wait till you see. It's all that people in this town talk about. Like high school basketball has suddenly become the company in a company town. *Newsday* is going to cover every game, according to Dave. Same with the *Press.* All of a sudden, the little town is big-time. You know I've lived here my whole life. I've never seen it like this. We were supposed to have a team like this a couple of years ago, when Glenn and this other big sophomore stud, Kyle Sheppard, were coming along. Glenn's best buddy, actually. Then Kyle tore up his knee in a practice game, him and Glenn got tangled up going for a rebound, never played again. Glenn's had to pretty much carry the load himself ever since. Till now, anyway."

Bender put big, rubber-soled black shoes up on his desk. "So, to what do I owe the honor of a visit from South Fork's former favorite son?"

"Bastard son is more like it."

"You been back how long?"

"Six months?"

"And I haven't seen you?"

"You have to get to Hiram's early, then ignore the 'Leave me the fuck alone' sign they post near my booth."

"Seriously, bud," Hank Bender said. "What's on your mind?"

"The Ferraro kid, what else? Your boy must be pretty shook up about it."

"Everybody's shook up about it," he said. "You know this town. Hell, you grew up here, too, till you went off to college. We don't see a lot of seventeen-year-old kids get beat up and then wash up across from Fogg Pond."

"What is the extent of the injuries?"

"Some head trauma, like somebody cracked him with something to the side of his head. Cracked rib." Like he was reciting something in class. "Bruises on his stomach and back." He rubbed his eyes hard, with both hands. "Jesus H. Christmas, somebody doing something like that to a nice kid like Bobby."

"How many detectives you got here?"

"With the official rank? You're looking at him. My help comes from the rest of the force, most of it from a sharp young guy I think you might've met over at River Road last night. Carl Bowdoin. His cousin's a forward on the team. Christian Bowdoin."

"Got any leads?"

Bender did something with his face that was somewhere between a smile and a frown. "Okay, I gotta ask you now," he said. "Is this some kind of official interview? 'Cause I'm under orders from the mayor . . . "

"Unofficial," Mitchell said. "I got no status anywhere."

Mitchell looked around. There were only two other people in the room at nine in the morning, both of them in uniform. Everybody else was probably out working on Bobby Ferraro. There were suspicious circumstances about a death in South Fork, a place where a crime wave usually involved a wallet being snatched from an unlocked car while somebody went for a walk on Main Beach or the beach at the end of Ocean Road near where Mitchell lived.

Bender said, "Why are you so interested in this?"

"I've got a lot of time on my hands," Mitchell said. "I'm like you." He gave a little shrug to his shoulders. "Just wondering why somebody would do something like that here."

"Here or anywhere," Bender said. "Why does somebody grab somebody like John Walsh's kid out of a fucking Sears store? Why did somebody kill the little dancing blond girl in Boulder or grab the Smart kid out of her bedroom in White People, Utah? The world's a bad place, Mitch, filled with bad people. You found out when you did that book of yours." Bender smiled for real now. "One I actually read."

"In the old days, you would've asked me to read it for you."

"Is that why you're here? You got up this morning, felt the old bounce in your step, decided to do a book on a small-town murder?"

"Nah, but I'm still nosy," Mitchell said. "Tell me something about the dead kid I don't know."

Bender said, "Not much to tell. Parents are divorced. Mother's in Santa Fe, doing some kind of artist thing. The dad, Matt, used to be some kind of big-shot veep with Morgan Stanley. Or maybe it was Goldman Sachs. Gave it up a few years ago, went into business for himself, apparently kept enough high-end clients to stay on the high end himself. Wanted to live a quieter life out here, or so he told people. Except he's still at his office in the city, or in Europe, as often as he's here. Or in the apartment he keeps in the city. Someplace uptown, I've got the address somewhere."

Mitchell said, "How'd he end up with the kid?"

"You ask a lot of questions for a retired guy."

"Humor me, there's a long way between now and the six o'clock *SportsCenter.*"

"He got him because she didn't want him—she wanted to find herself. Get in touch with her inner alimony. What can I tell you? According to my kid, the Ferraro kid was alone too goddamn much."

"Alone enough to get into trouble?"

"Nah, everything I hear is good. Popular. Eager to please. A puppy dog. Not good enough to play ball himself, but wanting like hell to be a part of the team. Seemed like the team was the only family he had sometimes. Like that kid we had managing the baseball team, what the hell was his name?"

Mitchell said, "Ricky Fletcher," having the name right there and not knowing exactly why. Maybe because Hank Bender was sitting in front of him.

The shit you remembered.

"That kind of kid. Mascot almost."

"So," Mitchell said, trying to make the question sound off-hand, "you checking out the family members on the team?"

Bender had his Knicks mug all the way to his mouth, held it there, tilted his head slightly, curious, like he'd heard something from outside. "You asking me if the players are suspects? Players on a team my *kid's* a player on?"

Mitchell gave him a wave-off sign, saying, "I'm just an old reporter with too much time on his hands trying to understand how the manager of the high school basketball team ends up dead in the water."

"I'm gonna talk to everybody, players included. I was on my way over to the school this morning, just to get away from calls from hysterical parents."

"How's the father doing?"

"How would you be?"

Mitchell said, "Anybody in town remember seeing this kid from the time school ended on Friday until his old man came back?"

"That's why I was going over to school."

"You talked about chain of evidence before," Mitchell said. "Have you gotten a look at the phone logs yet, or whatever the hell they're called?"

"Before you showed up. No calls from either of the lines in the house. Nothing on the cell after Thursday night. For my kid, it would be an all-time personal best. I haven't checked his computer yet. My kid says that's how he used to send out messages to the team. Sometimes, just to goof around, he'd make a tape of himself with his phone, tell them what time practice was that way."

Bender looked out the window, toward the tiny cemetery behind St. Ann's Church, one that was as old as the church, headstones going back to the early 1800s, the grass around the headstones perfectly manicured. Mitchell, trying to keep everything casual, said to Hank Bender, "Everybody on the team get along with everybody else?"

Bender kept looking out the window. "Why would you ask that?"

"Because I played myself once," Mitchell said. "And because I heard a couple of guys got into it at that, what was it, like spring training over in Connecticut? Your boy ever mention anything about that?"

Bender turned back to Mitchell, a little half-smile on his face. "*Where'd* you hear that?"

"Couple of guys at Hiram's. I don't even know their names."

"All my kid said was that they didn't have any instant messaging or cable TV," Hank Bender said. Paused and said, "You're still asking a lot of questions for a retired guy."

"I just think it's kind of interesting, something like this happening around a team with a couple of star kids like you've got here."

Bender said, "Or maybe this kid dying doesn't have any-thing to do with the basketball team, we're just talking about a lonely kid who died of bad luck."

"If that's the case," Mitchell said, "then all I'll have done is waste my own time."

"Do me a favor, Mitch? Let me ask the questions. I got

enough trouble already with assholes who aren't from here poking around, pissing off the townies."

"I'm from here."

"A long time ago."

Bender stood up, as a way of saying they were done. "We'll go to a game, and then you and me and Anna will go out and have a burger."

They shook hands.

"Seriously," Ben Mitchell said, "who kills the team manager in South Fork?"

Bender said, "You sound like those TV reporters who've been shining their teeth into my eyes the last twenty-four hours."

"That's no way to talk to an old teammate," Mitchell said.

Bender clapped him on the back and said he'd walk him out. When they got into the hall, Mitchell leaned over and said in a quiet voice, "Officer Halsey doesn't like me."

"She's not singling you out," Bender said. "She just hates reporters in general."

"Who doesn't?" Mitchell said.

# 4

Mitchell turned to Sam and said, "Your coach?"

"Yeah?"

"Does he usually run the whole practice at the top of his voice?"

"Pretty much."

They were sitting in the top row of the bleachers in the South Fork gym. The coach, Ken Glass, didn't allow anybody, not even *The New York Times,* to sit much closer. Not that anybody needed to sit any closer, you could hear him just fine from up here. And, Mitchell had observed, probably from the parking lot.

Sam was allowed to attend practice because he was from the school paper, and also because he now had official status with the *Press.* When he and Mitchell were making their way up through the bleachers, Sam said to him, "I hope Coach doesn't ask who you are, he's not big on strangers."

Mitchell said, "It'll be fine."

Sam said, "I've seen him kick people out."

"Not me," Mitchell said.

Sam could see that Mitchell was different today, even more different than he'd been last night at their kitchen table, calmly backing his mom down, which Sam knew was no easy thing to do.

Mostly Sam saw how pissed Mitchell was about what had happened last night, to the car, to his mom's store. The last thing he'd said to Sam before mentioning he wanted to come to practice was, "Whoever did this is going to find out that the dumbest thing in this world is to fuck with a reporter."

In the gym now, Mitchell said, "You notice something? The coach yells at everybody directly except his stars. When they screw up, he yells at the whole team."

Sam had always thought Coach Glass looked more like a cop than a basketball coach, or some kind of Marine drill sergeant, all the way up to his drill-sergeant crewcut. His legs were so bowed it looked like a couple of the little guys off his bench could dribble right through him if they had to.

He had that amped-up voice even when he said "Good morning" to you in the hall. When he answered a question after the game, he sounded like he was still shouting out defenses.

But as much as Coach Glass yelled and waved his arms and held his head and kept stopping things in order to yell a little more, even grabbing some kids by the front of their jerseys, Sam was able to do what he usually did up here in the cheap seats during practice:

Watch Show and Glenn.

Glass wanted it to be about him. But it was always about them, at least when he wasn't blowing his stupid whistle and explaining basketball again.

Sam wouldn't ever admit this to Ben Mitchell, but he felt like some kind of groupie up here, getting to watch them practice for free. Knowing he would have paid to sit up here. He knew he wasn't supposed to be this excited about a couple of high school basketball players the same age as him. But there it was. They *did* have the kind of status that guys like Eric Daneko wished they had, or thought they had just because they were on the same team.

Sam wanted to step back, look at them with the detachment that good reporters were supposed to have. But he couldn't do that, no matter how hard he tried. Why? Beause he was going to remember watching the two of them play together, before they went off to the pros or college or whatever, for the rest of his frigging life, that was why.

Coach Glass had stopped yelling at Dave Bender down on the court, long enough for Show to sneak in behind Eric Daneko and steal the ball as Eric was trying to make a move down the baseline. Then, as Show was falling out of bounds in the corner—there was no way he could possibly know Glenn was breaking away like a wide receiver on the other side of the court—he turned his body and threw a pass Brett Favre would have killed for on his best day.

Glenn caught it one stride on the other side of halfcourt, took three dribbles, calmly dunked the ball with two hands, then turned and pointed down to the other end of the court where Show stood with his hands on his hips, bopping his head like, uh-huh, uh-huh, uh-huh, like he was listening to music.

It was as if the two of them were in the gym alone, just trying stuff.

Sam still couldn't tell how much they really liked each other off the court, what Glenn thought about having to share the ball and the spotlight and everything else after being the star of everything for so long. But for now anyway, maybe because of the media crowd watching, it was as if they'd grown up together playing ball.

"Sam?" Sam heard Mitchell saying.

"What?"

"Have you heard a word I've been saying the last couple of minutes?"

"I'm sorry, I was just thinking about something."

"Yeah, your two dreamboats down there on the court." Mitchell pointed. "I was just asking you, which one of them is really gonna be the man on this team?"

"Well, like, both of them are."

Mitchell said, "Jesus, you really are young."

It was right then that Drew Hudson, the smallest kid on the team, his spiky dark hair featuring those blond streaks you saw in guys' hair all over school now, hardly any upper body on him at all, threw away a no-look pass to Dave Bender, who was cutting down the baseline toward the basket, wide open.

Coach Glass blew his whistle, stopping everything again, and said, "Hudson, the *girls'* team practices right after us today, why don't you wait around and show off your cute little game to them?"

Then Coach Glass said, "Get out of my gym."

Only, Drew Hudson didn't leave.

"You hear me, Hudson?" Coach Glass said, not caring how many reporters were listening to his sudden rant. "Go take a shower and try to clean the *crap* off your game."

Drew Hudson still didn't move, or even acknowledge that the coach was dressing him down this way.

He just stood right where he was, from where he'd thrown the pass, about even with the foul line, and started to cry.

In front of everybody.

He stood down there to Sam and Ben's right, head down, arms hanging at his sides, his chest the only thing moving, going up and down. After hearing only Coach Glass's voice for almost the whole practice, now the only sound in the gym they heard was Drew Hudson, sobbing.

It was Glenn Moore, not the termite coach, who made the first move toward the kid. Moore looked like the only person on the court who seemed to understand how helpless the kid was, Mitchell thought. Naked, really. Moore got to him and put an arm around him and even looked like he was trying to hug him in close to his body.

Drew Hudson tried to shake him off at first. But Moore was bigger, and clearly taking charge the way he did when they were playing. So the smaller boy gave in to whatever this was now, kindness or compassion or pity or whatever.

Or maybe Glenn Moore was willing to do anything just to get them all past this.

Mitchell, motioning for Sam to move down the bleachers with him, watched as Glenn Moore kept his arm around Drew Hudson, who could not stop crying, walking him toward the bleachers on the other side of the court.

When Glass, the coach, started walking over there, Glenn Moore stopped him with a look, then a slow shake of his head. Like it was his team, and he was in charge now.

Maybe he had been all along.

"Hey, guys," Glass said to the rest of the players, as a way of being in charge of them at least, "why don't you shoot your free throws and we'll knock off early today."

In a quiet voice, Sam said, "What was *that* was all about?"

Mitchell didn't answer him, kept watching the scene on the court play itself all the way out. Eric Daneko and Dave Bender walked toward Glenn and Drew now.

Moore shook his head. As soon as he did, both of them stopped in their tracks, as if he'd yelled *Freeze*.

At the same time, Mitchell heard somebody bark out a laugh from the other end of the court, turned his head to see Show Watkins, left hand covering his eyes, make a free throw blindfolded with his right hand.

"Two for two," he said, and motioned for the white kid rebounding for him to give him the ball, as if what was happening to Drew Hudson was happening in somebody else's gym, to somebody's else's basketball team.

"You think Drew's still broken up about Bobby, or something?" Sam said.

"He's sure as hell broken up about something," Mitchell said. "When I was seventeen, eighteen years old, I would have wanted to wet my pants in front of the guys before I'd cry in front of them."

There was a whoop from the other end. Now the white kid was throwing lob passes to Show Watkins, who was dunking the ball like it was part of the NBA's Slam Dunk and Hot Dog competition.

"Your man Show is certainly a piece of work," Mitchell said.

Sam said, "Not much fazes him. You watch him during scrimmages, you can't tell whether his team's winning or losing."

"I think he knows."

"I think he's a lot smarter than he lets on. And not just about basketball."

Mitchell saw that Drew Hudson had finally started to calm down.

"The other guys on the team like Show?"

"They're, like, pretty much in awe of him," Sam said. "As cool as kids think they are out here, dressing the way they think cool kids are supposed to dress, Show is like the real deal. He grew up in the city. We heard that he saw a guy get shot one time, in the stairwell of his building."

"Wow," Mitchell said. "What could be cooler than that?"

"You know what I mean. You know all that men-among-boys stuff you hear from adults? He *is* like a man to the rest of us. Which is another thing that makes everybody want to be like him. Talk like him. Dress like him. Shit like that."

Mitchell said, "Reverse snobbery."

"Huh?"

"Usually it's the kids who have stuff—or at least a lot more stuff than Watkins must have had growing up—who get looked up to. But according to you, these kids worship a guy who practically grew up in a crack house."

"It is kind of funny."

"Yeah," Mitchell said, "one more thing to make it such a funny world."

Show Watkins caught a lob pass that should have been too far behind him to catch, reaching back, extending his arm as if it were attached to some kind of crane, catching the ball and controlling it at the same time. Then, in the same motion, he threw down a violent, one-handed dunk.

When he landed, he went right into a smile and strut and nod, giving a quick pound to his chest like there was a camera on him, even though there wasn't.

"It doesn't have to be today," Mitchell said, "but you have to find a way to get Drew Hudson alone and find out what this was all about. As a friend, not a reporter."

"I can do that. We actually worked together two Christmases ago at Bob's Sports."

"Maybe he just can't take it from a coach like this, it might not be any more complicated than that," Mitchell said. "But it would be nice to know for sure."

Glenn walked Drew Hudson to the locker room. The rest of the players shot free throws for a few minutes, then left the court. Sam headed for the locker room.

The last player shooting free throws was Eric Daneko.

Eric was the one who had gotten drunk at a party and said some things to Sam Perry, his ride home. When Sam had asked him about it afterward, Eric had denied everything and immediately tried to muscle him. And before you knew it, somebody had gone to work on Sam's tires and thrown something through the front window of Kate Perry's store.

Mitchell watched the kid go through his little routine, knock down his last ten free throws in a row, try a halfcourt shot and miss, disappear through a door at the far end of the court, oblivious to anybody watching him. When he was gone, Mitchell walked down through the bleachers and out to the parking lot, thinking that if Eric came out alone, maybe he could walk the kid to his car.

Get to know him a little.

# 5

Mitchell sat in the front seat of the Ford pickup, a Lariat F-150 he'd bought when he moved back, partly because he'd always wanted one, partly because that's the way he saw himself in South Fork, a townie in a used pickup and not the cool L.A. guy driving around in a BMW.

He'd already counted eleven players coming through the front doors of the school, plus the new team manager Sam had pointed out when they were in the gym, a transfer from Hawaii named Billy Mahalu. Still no Eric Daneko. Mitchell was starting to wonder if maybe Daneko had left by an exit on the other side of the building when he finally saw the kid come out wearing an oversized hoodie sweatshirt, cargo pants, high unlaced boots, probably Timberlands, just because they all seemed to wear their Timbies these days. Daneko looked as if he'd dressed himself by looking at black hip-hoppers on the cover of one of those *Vibe* magazines.

Mitchell didn't even know how big *Rolling Stone* was with kids anymore. He'd mentioned something to Sam about Hunter Thompson the other day and Sam had said, "You mean the guy who writes for ESPN dot com once in a while?"

One of the janitors poked his head out of a classroom window. "We lookin' good, baby!" the guy yelled. Daneko turned around and pounded his fist to his heart twice, then reached into one of the pockets of his hoodie, pulled out his cell phone, one that looked as small as a pack of matches, and flipped it open with a quick snap of his wrist. He must have been answering a call because he had the phone to his ear right away. Then he said something and laughed, leaned against an Explorer that had to be his.

Mitchell saw it was just the two of them now in the parking lot. He walked toward Daneko. As he got closer, he heard the kid say something into the little designer phone about how he'd gotten snapped at during practice just because he'd forgotten his gamers and worn his discount kicks instead.

Then he said, "Whatever," then "Peace out," snapped the phone shut, and pulled out his car keys. He must have hit his remote button, because the car lights went on.

A remote world, Mitchell thought, getting more remote all the time.

"Hey," Mitchell said. "Hey, Eric."

Daneko's head whipped around, as if he'd heard a bogeyman voice come out of nowhere in the empty parking lot.

The kid squinted in his direction. "Yo?"

"Wait up," Mitchell said.

Mitchell came out of the splash of light from the streetlight closest to Daneko's Explorer. The kid was still squinting. "I know you?" he said, like he thought he might.

Mitchell said, "Ben Mitchell," stuck out his hand. The kid gave it a half-shake, half-slap, as if Mitchell had just hit a big free throw.

Mitchell said, "I was in there watching practice today and, shoot, you guys could give the Knicks a game."

"Cool."

The kid casually moved toward the driver's-side door, but Mitchell moved right along the car with him.

Daneko took a closer look at him. "Wait a second, I think I *do* know you." Snapped his fingers and said, "From ESPN!"

Mitchell shrugged now, as if he'd been made. "Busted," he said.

Daneko said, "One of those shows where you all yell at each other, right? I *love* that shit."

Mitchell said, "I'm afraid you're going to have to narrow it down a little more than that."

Daneko, excited now, said, "No, no. I used to see you, I just can't remember whether it was the one with the two guys yelling at each other, or the four." Then he put up a hand, like, wait. "Or was it the one where they've got a bunch of guys in different cities and they keep score?"

"I was one of the four guys once in a while," Mitchell said. "On Sunday mornings. And some commentaries, like little opinion pieces, once a week."

Daneko pointed, like Mitchell had just thrown him a good pass. "I knew it!"

Television. It was their only reality. Their version of real life, just once removed. The only way to get their attention was to be on television. It was the same in a parking lot outside a high school as it was in the pros. Mitchell was hoping Sam Perry would figure it out sooner rather than later. You had real juice only if they watched you, not if they read you.

That was if they read you at all.

"You got me," Mitchell said.

Now Daneko shook his hand. "Well, it's nice to meet you, but I can't do any interviews, dude. Coach says any interviews, 'specially since Bobby, had to go through him. So maybe if you want to hook up you could, like, talk to him tomorrow or whatever. Though you probably just want to talk to Show or Glenn."

Mitchell smiled. "I'm not here to interview you."

Up close, even with Daneko in his boots, the two of

them were almost eye-to-eye. Maybe the kid had a couple of inches on him, though he probably outweighed Mitchell by twenty or thirty pounds of weight-room muscle.

Mitchell still figured the sides were even, Eric Daneko out here talking to an adult, all by himself.

"Well, nice talking to you," Daneko said, reached over, and got his door halfway open.

Mitchell gently shut it.

"We're not quite done," Mitchell said.

Daneko said, "Huh?"

Mitchell smiled again. "I think there was some confusion the other day," he said. "With you and a friend of mine? Sam Perry?"

Daneko didn't say anything. He seemed to be wondering how to play this, some guy from TV here acting like the one in charge.

"Anyway," Mitchell said, "I think he might have mistakenly given you the impression that he was asking questions on his own. About this and that."

Eric Daneko said, "This and that."

"But the truth of the matter," Mitchell said, "is that the kid is working for me."

"Sam and you? For ESPN?"

Mitchell nodded, as if nodding at that, and said, "I'm thinking about doing a piece on your team. The whole season, start to finish. Like they do on ESPN sometimes? I mean, I was going to do it before Bobby died, but now it just seems to have turned the whole thing into more of a circus, you know? Like the circus has come to town."

"Right," Daneko said. Like he understood where Mitchell was going with all this. "It *has* gotten, like, mad."

"Yeah, mad," Mitchell said. "Anyway, I'm going to be hanging around, and I thought we should get to know each other."

"Like I said," Daneko said, "for interviews, you got to go through Coach. . . ."

"Right, right," Mitchell said. "For *interviews*. But like I said before, this isn't an interview, this is just the two of us shooting the shit."

"Well, yeah, like right. But right now, I really gotta bounce, my parents are expecting me for dinner."

Mitchell was leaning against the car door now. "Well, I better get to it, then. It seems that after you and Sam had your talk, some numbnut pitched a brick through the window of his mom's store. And, and you're not going to believe *this*, but somebody else, maybe even the same numbnut for all we know, went into Sam's driveway and slashed the tires on that old red Volvo of his."

Eric Daneko said, "Hold on, dude, that's the first I heard . . ."

"Whoa," Mitchell said. "*You* hold on, dude. I'm not suggesting you had anything to do with it. Even Sam says you're solid."

"Sam and I go way back."

"I'm sure you do. But you know how it goes in school. How guys get shit wrong. Maybe you said something to somebody and somebody said something to somebody else? And every time it got passed along, there was some little element they got wrong." Mitchell smiled his biggest smile yet. "Anyway, I just wanted to say, for the record, that anybody fucking with Sam Perry or his family from now on is fucking with me. Is that clear?"

"Clear," the kid said. "Now, if you could move . . ."

Mitchell looked down, as if surprised to see where he was. He stepped back, opened the door for Eric Daneko, and said, "Oh, and one more thing?"

Daneko waited.

Mitchell said, "Don't put another hand on Sam Perry, Eric."

You could hear the car traffic from Farm Road. A small plane in the sky above them.

"Are you, like, threatening me? 'Cause . . ."

"I'm not threatening anybody," Mitchell said. "If I was,

I'd actually be telling you, and telling you to tell your friends, that if you lined up everybody in this whole town, the last one you'd want to fuck with the way somebody did with the Perrys is me."

Mitchell gave his chest a couple of short pounds with his right hand.

"Peace out," he said.

They were letting the cop, Dave Bender's old man, use the locker room.

That's where he was interviewing the guys on the team, one by one, the scrubs first, Show noticed, like he was working his way up from them to the big dogs.

That's how the starters thought of themselves, the big dogs, even though they understood there really were but two.

Show was scheduled for late morning, which was fine and dandy with him, at least he got something out of the deal, which meant not having to listen to that bitch Ms. Diaz in World History.

Even though.

Even though Show never wanted to talk to the cops anytime, about anything. He saw it with his brother Antoine, when Antoine was still working as a street cop, before he moved up to detective. Before he turned. Antoine would bring Show with him sometimes, let him see how the game was played, how cops had their ways of making you look guilty and sound guilty even when you weren't guilty of nothing more than standing *outside* when something was going down *inside*. How you had to watch yourself, or they could give somebody their shuck and jive and make them feel like a perp even when they weren't. *Mind* yourself. Maybe like today, Show thought. He was wondering already how he would present this to Two Mom.

Everybody else knew his grandma as Emmy. Emmy Watkins. Or Miz Emmy, which is what a lot of them called

her. But she had always been Two Mom to him. Always had
been, always would be, even now that his real momma had
passed. Two Mom had always been the boss of all of them,
him and Antoine and their momma, small as she was, cute
as a little bunny. Show hadn't wanted to tangle with her
when he was little, didn't want to tangle with her now. He'd
learned something the hard way, all the times when he'd
come at her wrong with something and she'd crack her
voice on him like one of those lion tamers with a whip:

Presentation was *always* the damn key with Two Mom.

Except she'd probably know about the cop being at
school by the time she was making him his dinner, Two Mom
cleaned so many houses in South Fork she had her radar going all the time. Show had only been living with her full-time
a couple of months. Already he could see that when anything
happened in South Fork, when it came to somebody's marriage breaking up, or somebody getting arrested for driving-
under, Two Mom was always ahead of the news.

Two Mom: the black maid who decided to come out
with the Park Avenue family after Show's grandpa died.
Only then the Park Avenue family left after a few years,
went back to the city, and Emmy Watkins decided to stay,
work for all the people in town who'd always said to her,
Emmy, I wish we had somebody like you-all. Now she had
all the houses she needed. And all the news. Old and new.
Coming home with it. Not telling it to him in a gossipy way,
just telling him what she picked up. Telling him always,
watch himself, this town she brought him to wasn't as nice
as she used to think. Like she was always telling him he better watch himself walking around with his shoelaces un-
tied, he was gonna trip one of these days.

What did they say on the news radio? Give us twenty-
two minutes, we'll give you the world? Two Mom always
seemed to know twenty-two minutes *before*.

Bottom line? Two Mom likely knew Detective Hank
Bender of the South Fork Police had set up shop in the

locker room while the coffee he'd brought with him was still hot inside his sippy cup.

Eric Daneko had been in the locker room with Dave's old man right before. Show got with him at their lockers before the bell ending second and Eric had said the whole thing was bullshit, strictly routine, that he thought Dave's old man was just going through the motions.

It was the first time Show Watkins had seen Eric all morning.

"You sure you didn't get in there and confess to everything except capping Biggie?" Show said.

"You know me," Eric said, giving him one of his sideways looks. "I don't talk."

Show said, "Not even to reporters?"

Eric, who'd been acting scared of everything lately, looked around to see if anybody else was listening. In a voice that wasn't much more than a whisper, he said, "I *told* you, Sam Perry must have found out, must have *heard* that shit, from somebody else. I keep telling you," he said, ducking his head, "there's nobody more a team man than me."

"My personal experience, yo?" Show said. "Everybody's a team man till they's not."

Eric looked like he might shit all of a sudden. "What's that mean?"

"Relax," Show said. "I'm just playin'." Then gave Eric a lean-in hug, one-handed, trying to end it light.

Show started down the hallway, to the stairs leading to the locker room, and Eric said, "Wait." There was still a few minutes before third period. Eric said, "We got to talking about Dave's dad and I almost forgot to tell you about this real reporter, from ESPN, waiting for me in the parking lot last night."

"ESPN guy wanting to talk to *you?*"

Eric said, "Did you hear anything about somebody throwing a rock through the front window of River Road? Store that Sam Perry's mom owns? Or dicing the wheels on Sam's car?"

"Fuck, no," Show said. "Two Mom doesn't do her shopping at River Road, she's over at the Big K."

"He started acting friendly, and then he acted like me rousting up Sam a little bit after the funeral that day might've gotten somebody to mess with Sam and his mom. Before he left, he told me to let everybody know that messing with them was the same as doing it with him."

"Boy got a name?"

"Ben Mitchell."

"Ben Mitchell of ESPN," Show said, standing there with Eric in the hall now, even knowing he was keeping the police waiting. "Which *SportsCenter* is he on?"

The bell rang then for third period. Eric said he had to go, they'd talk after practice.

Show walked down the stairs by himself, not thinking about Dave's dad waiting for him in the locker room. Just thinking about how fast things could mess up *generally* if you didn't watch your ass. Thinking how hard he had worked to stay clean, to not end up like Antoine, or his momma, keep his eye on the prize, like Two Mom told him. The two of them were talking about a different prize sometimes, he knew that, and so did she. But the real prize, to both of them, was this here: getting out of this life, and on to the next one.

And he wasn't talking about the hereafter, he'd point out to Two Mom.

"I already *know* what I'm here after," he'd tell her.

Show knew he wasn't perfect by a long shot. But he'd kept his grades, stayed out of the clubs he knew he could get into even though he wasn't the age, had been with only one girl in his life, back at DeWitt, even though he could have anybody he wanted. It was the same out here as it had been back there.

Now he was one year away.

That close.

Show knew where he was supposed to be going, had known for a long time, not needing a father to tell him, never needing his momma or Antoine, or even Two Mom.

But where was he *right now?*

That might be a harder question than any the cop might ask.

**D**ave says we're looking pretty damn good," Dave's dad said to Show.

Dave's dad was sitting on one bench, in front of one row of lockers. Show was on a bench facing him, a few feet away. The guys on the team talked about how they'd fixed up the locker room between last season and this, how you should have seen it before the fix-up. It still reminded Show of some of the little dink locker rooms he used to see when he was playing AAU ball back in the city.

Detective Hank Bender had one of those big wire notebooks and a cheap ballpoint pen. Big hands on him, big enough to palm a ball, Show figured. Hands he could probably do other things with, if he had to. Some parents Show had seen in South Fork, basketball parents, picking up after practice, looked old. Dave's dad looked younger than the rest, even with hair cut so close, what brothers would call nappy-like, Show wondered why he didn't go all the way bald.

They were talking ball before they talked about Bobby.

Even the cops wanted to talk about how we were looking.

*We.*

Show knew this was a day to use what he called his Two Mom English, not fuck around.

"It's just a question of us coming together," Show said. "As a team, I mean. And Dave's going to be a big part of it, you can count on that, Mr. Bender. You tell him I said that."

The cleaning people in town that Two Mom made a face about, even called house niggers, couldn't be politer than Show when he wanted to be.

"That's nice to hear," Bender said. "He's got a lot riding on this season, too."

"He's the kind of guy who knows where he's supposed

to be at all times. Where *everybody's* supposed to be. And I don't have to tell you, the boy can shoot. We'll get him that full ride he talks about, don't worry."

"Well, he certainly works hard enough."

Show sat there, wondering how long all the feeling-out was going to last, when Dave Bender's dad was going to get to it, stop acting like another mom-and-dad groupie.

Finally, almost like he was embarrassed, Hank Bender said, "I don't have to tell you why I'm here."

"About Bobby."

"Shame."

"I used to see stuff like this back in the city," Show said. "I never expected it to happen out here, once I came to live with my grandma."

"Tell me about it."

"Didn't know him all that long," Show said. "But he seemed like a good guy to me."

"When was the last time you saw him?"

"Practice Friday."

"He say what he was doing over the weekend?"

"It wasn't like that between Bobby and me. I didn't ask him about this, that, and the other. He didn't try to get himself on the inside of my business either. Maybe that's why we got on so good. He didn't need to be my best friend and I didn't need to be his best friend *for* us to be friends."

"So you wouldn't have been able to tell if anything was bothering him? Or if there was anything different about him lately."

He looked up now from his secretary-type notebook. Smiling like they were still talking about ball. Show knew the drill, from all those times when there were cops in the apartment.

Show thought: This is the part where he acts like he's *my* best friend.

"Just the same old Bobby," Show said.

"Can you think of any time over the last couple of weeks, since you guys got back from camp maybe, where he didn't seem like himself?"

It was all nice, casual, the cop-dad easing them both toward wherever it was he wanted to go.

"Nothing jumps . . . nothing that jumps into my brain," Show said. "But, like I might've mentioned, don't ask me what day it is when I've got my focus going on ball."

Show gave him the big smile. "My grandma, I was mentioning before? I call her Two Mom. She says she sees it come on with me when the season starts to come on. Like I put the whole rest of the world on some kind of mute button."

"I played some ball," Bender said. "I don't know if my kid mentioned that to you."

They always had to tell you, like there was some sign you were giving off that you gave a shit.

"And," Bender said, "I was never as excited about one of my own seasons as I am about this one." He closed up his notebook, even though Show knew that didn't mean anything. "By the way, was there some kind of problem with Drew Hudson at practice the other day?"

He knew there was, and Show knew he knew, or he wouldn't be asking. Detective knew about it from his own kid, and from every other kid who'd sat on the bench Show was on now.

"Oh *that*," Show said. "Drew gets all worked up sometimes when the coach gets on him."

"Upset enough to *cry?*"

"No, I can't say as how I ever saw him do that before, now that I think about it."

"You have to admit, it is a little unusual. Over the top, like they say."

He smiled at Show again. Show smiled back. Everybody smiling on everybody else.

Bender said, "You were talking about the coach getting

on his ass. Like coaches do. Did you hear about any of the
guys picking on Bobby, or Drew, anything like that, when
you guys were over there in Connecticut?"

"No, sir."

Shit. Did he answer too quick? Antoine always said if
you did that with a cop, they thought you were hiding something. Whether you were or not.

Hank Bender said, "You're sure?"

"Did somebody tell you different?"

"You mean, did my kid tell me different?" Bender shook
his head. "He doesn't talk about anything, ask his mother."
He shrugged. "I just remember how when I was on the
team, the older guys used to give the younger guys a hard
time. Just horsing around."

Show said, "Back in the day."

"I just thought you might have seen something. Or heard."

"No, sir." He paused and said, "But getting back to Drew
for just one second, that's just Coach's way. He gets on all
of us sometimes." Which was one of his good lies. "Me included. And," he said, "between you and me, he does go too
far sometimes. But that's probably just because I think he's
a little on edge, and whatnot, with the season coming on.
I'm just assuming, even though my Two Mom always tells
me that assume starts with ass, that he doesn't want to be
the coach known as the one who messed up me and Glenn."
Show held up a finger, like for emphasis. "*And* fine role
players like your Dave."

"Makes sense to me," Dave's dad said.

The cop trying not to act like a cop opened his notebook
back up then, made one more note. As he did, Show said,
"If I could make one more observation? Me and the boys
were saying that it was a little bit messed up to have that
ESPN guy around bothering Eric yesterday."

"What ESPN guy?"

"Ben Mitchell. Eric says he was waiting in the parking
lot after practice last night."

"I went to school with Ben Mitchell," Bender said. "But he doesn't work for ESPN anymore, as far as I know. He doesn't work for anybody."

"Eric didn't mention it to you?"

"No."

Show said, "Well, I'm just relaying what I heard, but Eric said this Ben Mitchell was acting like Bobby is almost like some case *he's* working."

Show was just going with it now.

"That's a little weird, don't you think?" Show said. "A guy waiting for one of the players in the parking lot and saying he's with somebody he's not with?"

"And he was asking about Bobby?"

"Along with this and that, at least according to Eric. I didn't get the whole story from him, he just ran it by me a few minutes ago."

"I'll have a talk with Mr. Mitchell, you can count on that," Bender said.

"My thinking? We got enough things, with Bobby and all, getting us all sideways. Don't *you* think? We don't need one more distraction."

This was more like it, Show watching Bender's face change, get set in a business way. He'd come in here asking the questions and now it was like Show was interviewing him.

Sometimes, Show thought, I got moves even *I* didn't know I had.

But to be honest, he'd been surprising himself for as long as he could remember, off the court as much as on. All the way back to when he'd first decided he was going to get off Gerard Avenue, not like gone-wrong Antoine, or fucking die trying.

Back when he'd first made up his mind that there wasn't *nobody* going to get in his way.

# 6

Drew Hudson didn't show up at school the day after he cried.

Not missing, Sam checked that out right away, just absent.

The only class he and Drew had together was Spanish, right before lunch. When it was over, Sam went straight to the list of Excused Absences posted on the big bulletin board outside the cafeteria. Drew's name was on it, which meant the school had been in contact with Shelley Hudson, Drew's mom.

That was Tuesday.

Drew Hudson missed school again on Wednesday. And Thursday.

For anybody else at school, it wouldn't have been a big deal. But missing school meant Drew was missing three straight *practices*. Sam knew that even for a backup point guard for Coach Ken Glass, it was a lot. Everybody who followed the team knew how things worked. It was cutthroat ball all the way. If one player moved out of the way, even if he got hurt, there was somebody waiting to move up.

The only ones safe were stars like Glenn and Show.

Bottom line? If Drew Hudson was sick with something, some kind of flu, he was *really* sick. Only he hadn't seemed to be suffering from any pulled muscles when he'd broken down in front of everybody.

Coach Glass had told everybody the day before that he had to be at some coaches' conference up-island, so basketball practice would be between seven and nine Thursday night. After school, Sam had driven over to the Tower Records in Shore Haven, next town over, bought the new Aerosmith, and come back taking the back roads so he could listen.

When he came up on the intersection of Whitaker and Church, the car seemed to take a right on its own.

Whitaker was Drew's street.

Sam had left a couple of messages on Drew's cell, saying he was just checking in, gotten no answer back. Now he drove slowly up Whitaker working out what he was going to say, that he was just driving by, bullshit bullshit bullshit. That they'd been friends for as long as either of them could remember. That he'd decided after what happened to Bobby that he wasn't going to wait around anymore when he wanted to do something nice for somebody.

Most of it was true. But only partly true. Sam had been waiting to talk to Drew for three days and didn't want to wait anymore. He stopped the car in front of 323 Whitaker, got out of the Volvo, now featuring the new radial tires his insurance had paid for, and walked toward the Hudsons' front door. Remembering as he did all the times he'd driven Drew home after work, right after Sam had first gotten his license, the two of them laughing their asses off about people who'd shopped at the store that day, turning into pretty good buds even if Drew was a year younger.

No cars in the driveway now. Garage door shut.

Sam walked up the front walk and noticed that even though the storm door was closed, the real front door, bright red, was wide open.

**H**e rang the doorbell anyway, waited.

He could see into the foyer in front of him, the stairs leading up to the second-floor landing, the small table against the wall, a vase of flowers on it. Antique mirror above the table. Around the corner was the door leading downstairs to the Hudsons' furnished basement, where Sam knew the plasma TV was, and Mrs. Hudson's Stairmaster, and the treadmill, and the Ping-Pong table, unless they'd changed things down there.

Sam knew this house.

Knew that if you walked up the stairs, you could look down over the railing to the immense living room and its high ceilings, the huge windows at the other end of the room facing out to the swimming pool in the backyard.

To the left of the living room was the kitchen.

No answer, no movement.

He rang the doorbell again and then tried the storm door. The handle turned. No big deal, he thought, the last person out had probably forgotten to close the red one, which really locked the house. Relax, for Chrissakes, this wasn't *Freddy vs. Jason*. Just because Drew was absent from school didn't mean he had to act like he was under house arrest. Maybe he had driven himself into town to get some meds at the pharmacy. Or his mom had taken him to the doctor's. Or he was in the shower and hadn't heard the doorbell.

People left their front door open in South Fork all the time.

Sam had been in this house plenty of times without even ringing the doorbell, or knocking.

He pushed the red door all the way open and stepped into the foyer.

"Hey?" he said. "Anybody home?"

Nothing.

He stared at his own reflection in the mirror in front of him. Like: Now what?

"Drew? You here, dude? It's me, Sam."

He heard music playing softly from somewhere upstairs, one of the bedrooms maybe. Go or stay? Sam stepped back and used the brass knocker on the red door, giving it a big rap, the sound of it like a gun going off.

"Helllllooo," he said.

He kept going. Past the open basement door, into the living room area. Kitchen table, one of those long butcher-block deals, to his left, still covered with the morning papers. An empty coffee cup on the counter next to the sink. Everything else pretty neat.

Message light blinking on the answering machine on the desk against the wall behind him, underneath a cork bulletin board. One of the things on the bulletin board was the full South Fork basketball schedule.

"Dude? You here?"

He started through the kitchen toward the front stairs, then stopped, because he thought he heard a voice from somewhere.

He knew Mrs. Hudson's bedroom, the master, was at the top of the stairs to his right. Down the hall were the kids' bathroom, a guest bedroom, the bedroom for Drew's sister, who was at Wellesley now, and Drew's big bedroom on the corner, facing out over the front yard. Where they'd played video games or instant-messaged guys after work. Or just laid around on the bed and the small couch in there and shot the shit.

The music was definitely coming from down there.

He walked down the hall to Drew's room, which they had changed around, Drew's desk against the wall as you came in now, a new bed, bigger than the one Sam remembered, along the length of the far wall.

Drew was on it, stretched out on his back, right arm hanging over the side of the bed, wearing a white South Fork t-shirt, the one Sam knew only the players got to wear. And oversized, down-to-the-knees white basketball shorts, the satin-y kind, with a black stripe going down the side.

His eyes were open, staring at the ceiling.

Or nothing at all.

"Drew?" Sam said. "You all right?"

Drew Hudson turned his head on his pillow, narrowed his eyes now, like he was trying to focus them.

"No," he said in a small voice.

Sam took a step into the room, pulled out his cell phone.

"*Don't!*" Drew said, his voice louder this time, stopping Sam in his tracks.

Drew tried to get himself up into a sitting position against the headboard. But when he did, his elbow missed the side of the bed and he rolled over, hard, to the floor, before Sam could get over to him.

When he did, Sam could see the blood on the back of the white shorts, and on the bottom sheet of his bed.

"Don't . . . tell," Drew said.

Sam stared at the phone in his hand, feeling like a dope, not sure if you could even dial 911 from a cell.

"What are you doing?" Drew said.

"We gotta get help," Sam said.

"Don't," Drew said again, looking at Sam with crazy eyes.

"Drew, I don't know what's wrong with you, but you're bleeding and I need to get you to the hospital," Sam said.

Drew said, "You take me." He looked up at Sam, eyes pleading. "Promise you won't call?"

Sam stuffed the phone into the pocket of his jeans. "Promise," he said.

Drew Hudson passed out.

---

Sam drove like a fucking madman to South Fork Hospital, calling ahead to tell them to meet him at the emergency room entrance.

This was after he had picked up Drew as gently as he could, put him over his shoulder, grabbed a blanket from the bathroom on the way by, cleared the garbage dump off the backseat of the Volvo and laid him down.

Then he had called Mrs. Hudson's law office, which was in town. The woman who answered said Mrs. Hudson was at a meeting out of the office. Sam told her to find her, and tell her that Drew had been rushed to the hospital, to get over there as fast as she could.

He'd called Mitchell then.

Now they were in the waiting room, Mrs. Hudson back somewhere with Drew and the doctors. Sam had looked at his watch when Mitchell got there. It had only been about forty-five minutes since he'd rung the Hudsons' doorbell.

Shelley Hudson had stopped in the waiting room only long enough to give Sam a hug and say, "I don't know how to thank you."

Sam said, "You don't have to."

Shelley Hudson said, "How did you even happen to be there?"

"I'll tell you later, Mrs. Hudson," he said.

Then she saw one of the doctors motioning to her, and ran.


Mitchell hung back while Sam talked to the kid's mother, then watched her run toward where he knew the two examining rooms were at South Fork Hospital, because the place didn't look as if it had grown much. It wasn't like *ER* on TV, not everybody's big-city idea about what emergency rooms were like. Mitchell flashed back to a touch football game when he was Sam's age, the day after Thanksgiving, one of the dads in the game rupturing his Achilles on the last play of the game. Even then, Mitchell knew things. So he knew that the cap-pistol pop he'd heard when he'd been guarding the guy meant to get him into the car and get him straight here.

When Drew Hudson's mother was out of the room, Mitchell came back over and said, "You did good."

Sam ran a shaky hand through his hair.

"When I saw the blood . . . "

"There was that much?"

Sam nodded. "He still didn't want me to call 911."

"His mom's a lawyer," Mitchell said. "Maybe he knows 911 brings the police into it."

"The first thing he said when I found him was 'Don't tell.'"

"Anything else?"

Sam shook his head. Mitchell saw how red his eyes were. Sam Perry was a cool kid, one who could handle himself with adults, who talked like an adult. But he wasn't cool now. Just a kid who'd seen bad things today.

Mitchell said, "You call your mom yet, tell her where you are?"

"*Shit.*"

"Call her."

Mitchell went over to the coffee machine, put his coins in, his theory always being that bad coffee was better than none. Sam was on the other side of the room, his little Nokia pressed to the side of his head, not saying much, mostly listening. When Mitchell got back over there, Sam flipped the phone shut and said, "She's pissed that I called you first."

"Don't worry," Mitchell said. "By the time she gets over here, she'll have figured out a way to blame that on me."

"Being a mom."

"Being a woman," Mitchell said. "Not that I'd ever want to be quoted on something like that."

They sat back down and waited. It's what you did, Mitchell realized, even when you were out of the game. He'd been talking to a journalism class once and one of the kids had asked him the secret of his success and Mitchell had said, "I lean against the nearest wall and wait for something to happen." So he had waited outside locker rooms, and outside courthouses after another famous athlete got busted for dope or sex or income taxes. Waited for buses to come at the Olympics.

Waited in some pressroom while the assholes from the players' union and the owners decided whether or not to shut down baseball again.

They sat there until Shelley Hudson came back, her high heels click-click-clicking as she made her way across the waiting room.

She ignored Mitchell and hugged Sam again. "If you hadn't been there . . . " she said.

Sam said, "I was worried about him."

Now she noticed Mitchell, staring at him until Sam said, "This is Ben Mitchell. He's a friend of . . . our family."

She gave him a strong handshake with her small hand. "Shelley Hudson."

Mitchell said, "Is he going to be all right?"

"Yes."

Mitchell said, "Do they know what caused it?"

She looked at Mitchell again, as if wondering why he got to ask the questions. "He's all right," Sam said to her. "You can talk in front of him."

She said, "They said something must have collapsed inside him. In there. Like a wall breaking down. . . ."

She bit down on her lip, but that was it, she started to cry.

"How?" Mitchell said.

He knew Sam wasn't going to ask her.

Shelley Hudson swallowed hard, started fumbling around in the bag over her shoulder, probably looking for a tissue. "They say it's too early to tell, that there could be a number of reasons. They can't even tell me when something could have happened to him. Or why the bleeding started now . . . "

Shelley Hudson dabbed at her eyes with the handkerchief

she'd finally found in her bag. Nobody said anything in the waiting room, until Mitchell finally spoke.

"Mrs. Hudson: Did you ask your son if someone . . . assaulted him in some way?"

"As a matter of fact, Mr. Mitchell, I did."

"What did he say?"

"He told me to get out of his room."

# 7

The black Ford Super Duty, DANEKO LANDSCAPING written in big block print on the side, was parked on the street in front of Mitchell's house when he got back from the hospital a little after six.

Behind the truck was a navy Taurus, Hank Bender leaning against the front of it wearing the same suit he'd been wearing in his office. With him was a big guy in an orange sleeveless parka, a beefy-looking guy with a day's growth of stubble, wearing a faded Yankees cap. The other guy, who had to be Eric Daneko's father, was taller than Bender, but fat.

At first glance, Mitchell thought Eric Daneko's old man would have had a better shot at climbing a fucking Alp than getting his parka zipped around that gut.

When Mitchell got out of his own truck, Bender and Daneko Landscaping were already walking toward him.

"Hank," Mitchell said.

"We gotta skip the preliminaries today, Mitch. This is

official business. Or at least semi-official." He nodded at the guy. "Got Art Daneko here with me. Eric's dad."

Mitchell nodded.

They all stood there until Art Daneko said, "Fuck this, Hank. Why don't you just get in your unmarked and leave me alone with this prick, so I can knock him on his ass."

"Or at least give it the old college try," Mitchell said.

Bender said, "Art, I told you I'd do the talking."

In a pleasant voice, Mitchell said, "Is there some kind of misunderstanding here, Officer?"

"Misunderstanding, my ass," Art Daneko said.

"Art, shut your pie hole," Bender said. "And Mitch? This is not the time to have a smart mouth of your own, trust me."

Mitchell could feel Art Daneko still eyeballing him. But Daneko shut up.

Bender said, "Art here has a mind to file charges for that little scene with you and Eric in the parking lot the other day."

Mitchell said, "Which statute about conversation in South Fork did I violate?"

"See what I mean, Hank?" Daneko said. "The wise fuck can't help himself."

"Hank," Mitchell said. "Seriously. I had a conversation with a kid after practice. Introduced myself. Explained a couple of things. He went home to dinner."

"Bullshit," Art Daneko said.

Bender closed his eyes. Said to Mitchell, "That kind of conversation is against school policy and against team policy."

"Policy I didn't know existed until after I started talking to the boy."

"The kid said you threatened him."

Even as juked up as the old man was, as ready to go, Mitchell said, "Then the kid is full of shit."

"The *fuck?*" Art Daneko said, and took a step toward Mitchell, meaning it.

Bender stepped behind them, put two hands on Daneko's chest and said, "The truck. *Now.*"

"But you're here on *account* of me," Daneko said.

"No," Bender said, "I'm here because your wife called and told me you were hot and on your way over. You're *still* here because you promised me you'd behave. Which I suspected was bullshit but was willing to have you surprise me on. But now that we're *all* here, I don't need any help. I got your version. I already had your kid's version. But you keep interrupting me. So now you go sit in your truck until I'm finished. Or just go home to Ellie, and thank her for calling me, because if she hadn't, I'd probably be booking you already on an assault rap."

Daneko stood there, chest heaving, said to Mitchell, "You go *near* my kid again . . ." left the rest of it hanging there, walked back to his truck, muttering to himself, fuck this, fuck that.

"It's not like when you used to piss somebody off in sports, but they couldn't touch you because you were a reporter. It doesn't work that way with the townies around here, you must've forgotten that."

"I've been threatened by worse—who didn't give a rat's ass whether I was a reporter or not, by the way."

Bender took Mitchell by the arm, walked him up on the front porch, as if it would be easier for them to talk if they put a little more distance between themselves and Art Daneko. Bender said, "Now, what the hell do you think you're doing trying to roust some high school kid?"

"He tried to roust a nice kid named Sam Perry first. And he tried to roust Sam Perry right before somebody fileted the tires of the kid's car and put a brick through the window of his mother's store."

"And you've decided to investigate on your own," Bender

said. "Since your most recent investigating in the newspaper business worked out so good for you."

"Hey, Hank," Mitchell said. "Go fuck yourself."

Bender let it go, like they were still kids in the locker room. As if any of them had ever left.

"Somebody reminded me the other day that only suckers believe in coincidence," Mitchell said. "I don't believe in it and neither should a good cop."

"You're saying I'm not? What, because your old man was a cop and you pretended you were one when you were still working for the newspaper? That makes you some kind of expert?"

"You know what I'm saying."

Mitchell turned around. Daneko was sitting in the truck, talking on the phone. Still eyeballing him.

Bender said, "Tell me about Eric and Sam."

Mitchell left out the part about Eric being drunk with Bender's kid at the girl's party, just said that Eric Daneko had let something slip about some sort of vague trouble over in Connecticut and Sam Perry had followed up on it, is all. "That was the trouble at the camp I asked you about before," he said to Hank Bender.

"And after we talked at the station that day, I asked my kid if there'd been any trouble over there. He said nothing he saw, or heard about. And when I went over to the school, I asked the other kids on the team, and basically got the same answers."

"And you believed them, of course. Because everybody in this town seems to be a team player."

"Hey, Mitch? Go fuck *your*self. And why'd you tell Eric you were with ESPN?"

"*He* told *me* I was with ESPN."

"You let him think that because you thought it might get him talking. These kids go weak at the knees if they even think a camera might come around, even when their coach tells them to zip it."

"Hey, Hank? Fuck Eric Daneko, too? It was easy for him to muscle a kid from the school paper. I wanted to let him know it was a little different with me, it doesn't impress me that he's got his varsity letter."

"That's what you do now? Settle schoolyard beefs?"

Mitchell said, "Can we talk straight for one minute?"

"Go."

"Something happened at that camp, whatever the kids are saying. Including your own. And it might be tied into the dead kid."

"You've been watching too many movies."

"I don't think so."

"You're calling these kids, mine included, liars?"

"I told you what I think," Mitchell said.

Bender said, "Now let me tell you what I think: Small towns like this get smaller all the time."

"Meaning what, exactly?"

"Meaning you got no status here. Far as I can see, as a matter of fact, you've got no place in this thing at all. No matter how many theories you got. And Art Daneko may be a hothead, but he's right, you got no right hanging around a school parking lot trying to scare some kid. Whatever that kid did to another kid."

Mitchell sighed. "For the last time, I didn't threaten anybody."

"You told him you were the last person in town to fuck with?" Bender said. "Guess what? You're not. But I am."

"I'm telling you, Hank, there's something going on around this team."

He'd promised Shelley Hudson he wouldn't say anything about Drew. Even though Hank Bender had to know by now. Along with half the town.

"If something is going on," Bender said, "I'll find out about it."

Mitchell said, "You sure you want to?" Then turned

around, not waiting for an answer, walked up the front steps and shut the front door.

**H**e fried himself a burger, with cheese and onions, ate it in front of the television while he watched Brokaw do the network news, paying no attention to the economy or Iraq, just thinking about Drew Hudson. Sure now that the kid had been violated in some way over at that camp.

Mitchell tried to put himself in the kid's shoes, imagine what he would have done at sixteen if it had been him. If somebody—one big guy, a bunch of big guys, boys who were supposed to be his friends—had held him down somehow. Because whatever the physical damage—enough that it had ended him up in a pool of blood before Sam found him—the mental and emotional had to be worse. You're going along, you're one of the cool kids in school because you've made the varsity, you're living out a happy life in Happyville. Then somebody puts you down and does something unspeakable to you while others watch. If that's the way it *all* went down.

Mitchell wondered if he would have had the nerve to come forward at that age.

Would he have wanted justice, or revenge?

Or just to have it all go away?

Would it be worth walking through the front doors of the school for as long as he was there and having every single kid and every single teacher know what had happened to him?

He turned off the television set and smoked a cigarette in his quiet house. Too much quiet in the house tonight, not nearly enough answers.

He went and grabbed the car keys off the kitchen table and drove into town and found a parking spot right in front of Jimmy O'Rourke's.

―――――――――

The original O'Rourke's, on East 50th in the city, had opened right after Mitchell got out of Syracuse. It had been an old-fashioned newspaper saloon that even the guys from out of town thought of as their New York headquarters, a place where columnists and reporters and TV guys and jocks and coaches and managers and stewardesses and models could drink and misbehave in a setting that the owner, Jimmy O'Rourke himself, said was completely off the record.

But then O'Rourke, who had no head for anything except big hair and big tits, took on some partners. Those partners decided to take the place upscale, expand, improve the food. O'Rourke liked things the way they were, thick steaks and cave lighting. They finally bought him out. He took his money and came back out to South Fork, where he'd first bartended as a kid. He'd even married the former United stewardess he'd taken back up with right before he left Manhattan.

Now the new O'Rourke's, which looked exactly like the original, was one of the places on Main Street that did good business year-round, even after the summer people had left. The food was decent, there was always a game on. Mitchell would sometimes come in late and sit with O'Rourke and talk about the old days, when Mitchell used to stop at O'Rourke's before he even checked into his hotel.

O'Rourke wasn't around tonight. The regular bartender, a funny little guy named Cal, said somebody had given the owner Knicks tickets, and he'd taken the train in.

Cal said, "He's got this thing for Marbury. It's the first Knick he's given a shit about since Clyde and Earl the Pearl retired."

Mitchell took a seat in the middle of the bar, making sure he had a good view of the game, ordered a draft beer, watched Marbury draw a double team and then throw a be-hind-the-back pass halfway across the court to one of his big guys, who said thank you very much, made a move on the guy covering him, drove down the lane and threw down a ghetto-fab dunk.

"Is this seat taken?" a woman's voice said.

He turned around and saw Kate Perry standing there.

"No," he said.

"Would you mind if I joined you for a minute? The rest of the girls in the book club are calling it a night."

"Please sit down," Mitchell said, and he motioned for Cal to come over. Kate Perry said she would have a glass of Pinot Grigio.

When Cal brought it, Mitchell clicked glasses with her and said, "Truce?"

She said, "I didn't know we were at war."

"I thought we got off on the wrong foot, and were just going to stay there."

"Sam's still a boy in a lot of ways, important ways, even if he thinks he's a man."

"I know."

"Now, after everything else, there's this thing with Drew."

"And you want to talk about that."

"Shelley Hudson is one of my best friends. Sam and Drew grew up together at our house, or theirs. She's in my book club, we play tennis twice a week. She was there for me when my husband died, I was there when Shithead left her for his Pilates instructor." She sipped some wine. "I had a long talk with her at the hospital after you left."

"She told you Drew won't talk."

Kate Perry nodded.

Mitchell said, "She told you she thinks somebody did something to him."

"Maybe even somebody on the team."

"And your son covers that team, and you think he's ask-ing too many questions and you're afraid for him."

"Don't stop now, you're doing fine," Kate Perry said.

"This really isn't a sociable drink."

"I want you to tell me, chapter and verse, exactly what you think is going on. And where it goes from here."

"I can do that."

"Then I want you to promise me my kid won't get hurt."

Mitchell said they'd probably have more privacy at a table.

Thursday was his mom's book club night.

Before she left the house, he'd asked who they were reading now, and she told him Elmore Leonard. She said it had been her idea, over the objections of the rest of them.

"Everybody else reads him for the bad guys," she said. "I like his bad girls."

She told him they were going to O'Rourke's for a quick bite afterward, this was the one Thursday of the month when they did that. She told Sam she'd be home around ten o'clock, and expected to find him studying.

He studied until seven-thirty, called the hospital and asked when visiting hours ended. The woman on the other end of the phone said eight-thirty. That was fine with Sam, he could go from there to the end of basketball practice.

Stay busy.

Even with the day he'd already had, the crazy shit with Drew, he was still hot-wired, knew he couldn't spend the night just sitting around on his ass. He left his mother a note saying he was going over to check out Drew, and promised not to be late.

"You always tell me there's nothing more important than being a good friend," he said at the end of the note.

You could never go wrong turning their own words around on them.

———

There were two wings at South Fork Hospital, east and west. The emergency room was part of the east wing. The receptionist there, pretty, with a Spanish accent, told Sam that Drew had been moved over to the patients' wing, which meant west. Second floor. The receptionist handed him a little site map, showing him how to get over there without going back outside in the rain that had started in the last half hour, one of those big storms that seemed to come out of nowhere off the water.

When he got off the elevator at Two West, the candy striper there said he had just missed Mrs. Hudson, she had left a few minutes ago.

"Is Drew expecting you?" the candy striper said. Her name tag read K. MORIARTY. Sam thought she might have been a couple of years ahead of him at South Fork, the face and name were both vaguely familiar.

"I'm the one who brought him in today."

"Oh, well, down the hall then, third door on the right."

Sam gave two quick raps on the door to 205, pushed it open, poked his head in. Tried to look happy to be there. Drew had his recliner bed propped up and was watching the Knicks on the small television on a shelf just underneath the ceiling.

Sam said, "Picking up pointers from Marbury?"

Drew looked over at Sam without changing expression, as if Sam were a nurse bringing a pill, then went back to the game. "Hey," he said.

Sam said, "I was driving by. You know, thought I'd check you out."

Drew said, "You didn't have to." He shot him another quick glance, said, "Thanks for this morning, dude."

Sam grinned at him. "You would have done the same for me. Except you wouldn't have been scared dickless the way I was."

Drew fixed his eyes on the Knicks. "I'm kind of tired right now," he said.

"I just wanted to stop by for a minute," Sam said. "I'm actually on my way to practice."

Drew said, "Kind of out of the way for practice." Then: "Practice tonight?"

"Coach had some conference in the city, and changed the schedule, just for today."

Sam stood in the same spot he always took in hospital rooms, about a foot inside the door. He hated hospital rooms, had hated them since his dad. He couldn't help himself, he went right back there now: All the hospital rooms at Memorial Sloan Kettering in the city, in Pittsburgh, Boston. Finally, at the end, here. He felt like he'd spent a whole stinking year of his life in hospital rooms like this one, watching his father get sicker and sicker, no matter how many times he was told there was a shot with this new treatment or this new medicine. Radical this. Alternative that. Trying every kind of shit under the sun, including something called sea cucumbers at the very end. Watching him get smaller and smaller, knowing every time he walked in that he was going to watch his father die a little more.

Sam said, "Well, I just wanted to see how you were doing."

If he didn't know better, he would have thought Drew had been crying again. Or maybe your eyes just looked this tired and bloodshot after you went through what he'd gone through today.

"Dude, no lie, they just gave me something and it's got me fixing to close my eyes."

Sam said, "Can I ask you something before I leave you alone?"

Drew closed his eyes. His expression saying: Shit, you too? "Would it help if I said, no, you can't?"

Sam played the only card he had, even if he felt like an asshole doing it. "I was even afraid to move you this morning. I didn't know how bad a shape you were in."

"I said thanks already."

"And what I've been wondering is, how come you didn't want me to call 911?"

Drew said, "I didn't want to make a big thing of it, is all." As if his ass was worn out from explaining the same thing all day.

"Were you scared of it getting out, or whatever?"

To the ceiling, Drew said, "You're a reporter now." Not even making it into a question.

"You know I'm your friend."

"Then be a friend and just bounce, okay?"

Drew had muted the sound on the game when Sam came into the room. Now Sam heard Mike Breen, the announcer, say, "*It's good!*"

"Drew," Sam said, "did somebody do some kind of messed-up thing to you that you couldn't talk about even if you tried?"

Drew whipped his head around, all filled up suddenly, eyes redder than before, and said, "Why can't you all just leave me the *fuck* alone?"

I've come this far, Sam thought, I might as well go for it. "Did something happen at camp?"

"You're talking shit you know nothing about," Drew said.

Sam said, "You sound like Eric."

"What did he tell you?"

"That I didn't know what I was talking about."

Drew said, "Just leave it alone, okay? Leave *me* alone."

"You ever think that maybe I can do more to help you than just give you a ride to the hospital?"

"How? By making me a story in the newspaper? Writing it all up?"

Writing *what* up?

Drew said, "You've helped me enough already, okay? Why can't you just leave it at that?"

Sam said, "I didn't come here to upset you."

"Whatever."

Sam opened the door, held it open.

"I'm going now," he said. "But I gotta be straight with you before I do: I think something happened to Bobby and that something happened to you."

"Just go. *Please?*" Drew's eyes and voice pleading with Sam.

Sam backed out of the room, the door closing in front of him. When he got outside, he leaned against the wall outside 205, next to the folder with Drew's chart in it, his heart pounding like a jackhammer.

Drew had said Sam was talking shit.

What he hadn't said was that the shit was wrong.

# 8

They were near the end of practice, the two teams on the floor going at each other hard, Coach Glass yelling at them like this was a real game, as Sam half-snuck up through the shadows to the top of the bleachers.

For once, Coach Glass had Glenn and Show guarding each other, and you could see they were taking it seriously, no bullshit or pretense that they loved each other like basketball brothers, just banging away at each other at both ends of the court, neither one of them backing up.

On the last play of the scrimmage, Show made this crossover move that not only beat Glenn but got his feet tangled up so badly he ended up on the floor as Show drove down the baseline and reverse-dunked the ball. When he came down, he turned at Glenn and pointed at him, like *Got you.*

Sam could see Glenn, still sitting there, glaring at him. He must have said something then, because Show stood under the basket, cupping a hand to his ear.

Even from the top of the gym, Sam heard Glenn shout, "You heard me."

"That's right, dog. And you *saw* me."

Glenn turned his back on him, nodding. Sam couldn't tell whether he'd said something more or not. But now Show was the one shouting all of a sudden. "You got something to say to me? Then say it to my face, yo!"

He started to walk toward Glenn now, but Glenn was already at halfcourt, shaking his head as he passed Coach Glass, who blew his whistle and told everybody to cut the shit and go shoot free throws.

Okay, Sam thought, so maybe they aren't Butch Cassidy and the Sundance Kid.

Glenn was with a group of shooters at one basket, Show with his own group at the other. Sam stayed at the top of the gym watching them, trying to think of a good reason for being here at this time of night, no other reporters around. Maybe the grown-up reporters had shown up before practice when they'd found out Coach Glass was going late tonight. Or maybe they just weren't interested in the South Fork players today.

Maybe everybody was starting to lose interest in Bobby Ferraro. Everybody except people in South Fork, anyway. Mitchell said it happened that way a lot. When you stopped advancing a story, coming up with some kind of new angle or wrinkle, you could see the thing start to run out of gas. Then there was a new angle, and all of a sudden it was bells and whistles all over again, and everybody came back on the dead run.

Sam's only thought tonight was to get a word with Glenn, who was more the team spokesman than Coach Glass sometimes. The sports editor at the *Press* said there was still time to add original reporting to the long piece Damon Wills was writing about Glenn and Show for the Sunday paper as part of their big high school basketball preview.

"If it's new, we want it," the sports editor said. "Even if it sounds old."

Maybe there was a way to get Glenn talking about what it was like not only to face the pressure of the town's expectations, but then have to face the pressure the media was putting on him and the rest of the players since Bobby died.

Mitchell said the questions hardly ever changed, but if you asked them often enough, sometimes the answers did.

Sam hadn't been in the locker room since he and Eric had had their little scene in the parking lot. He knew he was going to have to go back in there eventually. Just not tonight, when they were probably all rushing to get the hell out of there.

So he waited inside Mr. Doherty's classroom at the top of the steps leading up from the locker room. The classroom was even darker than the hallway. Sam thought: Schools are meant to be daytime places, loud and bright and busy. Not quiet like this. Spooky almost.

He saw Kareem Holyfield first, the other black kid on the team, a couple of inches taller than Show and Glenn. Then Christian Bowdoin, a small forward. Ed Fusco: a big blond backup center, a sophomore who was clumsy but still growing. Then Show Watkins, Show with that half-smile he always had on him, like there was some joke only he was in on, the smile seeming to go with the loose-neck way he had of walking, a slight nod going, as he walked toward the front doors. Sam wondered if this was a night when his grandma was picking him up, or if one of the other players was giving him a ride.

Drew had told him once it was weird with Show, even when he asked you for a ride he made it seem like he was doing you a favor.

He started to come out of the classroom, then saw Eric Daneko and Dave Bender, laughing about something, hoodie sweatshirts on them, too, Eric wearing an old Baltimore Orioles cap, ugly white-and-orange with the big ugly bird on the front, the cap turned slightly sideways on his head, Dave wearing a retro cap of his own, an old Astros cap that said "45s" on the front.

Sam had lingered a few minutes in the gym after practice, not sure if anybody had noticed him come in, not wanting to draw attention to himself as guys were leaving. Now he started to think Glenn had gone straight home without showering.

He came out of Mr. Doherty's classroom, and was standing in what felt like a small spotlight at the top of the steps when he saw Coach Glass coming toward him two steps at a time.

"Coach," he said.

Ken Glass wasn't as tall as Sam. But he was Coach Glass, feared by everyone in school whether they played for him or not, and it made him bigger. He had dark skin, blue eyes. Bright blue eyes that always seemed to be open wide. Everybody who followed South Fork basketball knew about The Look players or refs could get from him when he didn't like something on the court, which seemed to be most of the time.

Glass talked a lot about how much he loved South Fork basketball, but Sam always thought he had a funny way of showing it, going through life pissed off at just about everything and everybody. The only thing he really seemed to love about South Fork basketball, as far as Sam had ever been able to tell, was kicking the shit out of the other team.

Glass gave him The Look now.

"What are you doing, sneaking around here at this time of night?"

Glass's voice jumped at him like a barking dog.

Sam said, "I like to come to practice every chance I get, Coach. You know that."

"No interviews tonight, it's too frigging late. And most of the guys are gone, anyway."

Sam said, "Actually I was hoping to get just a second with Glenn. If that's all right with you, of course."

Glass was wearing one of those old-fashioned varsity

jackets, wool with leather leaves, SFHS on the front. "Glenn doesn't want to talk tonight," he said.

"He told you that?"

"Are we having a debate here, son?"

They were too close all of a sudden, Glass having moved in, gotten up on him, without Sam even noticing.

"I was just asking."

He could feel himself pressing into the locker in back of him.

"So then we must be done here."

Sam knew he should pack it in now, just get his ass the hell out of there. But for some reason, he imagined what Mitchell would think if he were watching the scene play out this way. So instead of leaving, he stood his ground and heard himself say, "With all due respect, sir, I was wondering how you could know Glenn doesn't want to talk to me if you didn't know I was here."

"Who said I didn't know you were here? Shit, this *is* starting to sound like some kind of debate."

Sam was determined not to look away, to stand his ground against the toughest guy in town.

"I saw you before," Glass said. "You don't have your friend with you tonight. The famous Ben Mitchell. Who thought it was okay to bust the balls of one of my players in my school parking lot."

"I think that might have been a misunderstanding . . . "

"You know what we used to call guys like that, back in the day?" Glass said, ignoring Sam's answer. "Shit-stirrers." Glass folded his arms in front of him, gave his head a tilt to the side. "You're not turning into a shit-stirrer, too, are you, son?"

He can't even remember my name.

"I'm just trying to do a good job covering the team."

"Is that so?"

"Yeah."

"Not *yeah*. Yes, sir. Or yes, Coach. I don't let my players talk to me that way and I'm not going to let you."

"I'm not a shit-stirrer, Coach."

"Well, if you're hanging around with somebody like Ben Mitchell, I think you are. I think you might be the kind of guy who wants to stir things up just because it makes a better story."

"No, sir."

"I was under the impression," Glass said, "that everybody in this town wanted this team to do well." Leaning forward now, his hand against the locker next to Sam, cornering him. The two of them nearly nose to nose now. "Apparently I was wrong about that."

Sam said, "I want the team to do well."

"And it's *going* to do well. So well that the whole country is going to know about South Fork High. And I will not allow anybody on the outside, and I mean anyfuckingbody, to get in my way."

"*Coach,*" Sam heard from the top of the stairs. "There a problem here?"

They both turned to see Glenn Moore standing there, smiling at them from underneath his turned-around Samuel L. Jackson cap.

Glass casually leaned back, smiled at Glenn, like there was no problem here. "Just having some fun giving the media a hard time," Glass said. "You know what you guys call me. King of the ball-busters."

"He *is* good at that, isn't he?" Glenn said to Sam.

Glass said, "You say good, or god?"

They all laughed, even though nobody seemed to mean it. When it was quiet again in the hall, Glenn said to Sam, "Did I interrupt some big interview?"

Sam said, "I was waiting for you, but Coach was telling me there's no interviews."

Glass said, "It's late, is all I meant."

Glenn said, "How about if Sam just walks me to my car? That would be all right, wouldn't it?"

Glass was looking at Glenn. Just not with The Look. A different kind of look now, one Sam wasn't sure he could identify. Curiosity, maybe. Because here was the coach of the team being told what to do by one of his players.

And going along with it.

"Fine with me," Glass said. "I was just looking out for the big dog." And he walked down the hall on his short legs, his sneakers making squeaky noises until he was gone.

That looked pretty intense," Glenn said when Glass was gone.

"If you hadn't come up the stairs when you did, I was afraid he was going to bite my nose off."

"He's a good basketball coach, but the man has his ways. You just have to get to know him."

"I do?" Sam said, and Glenn laughed his deep laugh.

They walked down the hall, took a right, heading down a longer hallway past the principal's office and the main entrance. When they were outside, Glenn said, "How's Drew?"

Sam looked at him. "You heard?"

"This is South Fork. You know. We're the kind of small town that makes other small towns look big."

"He's doing better. I just saw him, actually, before I came to practice."

"They know what happened to him?"

Sam said, "No. I think they've got more tests to run, or whatever."

Glenn said, "I might go by tomorrow. When I called him on the cell before practice, he said he didn't feel like talking."

"Same."

"So he didn't say how it happened?"

Sam said, "No. He kind of blew me off."

"Maybe something just went wrong inside him. Like a knee blowing out. Or one of those things like that actor, John Ritter, had? Where there's some kind of weak valve or whatnot, and nobody knows it."

Glenn made no move for his car. There were questions Sam wanted to ask him, but right now he couldn't remember any of them. Mostly because he couldn't get past the fact that he was standing here, shooting the shit with Glenn Moore, who'd always been the star of everything in South Fork.

"Did anybody on the team have a problem with Drew?" Sam said.

"This for print?" Glenn said, making it sound casual.

"That's up to you, I guess."

"Either way," Glenn said. "Because there was no problem I heard about."

"Nothing that might have happened over at camp? Something that started out as a joke and then got out of hand?"

Glenn smiled. "You know, ever since Bobby, we're kind of only supposed to talk about basketball. The coach said. I promised. And I don't break my word, to him or anybody else."

"I'm cool with that."

"But understand something: We're not trying to cover anything up."

"Understood."

"In answering your question, though, just speaking for myself?" Glenn said. "No, I don't know of anything."

Sam said, "How was it set up over there?" Push without acting like you're pushing, Ben Mitchell said. "Were you guys all in one big cabin?"

"No, it was a bunch of them. Small ones. Two guys to a cabin. I was with Dave. I think Drew might have been with Eric. Or maybe Christian. I forget."

"So something could possibly have happened in one cabin and just the guys there would know."

"*Not* for print now?" Glenn said. He was smooth with it, just sliding it in there. "I'm not saying something *couldn't* have happened. But I didn't see anything out of the ordinary. Or hear about anything."

"You think anybody on the team is mean enough . . . ?"

"Are we talking about Bobby here, or Drew?"

"I'm just wondering if somebody's mean enough to hurt somebody bad. Lose it all of a sudden."

Glenn said, "The only one with that kind of temper is Show. You saw practice tonight, right?"

"That little scene with the two of you at the end?"

"Show needs to do a better job of keeping his emotions under control," Glenn said. "He forgets he's not on the playground anymore, where anything goes."

"So you think maybe he's the type who could lose it?"

Glenn just smiled. "Oh, his bark is probably worse than his bite." He put his hand on Sam's shoulder. "Hey, we need to talk like this more often."

"When you're not rescuing me from the coach?"

"Now, Coach," Glenn Moore said, "his bite is much worse than his bark."


**M**itchell and Kate Perry sat at O'Rourke's a long time, past when the Knicks game ended. They both switched to coffee finally. He did most of the talking, laying it all out for her, though he had told her in advance he didn't have much more than circumstantial evidence. And gut feelings.

"Gut feelings," Kate Perry said. "I get a lot of that from my kid."

When Mitchell finished, she said, "So you want the doctors to tell you that even something done to Drew three weeks ago, or whatever, could cause a reaction like this?"

"I don't want anything," he said. "I'm just telling you that hazing is like some kind of epidemic on sports teams all across the country. High school, college, you name it.

And if that's what went on here with Drew, if somebody held him down and did something bad to him, then my theory, and your kid's, is looking better and better."

"You do want to be right."

"It used to be more important, frankly."

"But not anymore," she said, enough sarcasm in her voice that he knew she wasn't buying this.

He let it go.

"I've had these so-called gut feelings before," he said. "But they're the kind you only remember when you're right. It's like getting drunk. You only want to remember the times when you laughed your ass off all night long."

"I don't make you as much of a laugh-your-ass-off guy," she said.

"I wasn't talking about me, necessarily."

"Let's talk about you for a minute," she said. "And why you don't just cover this story yourself."

"It's not my story. It's Sam's."

"But if you called up some big paper and told them you were ready to get back in the game, they'd jump at the chance, wouldn't they?"

"If it were my story."

"You talk about it like it is."

"This isn't going to come as some kind of bombshell to you, but I see a lot of myself in your kid. At his age, I mean."

"Duh."

"So I want to help him."

"So help him by making him do the grunt work. You be the one out front." She leaned forward. "He's waiting to hear from Syracuse. He wants to go there like his hero, Ben Mitchell. He tell you that?"

"He just said it was one of the schools he'd applied to."

"It's the only one he cares about, the rest are all backup."

"He'll do great."

"If nothing happens to him."

"Nothing's going to happen to him," Mitchell said.

"Can you promise me that?"

She was a pretty woman with dark pretty eyes, locked on him now.

"No," he said. "I can't."

They sat there, like they'd reached some kind of impasse. Finally, he said, "I told the Daneko kid that anybody who messes with the Perry family from now on is messing with me. Though not exactly in those words."

"Not good enough."

Mitchell said, "Listen, Kate: I'm crazy about your kid, but that's the best I can do."

"If you tell him this whole thing is a dead end, he'll believe you."

"No, he won't. Not as long as shit keeps happening."

She gave him a long look and said, "To be continued."

She said she had come with one of the other women in the book club. Mitchell said it would be no problem to drive her home. When they got there, Sam's Volvo was in the driveway behind her newer Volvo, one that looked like a cross between a station wagon and an SUV. She said he didn't have to walk her in. Before she closed the door, she said, "I can't say it was fun."

Mitchell smiled. "You're tough."

"My husband was stubborn like you," Kate Perry said. "Then he died."


**H**e drove through town and up Ocean and parked the pickup in his own driveway.

He put his key in the lock, except he didn't need the key, the door opened as soon as he gave it a little push.

When Sam had told him about going to the Hudsons', he said that he hadn't been shocked to find *their* front door open, that was just the way it was in South Fork, people left their houses unlocked all the time.

Mitchell had said he didn't want to sound like a bad neighbor, but he always locked his own goddamn house when he left.

He stepped inside and before he even turned the lights on, he reached into the front closet and grabbed the Mattingly bat from just inside the closet door, where it always was. He'd never considered himself a big Yankee fan, he was always more a National League guy. But Don Mattingly was his all-time favorite ballplayer. One day in Fort Lauderdale, back when the Yankees used to have spring training there, he'd asked Mattingly for a bat and asked him to sign it. Explaining that he'd never asked anybody for an autograph in his life. Not even Koufax, after he'd gotten to know Koufax a little.

"You got it," Mattingly said. "But why do you want it?"

"Because they should all be like you," Mitchell had said.

He stepped out with the bat and turned on the lights in the front living room. The front room with its high ceilings in much more house than Mitchell could ever possibly need. It had been an old-fashioned Long Island saltbox when it'd been built back in the '80s: two stories, two small bedrooms upstairs, a small den downstairs, to your left as you came in. But then a German family had bought it from the first owner, at least according to the real estate woman who'd sold it to Mitchell, and the Germans had built an addition that was the same size as the original structure, same basic shape. Now the two wings were connected by the kitchen and Mitchell had more bedrooms and more space than he needed. But he liked the neighborhood, he liked the acre of land in back, he liked the view from the deck, he liked being able to walk to the Atlantic. He had turned one of the back bedrooms into his study. The front bedrooms had been turned into his television-watching area, and the exercise room, where he had some weights and a rowing machine he hardly ever used, and a fast bag hanging from the ceiling that he liked to use.

Lots of places to hide, if somebody wanted to.

But why would they want to?

In the waiting room at the hospital, Sam had told Mitchell that when Drew Hudson hadn't showed up for school that first day after he cried, Sam had practically run to check out the list of excused absences they posted someplace at school. "Not that I'm getting paranoid about this shit," the kid had said.

Mitchell thought: Who's paranoid now?

He carried his Mattingly into the big house with the creaky floorboards.

He put on the lights in the front stairway, walked upstairs, hit the light switch at the top. Nobody in the TV room, nobody in the exercise room. And who was he expecting to find, for Chrissakes? Some kid from the high school team trying to put a scare in him? A lard-ass like Art Daneko? From the start, Mitchell had wanted to make himself feel as if he were chasing bad guys. The problem was, he had no idea who they might be.

Maybe he'd just left the fucking door open for once.

He went through the kitchen now, put on the lights in the back living room, the ceiling just as high in there, all the way to the huge skylight the Germans had built in the center of it. Clear night, Mitchell saw, full of stars. He loved the sky out here, believed it got bigger, took on more definition and clarity, the closer to the ocean you got.

He went upstairs to his bedroom. He wondered if he should check the basement, too. If he needed to go down to where he had the washer and dryer and way too many boxes filled with too much stuff he didn't need before he'd totally convinced himself the house was secure. But he'd already acted like enough of a candy-ass for one night.

Hadn't he?

The last room to check was the study, before he looked outside on the back deck.

He was reaching around for the light switch in there when he saw the light from the screen of the laptop.

Something he never left on when he left the house.

Any more than he left the front door open.

Whoever it was had used a big font to put the message up on the screen. And done the right keystrokes to make sure the screen didn't put itself to sleep.

The letters were very big, in bold type.

**IF YOU HURT OUR KIDS
WE WILL HURT YOURS**

Mitchell sat at the desk and looked at the words for a long time. Wondering if whoever had written it thought he'd scare off like some high school kid.

Like Sam was supposed to have gotten scared off with slashed tires and a brick thrown through his mother's store window.

Sam: The high school kid was being threatened now, even if his name wasn't on the message.

A kid he hadn't known a week ago was *his* kid now.

Mitchell got up finally, checked around the office, without knowing what he was looking for, wanting to see if there was any other evidence that somebody had been in here. But somebody *had* been in here.

A ghost typist.

He'd deal with it in the morning. Maybe when he woke up, he'd have a plan for fighting ghosts.

They'd come to his house this time.

It should have been enough excitement for one day, starting with Sam finding Drew Hudson. Mitchell backtracked his way through the house, shutting off most of the lights, making sure the doors and tall windows in both parts of the house were locked down solid.

One thing about the house: If you were in the back, especially upstairs in the back, you couldn't hear anything from the other side, not unless Mitchell had the speakers on in the front living room. So there was no reason why he should have heard the other truck. And there was certainly no reason to expect that Art Daneko would be standing on his front porch when Mitchell opened the front door, Art Daneko not even having to ring the bell or knock before hitting him with a right hand that drove him back inside and put him down hard.

"I just wanted to make sure," Art Daneko said, standing over him, "that you got the message about leaving my kid alone."

# 9

Two Mom said to him, "How come you didn't tell me the police were at school?"

She had been watching Larry King but turned the sound down when he came in. Show didn't recognize who Larry was talking to, some older woman with blond hair the color of popcorn, the woman looking like she couldn't stop smiling even if she wanted to. Even when her name went up on the screen—"Barbara Eden"—he still didn't know.

"Wasn't no thing."

"Ex*cuse* me, Mr. *Wasn't* No?"

"Was just Dave Bender's dad."

"*Was* just?"

"I was just saying. You know."

"Oh, I know more than you think. See more than you think I see. Hear more than you think I hear. More than *any-body* in this town thinks I hear."

"Mr. Bender was just asking about Bobby, is all. Just doing what cops do. You know. Going through their motions.

He wanted to know if I'd noticed anything different about Bobby, there at the end. I told him Bobby had never been one to show you no moods."

She sighed. "Another double negative. How many times do we have to go over this? You want to *be* successful, you've got to *sound* successful. And successful is a whole different language."

She *thought*. But Show knew better. Show knew his sweet Two Mom would have a stroke right there in front of the television if she ever watched any music awards, listened to some of those successful rappers and their acceptance speeches.

He said, "Can't we be done with English for tonight? I just came out here to fix up a snack."

"All's you do is snack. I went to the IGA three times last week, trying to keep you stocked up on your twenty-four-hour buffet."

"Pretty soon," he said, "you'll be living large and I'll have people to shop for you."

"After college."

"We still got those good cold cuts?" Changing the subject like he was crossing over on her, bam bam.

Two Mom got up. "Let me, I know where everything is."

She followed him into the kitchen. She was in her robe and the slippers he got her last Christmas, the Uggs the girls at school told him she'd love because of their sheepskin lining, no backs to them.

"I want to ask you something now," she said, putting Zip-locked ham and turkey and roast beef on the counter.

"One second," he said.

He took her gently away from the counter now, sat her down at the table, while he started to get the rest of what he needed for his sandwich: tomato, lettuce, pickles, mayo, some hot sauce. Even the potato chips he was going to crumble in there once he got her out of the room. Lining up everything neat, in the order he was going to lay them on the bread.

He had to have things lined up.

It had been that way from the time he really started re-membering things, which meant the sixth-floor apartment on Gerard, 825 Gerard, him and Antoine, right before An-toine moved out, got his own place as soon as he graduated police academy. The two of them and Shadeeka Watkins, their mom. Looking back, he knew she had already turned herself out by then, that she had to be day-tricking even as she was telling him she was going from one waitress job to another. But then she lied to his face to the end, till he got the call telling him they found her in a room at the Milford Plaza, over there by the theater district. . . .

Antoine, ten years older, still hadn't come up on his own trouble yet, even if Show knew he should've seen it com-ing, just because of how mean Antoine could be, to him and everybody around, when he was of a mind. Because of the way he was always working his angles, even after he got his badge and all.

And still.

Even in that little apartment, a block up from Yankee Stadium, Show could still convince himself he was normal if he just could keep his shit *organized*.

Maybe that's why he always liked doing his big puzzles on the folding table in his bedroom, no matter how many pieces, no matter how long it took him.

Ninth grade was when Show had his big growing year, shooting to six-four, right past Antoine, a big boy himself. That was the year he finally gave Antoine his first good beatdown. Which had all started with Antoine messing with Show's side of their room one day before Show got home from school, taking his CDs out of their cases, mov-ing them all around, rearranging all the basketball trophies Show had already won on the top of the cheap bookcase. Just to fuck with his head.

Making a mess of one of his puzzles, leaving the pieces all over the floor . . .

Then Antoine had laughed when Show called him out on it. As soon as he did, Show had taken a big step and was on him before his brother knew he was coming, putting him down, until Antoine promised never to touch his shit again.

Things got turned around that day, and they both knew it. Knew that Show would be the man of the house after that, till Antoine left the house for good.

Show always said he was going to go visit him at Green Haven, never did.

Now Antoine was out, and things were better between them, even if there was a part of Show that knew Antoine only wanted to be his big brother and protector again because Show was about to make enough money to set all of them up for the rest of their lives.

Once Antoine was out, Show was afraid there'd be all these stories about the guy they called Antoine the Cop, but somehow his brother had kept himself under the radar for a change. After Green Haven, he'd done the rest of his time at a halfway house over by Rosedale Park, the other side of the Bronx from where they'd grown up. No job yet, even though he said he was on the lookout, you bet, looking for a new life 24/7. He'd call Show and start talking about family again, how that was all you had, how he was here for his baby brother now, whatever he needed.

Sometimes he'd take the LIRR out and Show would take Antoine over to Mallozzi Park and the two of them would shoot some hoops.

When he was gone, Two Mom would make this sniffing sound and say that was her impersonation of Antoine Watkins, the money-sniffer in the family.

In the kitchen now, she said, "You ready to talk now, or do you need all your focus on your Dagwood sandwich?"

"What's a Dagwood?"

"What we called a fancy sandwich like the one you're making yourself, back in the day."

"I was just thinking on Antoine."

"The brother who was supposed to keep the law, then broke the law," she said. "What was that movie that won Denzel the Academy Award?"

"*Training Day*," Show said.

"I saw the end on cable the other night. All that shooting in the end, I was afraid the blood was going to come squirting right out of the set. Your brother is lucky he didn't end up *shot* up like that."

"He'll be all right from now on. No lie."

"You better not lie to me. About anything."

"Two Mom," he said, feeling a smile come on and meaning this one, "it wouldn't do me any good to lie to you, you know more than *Extra* and *Access Hollywood* combined."

"That's why I know about Drew Hudson," she said. "The one I really want to ask about."

He kept on with a sandwich he knew would do Subway proud, laying in the turkey, then the ham, then the roast beef, a slice of cheese between them.

"Whatyouwant . . . What would you like to know about Drew?"

"I heard somebody did something to him."

"Where'd you hear?"

Two Mom said, "Around."

He dropped his head to the side. "You eavesdropping on folks, Two Mom?"

In her snippy voice she said, "I was doing my *ironing*. Mrs. Hudson called over to the Mayers' when I was there."

He knew not to go any further with it. Show wanted to laugh sometimes: They called him one of the big dogs, but he never felt that way when Two Mom came at him.

Two Mom could boss him better than any coach.

"So?" she said.

"All I know is what I know," he said. "He ended up in the hospital. Some kind of bleeding out his back end."

"Did something happen over there in Connecticut?" She was looking at him now, eyes lit up like the sparklers somebody usually had back on Gerard Avenue for Fourth of July.

"No."

"De*Shawn?*"

"I told you," he said, careful not to sound like he was backing up. "I know *why* he got to the hospital. I didn't say I was a doctor, Show, tellin' you what caused his situation."

He was done with the sandwich now, starting to put everything away. He never started in on one of his masterpieces until he cleaned up.

"You sure?"

"Yes."

"You watch yourself around here."

"You never stop worrying about me, do you, Two Mom?"

"Sometimes I worry that I ever brought you out here in the first place," she said, and then said she was tired of talking, she was going to watch the end of Larry and go to bed.


**M**att Ferraro wanted to explain that he hadn't been a bad father, as if Mitchell had been taking out ads in all the local papers saying he had.

"I spent more time with him than a lot of parents around here who act as if they should get medals because they coached their kids in soccer once," Ferraro said.

"You don't have to convince me," Mitchell said.

"Humor me," Ferraro said. "I'm trying to convince people one at a time."

Saturday morning. Back deck of the Ferraro house, the perfect backyard stretching all the way down to the little dock on Fogg Pond. In the distance, on the far side of the pond, Mitchell could see the beach, a single Jeep of some kind outlined against the backdrop of the ocean. They found Bobby over there, Ferraro said, gesturing vaguely in that direction. He said the tide had decided where, and when. Mitchell said he knew exactly where, he'd walked the beach the day after the police found Bobby, just to get a sense of the place.

"A friend of mine told me that if you're born Catholic, you die Catholic, whether you go to church or not," Mitchell said. "Reporters are reporters. I just wanted to see for myself."

"Are you reporting today?"

"That's hard to explain, too, since I'm between jobs right now."

He looked more closely at Bobby Ferraro's dad. Gray hair getting closer to white, cut short. One of those expensive short haircuts, not like the one Mitchell got every few weeks at Vinny's. A good tan. A handsome guy who didn't look much like his son, at least not in the pictures Mitchell had seen. Kate Perry said the boy had favored his mother more. "The art ditz from Santa Fe," Kate had called the mother at O'Rourke's. "Her new religion involves Southwestern desert blooms. It was yoga before that. The homeless before that. How far back do you want me to go?"

To the father now, Mitchell said, "I think maybe we can help each other, like I told you on the phone."

"I'm still not sure I understand how."

Mitchell had been awake since six, mostly because of the throbbing on the right side of his face. He was surprised not to find more swelling, more color under his eye. There was just a slight bruise, like he was a hockey player who'd gotten an elbow in the corner. The ribs on his left side hurt where Art Daneko had kicked him before telling him again that this was what would happen if he didn't leave his kid the fuck alone, stop poking his nose where it didn't belong.

He thought about calling Hank Bender, but had a feeling Bender might tell him he had had it coming. He called Matt Ferraro instead, because he had been planning to for a couple of days, not even sure if Ferraro was in South Fork or the city. Matt Ferraro picked up on the first ring. When Mitchell started to explain who he was, Ferraro cut him off, saying he remembered the name. He asked what Mitchell wanted and Mitchell said that maybe they could help each other out, but the best way to do it was in person.

Now here they were, each of them, with the steaming cups of coffee Ferraro had fixed for them in the kitchen. Matt Ferraro said the morning sun hit this deck perfectly, just the way the goddamn overpriced architect said it would, that you could sit out here in the dead of winter and if the sun was high up in the sky the way it was today, it felt like August.

"Sometimes on the weekends, Bobby and I would sit out here and he'd go through the sports section and tell me everything that had happened the night before," he said. "When I was here." He looked sideways at Mitchell. "We got along very well. More like friends than father and son."

He went back to staring at the water.

"In the summer, I have a Dauntless, little sixteen-foot whaler, and we'd take it out fishing sometimes."

"It's a beautiful spot," Mitchell said.

Ferraro said, "I'm thinking of selling. It's not the same view anymore. And isn't ever going to be."

They sat there sipping coffee until Mitchell said, "I've got some questions about the last few weeks of your son's life."

Ferraro made a little snorting sound through his nose. "Me, too. Unfortunately, he spent more time with the coach of the basketball team than he did me. Maybe he's the one you should be talking to. Sometimes I think Bobby looked up to Ken Glass more than he did to me. You know my kid's dream was to be a coach someday, right?"

Mitchell said, "I hadn't heard that."

Ferraro managed to squeeze out a small smile. "And I still haven't heard why you're here."

"I've got some theories," Mitchell said. "After you hear them, you might think I'm just an ex–newspaper guy with way too much time on his hands. But for now, I'd like what I'm about to tell you to stay between the two of us."

Mitchell told him all of it then, everything he and Sam

knew, everything they'd heard, starting with drunk Eric Daneko and all the way through Mitchell getting popped by Daneko's old man. He didn't rush, didn't stop to see if he was getting a reaction from Ferraro, just went through it like he was telling him an interesting story.

"You think Art is the one who left the message on your computer screen?"

"I was still lying on my back when he walked out the door, and asked him why leaving the message on my screen wasn't enough. He told me to go fuck myself," Mitchell said. "But the more I thought about it afterward, the more I didn't think it was him. I don't think he wanted to scare me, I just think he wanted to hit me and had been waiting all day to do it. Then he got a few pops in him and came over and did it."

Ferraro said, "Then somebody else wanted to scare you away from what . . . asking questions about that preseason camp?"

"Yes."

"And you think that whatever went on there might have gotten my son killed."

"With absolutely no proof or evidence of that. It's why it took me so long to come to you, and made me reluctant even to do it today."

Matt Ferraro stood up, mug still in his hand, walked over and leaned against the railing so he was facing Mitchell, all the water, the pond and the ocean, behind him. His sweater was as blue as the sky. It looked like cashmere. Everything about the house, the property, this setting, the guy himself, was money. The feel of it was in every room they'd walked through to get out here. Mitchell wondered if Bobby Ferraro used to feel rich here when he wasn't reading his father the sports section or getting ready to fish the pond with him, or just felt like the loneliest kid in the world.

Mitchell said, "I need to know if there was any evidence in the full autopsy report about anything being done to Bobby. Like what I believe was done to Drew Hudson."

"Anything," Matt Ferraro said.

"Something bad."

Ferraro said, "I never even asked . . . They said it looked like he'd been in a fight, but the official cause of death for now is still drowning."

"I'm not disputing that."

"Wouldn't something like you're asking about have been in the original medical examiner's report?"

"Not necessarily. If there's no reason to suspect, well, rape you'd have to call it, I'm not sure they would have had a reason to check. I called a retired detective from the city I know. Mick Dunphy. Lives in Florida now. He said that sometimes they do, sometimes they don't, depending on the profile of the victim."

"If I come around asking questions like this now, won't they know I've been talking to you?"

"I don't give a shit," Mitchell said. "If they give you a hard time, tell them you think the *Long Island Press* would probably find it fascinating that Bobby Ferraro's dad thinks the local cops might have overlooked something. Watch how fast that gets their attention."

"I'll talk to Hank Bender first thing Monday about the autopsy," he said.

"Thank you," Mitchell said. "I know you want this to be over."

"I wish." Ferraro turned toward the water now, giving Mitchell his back, taking it all back to where it started.

"One too many weekends away," he said. "That's the bottom line, no matter how much I rationalize it."

"You could beat yourself up about that forever and not change anything," Mitchell said.

Ferraro turned back around.

"And don't get yourself too worked up about Art Daneko," Bobby Ferraro's dad said. "At least he's here."

———————

Mitchell drove around the corner, stopped the truck, grabbed the notebook and pen he kept in the glove compartment, and did exactly what he'd used to do: He wrote down details about the house, the deck, the water, the design on the coffee mugs. He wrote down what Matt Ferraro said about not being there for his kid. There were times in the old days when he'd interview somebody and not even take his notebook out. Mitchell knew he'd remember what was important. When he was with them, he just wanted them to talk to him, not the notebook.

Don't get yourself worked up about Art Daneko, Matt Ferraro had said.

The funny thing was, Mitchell wasn't that worked up about it, even though he figured that somewhere down the line there would be a day when it would be just the two of them again, when the whole thing wouldn't start with a sucker punch.

He still didn't think Art Daneko had written the note on the computer.

Daneko just wanted Mitchell to leave Eric alone.

Whoever else had gotten into his house wanted him to leave it all alone.

Somebody in South Fork, somebody around the South Fork basketball team, was worried about what he was going to find out about Bobby or Drew. Or both. What he was going to find out and *who* he was going to find out. And maybe how it was going to affect the precious basketball season.

Maybe even put the season in jeopardy.

When those football players had gotten found out at Mepham High, they'd canceled the season.

Mitchell fixed himself a pot of coffee. When it was ready, he poured some into a tall thermos so he wouldn't have to keep coming down to the kitchen, and brought the thermos up to his study. He set it on the desk, turned on the computer, lit one cigarette the way he used to, just to get himself started, like he was using it to get an engine to kick over.

Then Mitchell went into Microsoft Word, opened a new file for himself—"South Fork"—and did what he hadn't done in a long time.

He wrote.

He knew he wasn't even close to having all the facts, so he'd write it like a short story, or like a treatment for a book. He didn't know who he'd even show it to once he was finished, other than Sam. And maybe Shelley Hudson, just because if he was ever going to advance this thing, he was going to need her son. But he wasn't going to worry about that for now.

Mitchell wrote.

# 10

This is, like, awesome," Sam Perry said when he finished reading it. "What are we going to do with it?"

Mitchell said, "Nothing."

Sam looked at him. They were in the front living room. Mitchell had a fire going. He was drinking a real drink. Sam had a Coke. Art Pepper was working his way across one of the great jazz albums, *Winter Moon,* as if playing for the championship of all the sax players who'd ever lived.

Mitchell had called and asked if there was anything new with Drew. Sam told him he was going home from the hospital tomorrow, at least according to Mrs. Hudson. Then Mitchell said he had something he wanted Sam to take a look at, and could he come over?

Sam said, "But when you lay it out this way . . . " He waved the ten pages in his hand at Mitchell, like he was in one of those old newspaper movies and something was hot off the presses.

"You could drive an SUV through the holes in it," Mitchell said.

"But it all makes perfect sense."

Mitchell said, "To us."

"But this is the best thing anybody's written so far on Bobby's death," Sam said. "Nothing else is even close."

Mitchell said, "Yeah, it's like one of those fake stories guys used to win Pulitzers for."

"What about if Mr. Ferraro gets what we want out of the autopsy report?"

"It will confirm what we already believe is true. But it still won't prove shit. It sure as hell won't prove that somebody on the team did it to him over in Deliverance, Connecticut. We're going to need an eyewitness for that. Which means somebody on the team giving somebody else up."

Sam leaned back in his chair and stared up at the tall ceilings of Mitchell's front living room. "So we may never find out why he died."

"Not without help."

"Where's that coming from?"

Mitchell said, "Drew Hudson has to tell."

Mitchell got up and put another log on a fire that seemed to be going pretty good to Sam already. Sam remembered it being this way with his dad. It must be something that kicked in for guys when they got older, constantly screwing around with fires that already looked like the end of a disaster movie.

Sam said, "Can't the police make him tell?"

"You mean because they're so hot for our theories already?"

"You think Mr. Bender doesn't want to know the truth?"

"I think Hank Bender's a good man. I think he wants to be a real detective on this. But you can't be if you're afraid of what you might find out."

Sam said, "You think he's afraid Dave might be involved?"

"Put it this way: It were me? My kid on the team?

Somebody going around asking the questions we're asking? I'd be very afraid."

"They all should be afraid of Drew, then. The one who did it to him, I mean."

"You bet. That's why I want you to go see Drew again, first chance you get. You know the kid. Get a read on where he is after spending a few days lying on his back. Then, when the time is right, maybe we need to try an intervention with him, if I can convince his mother to go along."

"I know I should know what an intervention is."

"Like when somebody has a drug problem, or the kind of drinking problem my old man had. It's sometimes a last resort, you gang up on them. Get the people closest to him in a room. Surprise him with it. Then try to convince him to get help by telling him he's not just ruining his life but everybody else's around him."

"Did that work with your father?"

Mitchell shook his head.

"He just kept coming home drunk and pissed off and cuffing me around until he finally flipped his car one night over in the Bays, on that hard curve before you get to the Rusty Nail."

Mitchell got up and screwed with the logs again.

Sam said, "You think that will work with Drew?"

"He's the only one who can tell us the things that Bobby can't," Mitchell said.

Then he said that on Monday, he might go have the kind of chat with Coach Ken Glass that he had had with Eric Daneko the other time.

"But they don't want you around the team," Sam said.

"He's not the team," Ben Mitchell said. "Even though he thinks he is."

**M**itchell suggested Sam call his mother to see if the three of them might catch an early dinner at O'Rourke's, but

Sam told him she was having dinner with Mrs. Hudson at some new restaurant over in Two Mile Harbor. And that she damn well expected him to be home working on his English paper when she got home.

"It sounds like you and my mom have stopped fighting," Sam said.

"It's more like we're negotiating the terms of the cease-fire."

"She said you guys had a good talk the other night."

Mitchell said that a more honest analysis, in language Sam could understand, was that the evening didn't suck.

When the kid was gone, he fixed himself some pasta with Rao's sauce, checking every so often to make sure that the fire was still going. When he'd finished cooking up the pasta, he poured himself a glass of red wine, set himself up in front of the television, and watched Jason Kidd. Mitchell loved the young guys in basketball like LeBron and Carmelo. The NBA's version of Show and Glenn, he thought. LeBron from the projects, Carmelo with the smart sound-bite momma talking about how her boy was always going to college, even if it was only for a year. But Mitchell still liked watching Kidd play the point more than anybody else, at least when he wasn't staying with a women's game on television because Diana Taurasi had the ball.

When he was done with the Nets game and with dinner, he went back upstairs and fooled around a little more with a piece only Sam might ever see, trying to get it just right. Mitchell always loved rewriting long pieces, after all the times—what felt like a thousand nights of his life—he tried to make some column perfect over the phone, five minutes past what was supposed to be his deadline.

He got tired of staring at the screen finally, at the story he couldn't prove, went back downstairs, secured the house, and even set the alarm, using it for the first time since he'd moved in. He'd even had to call Bellringer Security to find out what his password was in case he set the sucker off. He went to bed and was shocked to discover when he awakened that he had slept until noon.

He took his sweet time showering and getting dressed, then put on an old Syracuse windbreaker and took a walk to the beach. When he came back, it was almost two o'clock. He drove to Hiram's, found a parking space right in front, went to the back booth, ordered himself up a late breakfast of eggs and ham and toast, with even a plate of pancakes on the side.

When he'd finished ordering, Laurie the waitress said, "Are you going to the chair later?"

He was reading the sports section of the *Times* when he looked up in time to see Sam Perry come charging through the front doors, nearly taking out a small blonde in black exercise tights, spilling some of her takeout coffee on her.

When the blonde turned around and Mitchell saw the way she filled out the exercise tank top underneath her un-zipped sweatshirt, he thought about going over and volunteering to help pat her down.

Sam was still apologizing when he spotted Mitchell in the back.

When Sam got to the table, Mitchell said, "That's the same move I used to make when I wanted to meet flight attendants."

Sam was out of breath.

"You haven't heard, have you? I left a message."

Mitchell said, "I slept in, then took a long walk on the beach. I forgot to check my machine before I came into town."

Sam leaned down, hands on the table, trying to keep his voice low.

"Drew tried to kill himself," he said.

# 11

Sam's story:
It turned out the hospital had sent Drew home early Saturday night, telling him to go get a good night's sleep in his own bed.

Shelley Hudson had called Kate Perry with the news. When she told Sam, he asked if it would be all right to call Drew. She said she couldn't imagine why not, unless Shelley answered the phone and said it wasn't. But Drew picked up the phone himself, saying his mother was out buying supplies. Sam took a deep breath, asked if he could come by in the morning, just to check him out.

To his surprise, Drew said sure, why not?

Sam went over about ten. Drew was in the living room watching ESPN. He seemed to be in a much better mood than when Sam had seen him at the hospital. And looked better, his eyes not as bloodshot, his face with some color back to it.

Mrs. Hudson came in after a while, said she was going to

the store, do the kind of real shopping she hadn't had time to do last night. Said she'd leave them alone to have a real visit and that she had her cell with her in case they needed her.

When she was gone, they bullshitted for a while, Sam asking when Drew thought he might be able to practice with the team again, Drew saying maybe as soon as the end of the week, according to the doctors. Depending on how fast his legs came back, he said, he figured he'd be ready for the start of the season for sure.

He said he'd talked to the coach, and that his spot would be waiting for him when he was ready.

"That sounds way too nice for Coach Glass," Sam said.

Drew said it shocked the shit out of him, too.

Sam said, "Maybe he's the one on some kind of medication, not you."

Drew said that some of the other guys had been by the hospital. Christian and Glenn. Dave and Eric. Ed Fusco and Tommy Mayer. A couple of other guys from the second unit.

When Drew got up to go get them a couple of Cokes from the kitchen—"We'll hide the evidence before Mom gets back"—Sam observed how slowly he was still moving. Stiff. When Drew came back with the Cokes, he grabbed the TV remote and zapped his way through the channels until he stopped at MTV, where Sam saw that Nelly was trying to break all his own crotch-grabbing records.

Finally, Drew said, "I acted like a dick the other night when you came by to see me."

"You had a right."

"No, I didn't."

Nelly's face on the screen was replaced by Andre 3000. When they went to a wide shot, you could see the rest of the guys in the Outkast video, all wearing purple suits with green hats.

Drew said, "Anyway, I've been thinking a lot about what you said."

Sam waited. Remembering, he told Mitchell now, how Mitchell had once told him that sometimes the best way to get the other guy talking was to keep your own mouth shut.

"I've had, like, way too much time to think, dude," Drew said.

Sam was careful, not wanting to make it sound like he was pushing. "If somebody messed with you . . . in some way . . . they shouldn't get away with it."

"It's not that simple."

Sam said, "I've got a pretty good handle on this."

Drew said, "I know you *think* you do."

It was there that Sam, on an impulse he said, told him he had something in the car he wanted to show him.

He ran out and got his copy of Mitchell's piece, came back and handed it to Drew. He read the first page, looked up, and asked who had written it. Sam told him Mitchell had. Then Drew turned down MTV and sat on the couch and read all ten pages while Sam flipped through the sports section of *Newsday*. Every once in a while, Drew would look up. "Eric?" he said at one point. Sam nodded.

Or: "Mr. Daneko popped him?"

Sam told Drew that Mr. Mitchell's version was that it was a sucker punch.

A couple of times, Sam was afraid Drew might start crying, like he had in the gym that day.

When Drew finished, he put it down on Mrs. Hudson's antique coffee table and said, "He writes a lot like you."

"No, I write a lot like him."

"It's really good," Drew said.

"Yeah," Sam said, "but is it *right?*"

Sam said that Drew nodded his head. "The right *track.*"

Neither one of them said anything, until Sam, in a soft voice, like he was trying not to wake anybody in the house, said, "Who?"

He saw Drew staring off, like he was looking at the

house across the street. Almost to himself, Drew said, "I've got to think about this a little more."

Sam said, "But you're telling me that the bare bones of it are true? They did something to you?"

Leaving Bobby out of it.

Sam told Mitchell that Drew nodded again.

"This isn't the time," Drew said. "My mom'll be back any minute . . . "

"But you're not going to let whoever did this get away with it, right?"

There was another long pause, Drew with his eyes closed, Sam worried that he'd fallen asleep, before Drew said, "I can't."

Drew pointed at Mitchell's piece.

"How many people have seen this?"

Sam told him no one except the two of them.

Drew said, "I'll call you later, I promise."

Sam said that Mrs. Hudson wanted him to stay until she got back. Drew said he was good, don't worry about it. As Sam started to walk out of the room, Drew held up Mitchell's story and Sam told him to keep it.

"Have you told your mom any of it?"

"No."

"Maybe it would be easier telling her with Ben's story," Sam said.

Drew said he would think about that, too.

It was nearly eleven o'clock by then. Sam went home, decided to go for a run, get his head clear on what had just happened. Second-guessing himself that he hadn't come at him a little harder, got more out of him. When he was finished with his run, he did what Mitchell had done, wrote up the whole scene, what they'd said to each other, just so he wouldn't have to remember it later.

It was around an hour later, Sam said, when Kate Perry picked up the phone and it was Shelley Hudson screaming at her, wanting to know what Sam had said to make her kid swallow a whole fucking bottle of her fucking Valiums.

**M**y son is out of this now," Kate Perry said to Mitchell across her kitchen table.

She'd finished telling Mitchell, and Sam, about going straight over to the hospital and finally convincing her friend Shelley Hudson that Drew was fine when Sam left the house.

"I know she's just being a mom," Kate said. "And I know she wants to blame somebody. I just didn't want it to be my kid."

"So *you* were being a mom," Mitchell said.

"It's why I want you to tell him to quit now," Kate said. "You know everything Sam knows. You take it from here."

Mitchell and Kate were drinking coffee in the late afternoon. Sam had a hot chocolate in front of him that he hadn't touched. He was mostly watching his mother and Mitchell go back and forth.

Mitchell was being careful with everything he said, afraid Kate Perry would jump on the first wrong word that came out of his mouth. Like some sleek-looking cat, ready to pounce.

"This isn't Sam's fault," Mitchell said.

"But when Shelley says that Sam was the last person to see Drew, what do I tell her?"

Mitchell said, "Tell her she has absolutely no way of knowing that right now."

Kate Perry started to say something, then drank some coffee instead. Mitchell noticed that her dark hair had a shiny look to it, mussed a little, as if she'd just come out of the shower before he and Sam got there. There was also a scrubbed look to her face. If she used makeup, she didn't use much. "Another visitor to the Hudsons is just more the-

ory you can't prove," she said. "Which makes it like most of
your other theories."

Mitchell said, "Does it sound to you like Sam was pushing so hard he pushed him right over the edge?"

Kate Perry said, "How do you know what it takes to
push somebody over the edge, exactly?"

Mitchell said because he had done it himself once, then
told her about Tom Robards.

When he finished, there was just the sound of the wind,
coming from the north today, against the kitchen windows,
and the tick of the big antique clock over the telephone.

"I'm so sorry," she said. "I never knew the whole story."

"Neither did I," Sam said.

"Robards knew and I knew," Mitchell said. "Then he died."

"And you quit because of that," Kate said.

"It wasn't the only reason," he said. "Just the last one."

He sipped some coffee now, his mouth dry. "I told myself at the time that if I could find out Tom Robards's secret, somebody else would, too, eventually. If there's one
thing you learn in this business, it's that somebody always
finds out your secrets. Even in South Fork."

Kate said, "You really think somebody else could have
been with Drew after Sam left?"

Mitchell said, "Or he could have gotten a phone call.
One of his buddies threatening him all over again."

"Mom, I'm telling you," Sam said, "when I left, it was
almost like Drew was on my side."

"I don't care!" Kate Perry slammed her mug down,
spilling coffee on the table in front of her. "This thing is
taking over our goddamned *lives!*"

"It's what happens when you're not willing to let things
go," Mitchell said.

"Well, I want Sam to let go."

Mitchell said, "Sam is in this because he doesn't want some punks to get away with this. That's what he told Drew. Not to let somebody get away with something. And today, Drew was nearly on board with that. Then, a couple of hours later, he changes his mind and decides to end it all? Does that make *any* sense to you?"

Kate said, "He's clearly unstable."

Mitchell reached over and covered her hand, doing it before he even knew he was. "He's unstable because they *did* something to him."

Kate Perry didn't move her hand. "I understand why my kid's obsessed with this. These are his friends. His school. But why won't you let go?"

"Because too many people want me to all of a sudden," he said. "Somebody thought it would be easy to run Sam off. It's harder with me."

Then he told her about the piece Sam had left at the Hudsons', that Shelley Hudson would understand everything a lot better if she took the time to read it.

"What piece?"

"Something Ben wrote," Sam said. "About the whole thing."

Mitchell said, "It's no work of art. Just tell her to read it when she gets a chance. Then we'll see who she wants to blame."

She said she'd do that when Shelley Hudson called. If she called.

Then said she'd walk Mitchell to his truck.

"I'm sorry I yelled before," she said.

"Tell your friend to read the story, it's pretty good."

"I'd like to see a copy of it myself. When you went to the bathroom, Sam said he'd never be able to write that well."

"Yeah, he will. An old columnist I knew once told me the whole trick was finding your voice."

Then he told her not to let Sam beat himself up and went home.

Kate called a few hours later, saying she had just talked to Shelley Hudson, the doctors had finally told her to go home, that if they were lucky, Drew would wake up tomorrow, that Valium comas like the one he was in usually lasted for only one to three days.

"So they think he'll come out of it."

"Fingers crossed." There was a pause. "But that's not why I'm calling."

Mitchell waited.

"I just got off the phone with her. We had a good talk. I explained about Sam all over again. And that he doesn't lie. So if he said Drew was fine when he left, Drew was fine when he left."

"She okay with that?"

"I think they might have given her a couple of happy pills to take when she got home."

"Just to take the edge off."

"Anyway," Kate said, "here's the thing. Your piece? The one you wanted her to read? It's gone."

"Maybe Drew threw it away. She check the garbage?"

"She said the garbage guys had pushed everybody back this week. So they just picked up at her house yesterday. The only garbage bag is in her kitchen. She checked the wastebaskets all over the house. Nothing."

"Maybe he hid it."

"She needed something to get fixed on tonight. It sounds like she turned the house upside down looking for it. Ben, she's convinced it's not there."

"Which means somebody took it."

"So somebody else *was* there after Sam," she said. "That's a big deal, right?"

Mitchell said, "Only if we find out who."

# 12

Mitchell knew the drill. Suicide attempts resulted in police reports. Police reports, especially in small towns like this, ended up in the newspaper. So the news about Drew Hudson got out fast.

The next morning, the media came back.

Near-death gave life to a fading story.

Drew Hudson's overdose didn't put the story back on Page 1, but it moved it back toward the front of the paper in the Monday editions of *Newsday* and the *Press*.

After breakfast at Hiram's, Mitchell walked down Main the way he had the first time he'd gone to see Hank Bender, took a right, and saw that a couple of satellite trucks were back, one of them from Channel 12, the other unmarked, which made Mitchell think it might be from the smaller cable station in Two Mile Harbor. He went inside the police station and asked the young cop at the front desk if Hank Bender was around. The cop said no. Mitchell asked if he had any idea when Bender would be back. The cop said no.

Would you like to leave a message? Mitchell said no, and left. On his way back down Main, he saw a news bunny interviewing the elderly woman who worked part-time at the front desk of the South Fork Library.

He was in front of Mayer's Hardware when he saw Coach Ken Glass come out of the Starbucks next door, Glass carrying a big cup of what Mitchell assumed was some kind of tricked-up coffee. Grande or vente, he could never keep the Starbucks size chart straight.

Mitchell hung back and watched Glass cross the street toward Hiram's like somebody was timing him, even if there was no traffic coming from either direction on Main. Glass came out of Hiram's a minute later with newspapers under his arm, walked around the corner, past the firehouse, and took his coffee and his papers to the bleachers that were on the third-base side of the better of the two Little League parks in South Fork, this one with local advertising on the outfield walls. It was a good morning to sit outside and have a grande or vente Starbucks and read the papers, the November sun high in the sky.

Mitchell had been wanting to talk to Ken Glass and now here he was. It was the closest thing to good luck he could remember lately.

"Morning there, Coach," Mitchell said.

Glass had the *Daily News* opened in front of him. He pulled the paper down as if Mitchell had startled him.

"Good morning doesn't mean sneaking up on people," Glass said. "Christ."

"Sorry."

"And don't bother introducing yourself, I know who you are."

Mitchell smiled. "Well, now that we've got all the awkward ice-breaking out of the way."

Glass shifted uncomfortably on the bench, as if Mitchell standing over him this way made him feel even smaller than he already was. He made a motion like he needed to move his coffee out of the way and rearrange his papers, and as he did, he moved up about three rows, then sat back down.

Now Mitchell had to look up to talk to him.

"I don't know why you're here," Glass said. "I have nothing to say to you, except to remind you to stay the hell away from my players."

Mitchell stood there, hands in his pockets, still smiling at him.

Glass said, "Oh, and by the way, not bothering them means not bothering me."

"It's too nice a morning for me to be bothering anybody."

"I talk to who I want to talk to."

"Sam Perry, for instance."

"Now, what is *that* supposed to mean?"

"It means I heard you ran into him after practice the other night."

Mitchell really wanted to talk to him about Drew Hudson. But there was plenty of time for that. And this seemed like more fun.

"So?" Glass said. "He covers the team. I saw him in the hall, it was late, I have a right to ask the kid what he was doing there that time of night."

"Covering the team, I imagine."

"There weren't any other sportswriters around, I was just curious."

"He said you didn't act curious. He said you acted pissed off."

Glass put his thumbs against his temples and rubbed them hard, as if trying to get a headache to go away. "Do I have to go someplace else to read my papers in peace?"

Mitchell nodded at *Newsday,* on top of his pile. "You read about Drew?"

"I didn't need to read about it, I heard yesterday almost as soon as it happened. I was over to the hospital last night, sitting with Shelley. His mom."

"Coachly of you."

"Is that supposed to be sarcasm about a kid in the fucking hospital?"

"I was just pointing out it's what any good coach would do."

"Can I ask *you* a question?" Glass said.

"Shoot."

"Where we goin' with this?"

"I was just thinking that you're probably wondering what I'm wondering," Mitchell said. "A normal kid, a kid who's got the status of making your team, suddenly tries to kill himself?"

"Is this an interview?"

"I'll tell you what I tell everybody else: I've got nobody to interview *for*."

Glass said, "Who knows why teenagers do what they do these days? I saw some piece on one of those cable networks the other night, one of those NNs, about how the suicide rate for kids is way up. You think they all wear a sign beforehand, they're gonna do it?"

"See, but that's the thing. There *were* signs with this kid."

"'Cause he cried that day?"

"He cried. Then gets rushed to the hospital after Sam Perry finds him. Comes home. Seems perfectly fine yesterday morning. Next thing you know, he's throwing Valium down his throat."

Glass sipped some of his Starbucks. "Even if I did know, which I don't, I wouldn't tell you. Not after the way you acted with Eric."

"I just told Eric not to get in Sam's face again. Which I consider outstanding advice for anybody, by the way."

"We talking about Eric now, or me?"

Mitchell heard the loud wail of the ambulance siren, turned and saw the flash of red lights flying east on Main Street.

"I hear you're the kind of coach who likes to know

everything about his players," Mitchell said. "I read in the clips, you said one time that the more you know, the easier they are to control."

"Kids want structure. They want to know where the line is, the one they can't cross. It's my job to show them. Because some of them got parents who don't have the time, or who just don't give a shit."

"What happens when somebody crosses the line?"

"I deal with it and move on."

Mitchell took one step up, leaned in, so now he was in Coach Ken Glass's space. "I think some of your guys crossed the line in Connecticut. I think they crossed it with Bobby somehow, and crossed it with Drew Hudson so badly he'd rather kill himself than deal with it. And I'll bet everything in my wallet and yours that if they did, you knew about it."

"I don't know what you're talking about," Glass said, sliding to his left and standing up.

"I think you do."

"Well, fuck what you think you know, and fuck you," Glass said.

His feet made loud noises on the aluminum as he made his way down. "Hank Bender's going to hear about this, you can count on that."

"Hear about what? A talk in the park? A rough, tough guy like you is going to run to the cops with that?"

"You're pushing the wrong guy in the wrong town," Coach Ken Glass said.

"I doubt that very much."

"Stay out of my season."

Mitchell said, "When the shit came out about the football team at Mepham High, they canceled the season."

Glass opened his mouth, closed it, walked back up the street, past the firehouse, and got into the black Lexus he'd parked on the side street next to Hiram's. He opened the driver's-side door, gave Mitchell that Look everybody in

South Fork talked about, the one that was supposed to make him go weak at the knees, then drove off, alone in the sleek car with his bad self.

There was a message to call Matt Ferraro when Mitchell got back to the house. A 212 number he said was the direct line in to him at his firm, and also a cell number in case he was out to lunch. Mitchell called the office number and a woman with a British accent answered and Mitchell told her he was returning Mr. Ferraro's call. Could he possibly hold for a moment?

When Ferraro came on, he said, "I heard about Drew this morning," before he said hello. "How's he doing?"

"Still sleeping, as far as I know."

"But they expect him to wake up, don't they?"

"In theory it could be any time now. I don't know what the exact amount in grams or milligrams it was, but the doctors keep telling his mother it wasn't enough to do the job."

"Why'd he do it?"

"Maybe he'll tell us when he wakes up."

"Okay, then," Ferraro said. "I talked to Hank Bender and asked him what you wanted me to ask him."

"He ask why you wanted to know all of a sudden?"

"Your name didn't come up, if that's what you're asking. I just told him I've had a lot of time to think, and that maybe I didn't ask the right questions at the time."

Mitchell said, "So did they check him internally?"

"They did."

Mitchell was upstairs on the outside deck, clouds off the ocean having erased the sun from the afternoon, his fleece on, noticing this had become one of those late-fall, early-winter days when the water and the sky seemed to be the same pale shade of blue.

He waited.

"They didn't find anything," Matt Ferraro said. "Then he

told me more than I ever needed to know about the lining of the rectum and how the soft tissue in there is a little bit like the tissue at the back of your throat."

"I could have gone my whole life without knowing that," Mitchell said.

"He said that he couldn't rule out that something might have happened a few weeks ago, depending on what kind of, ah, object was used and how hard they, ah, put it in there. But that depending on the angle and how high up, ah, even if something did happen, it could have healed."

"Son of a *bitch*," Mitchell said.

"You make it sound like bad news."

"I didn't want anything like that to have happened to your son. It just would have made things easier to understand."

"Don't you mean your *version* of things?"

"Something like that. But it doesn't mean it didn't happen. And that he didn't know about it."

"At least we know something," Ferraro said.

Mitchell lit a cigarette, early today. "Did you mention hazing to him?"

"I did. He said he knew the question was out there. And I said, 'Let me ask it in plain language: Did some of these kids go too far with some hazing in Connecticut?'"

"What did he say?"

"He said that he was a good cop, and if something did, he'd find out about it."

"Nobody said he was a bad cop."

Matt Ferraro said, "I was thinking the exact same thing after I got off the phone."

**T**he Blue-White Game, the glorified scrimmage that kicked off the varsity basketball season, was that Tuesday night.

Every year, they'd divide up the South Fork team into two squads, the Blue Team and the White Team, and play a scrimmage in front of the public at six o'clock. Then everybody would go into town afterward, the length of Main Street closed off to cars for a combination of street fair and pre-winter carnival and pep rally. The restaurants on the street, including Hiram's and O'Rourke's, provided the food; Jimmy O'Rourke set up a wine-and-beer bar for the adults in front of his place. A local garage band provided live music. At the Hiram's end of the street, the South Fork Booster Club had set up carnival-like booths where you could win stuffed animals.

The players picked the band following a Battle of the Bands the previous weekend at school. They also got to choose up the sides for the scrimmage. Glass coached one team every year. The South Fork captain—Glenn Moore in this case—coached the other.

A town meeting of high school basketball, Mitchell thought.

Sam sat at the press table. Mitchell sat with Kate Perry in the stands. Glenn's Blue team ended up winning 81–66. He had Dave Bender and Christian with him. Show Watkins had Eric Daneko, who played like a mutt the whole game, and a tricky little white kid, a wizard with the ball, Tommy Mayer, whose family owned the hardware store and who would have been the star of any team that didn't have Glenn and Show on it.

With two minutes to go, Glass called a timeout and they made a big production of Show taking off his white jersey and putting on a blue one, so he could play a little bit with Glenn and give the people what they wanted, a snapshot of what they could expect when the regular season officially began on Saturday night.

It took about twenty seconds for the two of them to blow the roof off the place.

Show started it, rebounding a missed shot by Eric,

whipping an outlet pass to Glenn. Who tip-passed it right back to Show as if the ball had never touched his hands at all. Show was coming hard up the middle and started high-dribbling the ball, hot-dogging it the way Magic Johnson used to when he led the fast break for the old Lakers. At halfcourt, he suddenly went behind his back to elude one defender, without missing a step, and as he did, Glenn cut behind him.

Show got double-teamed just inside the top of the circle by Eric and one of the backup forwards, a white kid in glasses named Chuck O'Neill. As Show split them, he stumbled a little bit, as if he was about to go down.

Everything that happened next seemed to happen in one motion. Show put his left hand on the floor to keep himself from falling as his right hand underhanded the ball toward the basket. Like it was going to be an air ball.

Two people knew it wasn't.

Knew that Show wasn't out of control, and wasn't just throwing the ball up for grabs:

Him and Glenn.

Glenn, who had slowed up slightly while everybody watched Show do his basketball pratfall, was flying in from the left side now, catching what wasn't an air ball but a slick little lob pass instead, still on the way up as he caught it before throwing it down, making it into a spectacular two-handed dunk.

Madness in the little gym, from everybody except the two guys who'd caused it, who didn't even look at each other when the play was over, didn't acknowledge each other or the noise all around them.

"You're still telling me they didn't plan that," Kate Perry was saying now on Main Street, the two of them standing in front of her store. She'd decided she needed a hat in the cold night air and had run into the store and come out with some kind of black beret that made her look like a high school girl when she put it on.

"Maybe they did it once in practice," Mitchell said. "Or maybe it was just something they both knew was going to happen because it was supposed to happen that way. Like when Miles Davis would riff with Coltrane."

"I don't watch much basketball," she said. "But whatever it was, it was beautiful."

"When it's right, it's like any other kind of art," Mitchell said, surprised to find himself trying to explain it to her, what he'd always loved about sports. What he loved about it even now. "Half the time when I used to walk around the Met, I didn't know what I was looking at. But then I'd get in front of a Matisse and come to a dead stop. Because I knew what he was doing was sure as hell different from the other stuff hanging in the room. You didn't have to know anything about basketball tonight to know those two kids are special."

Kate Perry turned, like he'd stumped her suddenly. "Mitchell of the Met?"

Without thinking, he said, "Maybe I'll take you sometime."

"Maybe I'll go," she said.

They made their way through the crowd on the cold night, the chatter of the game and the upcoming season and Glenn and Show all around them, lighting up the street as much as the Christmas lights the merchants had strung from tree to tree all the way down to the World War II monument at the intersection of Main and Ocean. When they got to O'Rourke's, Mitchell got them each a glass of wine and then they sat down on an empty bench in front of the library. They could see players starting to show up now.

Kate Perry said, "Sometimes it's not such a bad little town."

She had the collar of her black leather coat turned up, so mostly what you could see of her was her eyes.

"Except when it's a very bad little town," he said.

They sat and sipped wine. Sam said he'd find them when he finished filing his game story for the early edition of the

*Press*. Across the street from them, Mitchell saw Art Daneko and Hank Bender with their sons, all of them having a good laugh about something.

As much as Mitchell wanted to square the books with Art Daneko one of these days, he could still look across the street and see them as fathers, proud of their kids being on this team, the status it gave them with all the people on Main Street.

If I'm a dad in South Fork, if I've got a kid on the team, Mitchell thought, what would I think about some asshole reporter showing up and trying to piss in everybody's beer?

He found himself putting himself in their shoes more and more.

In the middle of the street, Mitchell saw Show Watkins and a big black guy Mitchell didn't recognize, the other guy with a shaved head and goatee, wearing a black leather Shaft coat, the two of them walking from the direction of the monument.

Mitchell got up and said to Kate, "You mind if I leave you alone for a few minutes?"

"Meet me in front of Mayer's," she said. "I told Ginny I'd come down and help her with the world-famous milk carton toss."

They had set up Portosan toilets near Ocean, but Show and the guy in the Shaft coat made a right turn when they got to Mayer's, then walked through the parking lot and up the steps of the little prefab house that had Main Street's obsessively clean public restrooms.

They came out a couple of minutes later. Show was wearing a Knicks hoodie and baggy-ass jeans that looked brand-new and even brighter white high-top sneakers. Mitchell was waiting for him at the bottom of the steps, smiling as he said, "Kid, you're one of the best ballplayers I've ever seen."

Show looked right past him, as if he'd barely heard. Just gave Mitchell a couple of head nods as he said, "Thanks, yo."

"Got a second?" Mitchell said.

The other guy, in a deep, gravelly voice, like he was imitating some old jazz man, said, "You know this guy, little brother?"

"You must be the famous Antoine Watkins," Mitchell said. "All the reading I did on your brother, I feel like I know you, too."

"But we don't know y'all," Antoine said. "Do we now?"

Mitchell put his hand out between the two of them. "Ben Mitchell," he said. Antoine reached out first, gave him the kind of shake that probably brought weaker guys to their knees at Green Haven. When Mitchell had read back on Show Watkins, he had read stories about his brother, too. Antoine the Cop Watkins: who had made a career out of busting drug dealers at his precinct in East New York, and then selling the dope at a tidy profit out in the suburbs. Long Island, mostly. On Nexis, he hadn't seen anything about Antoine getting out. Or maybe hadn't noticed.

Show didn't even bother to shake Mitchell's hand. Just gave him another nod.

"Oh, yeah, you the bad man," he said. "The reporter's got the coach all yanked up."

"Not me, baby."

Antoine said, "Coach told you not to be talking to no press, right?"

Show gave Mitchell his big-dog smile. "I even get seen with y'all, Coach'll have my dick in a wringer."

"Somehow I doubt that," Mitchell said.

Show said, "Understand, I don't personally got no beef with you. But Coach does."

"The coach and I are trying to work through it without counseling."

"Don't matter either way, at least right now, because Antoine and me gotta bounce, he's lookin' to get the last train back."

Mitchell looked up at both of them. Antoine was a few

inches shorter than his brother, but still looked to be six-four or -five.

"I just need a minute," Mitchell said.

Antoine said, "Like every reporter I ever met. They say they listen, but they don't. They say they got questions, but what they really think is that they already got all the answers."

"I just want to ask your brother one question," Mitchell said to Antoine. "If he knows anything about some bad shit that might have happened when his team went over to Connecticut a few weeks ago."

Show started to say something. Antoine put a hand on his arm to stop him. "He's got nothin' to say."

Mitchell ignored Antoine. "Because if something *did* happen over there and you were a part of it, man, that's the kind of thing that can take you down hard, whether *you* did something or not. Just ask Kobe."

Show said, "You're askin' if we put some girl down over there . . . ?"

Antoine said, "You're askin' about that boy in the hospital, aren't y'all?"

"You know about him?"

"You hang around here in Smallville, you hear things."

"You know anything about what happened to Drew, Show?" Mitchell said.

Antoine stepped between his brother and Mitchell now. "Is there some part of he's got nothin' to say you can't hear?" he said.

Show was smiling now, playing it cool, acting as if he were enjoying a different kind of show, the one with Antoine and Mitchell. To Antoine, he said, "Maybe we better ask to see his badge, brother?"

"Uh-uh," Antoine said, "'cause we all done here."

Mitchell stepped aside, let them pass. To their backs he said, "Somebody's going to talk eventually. And when he does, everybody on the old Blue and White better know something: It's gonna be every man for himself."

Show kept walking toward the street fair. Antoine Watkins stopped, turned around, came back to where Mitchell stood in front of the restrooms.

"My baby brother's a good boy," he said. "I'm not. Anybody comes at him right now comes through me, whether I'm around or not. We clear on that?"

He sounds like me, Mitchell thought, talking to Eric Daneko about Sam.

Antoine got one step closer to Mitchell, crowding him now in the empty parking lot.

"I asked you, are we *clear?*" he said.

"Clear," Mitchell said.

"Thought so," Antoine said. "Enjoy the rest of your evening."

He jogged to catch up with his brother.

# 13

Sam wrote until about ten minutes before his ten o'clock deadline, paranoid as always about being even one minute late. Then he did some minor editing over the phone with the copy editor he hoped he'd get, Bill Price, a young guy only a couple of years out of Fordham himself, one who never acted as if he was doing Sam a favor even by talking to a high school kid.

Price seemed to have this idea that even an eight-inch story about a high school scrimmage ought to be as good as it could possibly be.

Sam had written it in his cubby in the *Breeze* office. When he finished, he hooked up his laptop to the one phone they had there and listened as the computer dialed in to the *Press*'s 800 number.

Somehow the whole process was still magic to Sam, even though he had grown up on computers the way everybody else his age had. Hear the modem hook up, hit the SEND button, pick up the paper in the morning, there was what he wrote, whether he got a byline or not.

He was going to have a byline tomorrow, Price said. Underneath the names of the *Press*'s regular reporters it said, "Press Staff." Underneath Sam's, and all the other regular stringers like him, it said, "Press Correspondent." Like the other guys were the varsity and he was on the JV team.

He could not have cared less.

Sam Perry, Press Correspondent.

Worked for him.

When he was done with Price, he packed up his computer, turned off the lights, locked the office and called his mom on her cell, wanting to know if she and Ben were still on Main Street at the fair. She said they were, but to move it, she couldn't hold out much longer waiting for Mitchell to hit something with a ball and win her a stuffed animal. Obviously saying it for Mitchell's benefit. "He may be able to write," his mom said, "but he couldn't hit the sidewalk if he fell out of my front window."

Sam laid his computer bag in the backseat, pulled out of the parking lot, then heard his cell go off. He picked it up from the console between the front seats, thinking it was his mother telling him to forget it and go straight home.

"Sam Perry?"

He could barely hear the voice at the other end. He quickly put the phone into the dashboard lights to see the callback number, but all it said was "Unknown."

"Who's this?" Sam said.

"A friend."

It wasn't anybody he could recognize, whoever it was talking in a raspy whisper, like somebody trying to disguise his voice.

"Wait, I can't hear you very well."

He pulled to the side of Farm Road, stopped the car, turned off the engine. Waited.

"I have some information you might be interested in."

Sam said, "About what?"

"Your story."

Sam could hear his own breathing in the front seat.

"What story?"

"C'mon, Sam. My friend. You know what story."

"You mean Bobby?"

"Among other things."

Sam waited.

"I'm here," he said.

"We should meet."

"It's kind of late."

"I could call somebody else at the paper, be their friend."

"It's just that I've got to be somewhere."

"Everybody's got to be somewhere, Sam."

He thought about telling whoever this was to call back in two minutes, so he could call his mom, have her put Ben on the phone. So he could ask Ben what he should do.

But he already knew what Ben would *tell* him to do:

Stay right where he was, he'd come meet him.

And do not go anywhere alone.

"Meet me at Mallozzi. The basketball courts."

Mallozzi Park was the big public park you saw as you came into South Fork from the west. Two lighted basketball courts, four clay tennis courts. In the summer, the best kids from all the local high school teams would play under the lights at Mallozzi until the town's eleven-o'clock curfew.

"Fifteen minutes," the voice at the other end said. "And Sam? Come alone. If I even think you're bringing your friend, the one walking up and down the street right now with your momma, I'm gone."

"Why me?" Sam said.

There was a pause that lasted so long Sam thought the guy might have hung up.

"You want to *know,* don't you?"

Now he hung up.

He felt the tip of something hard. Something cold.

Pressing up against him.

Like they were about to put it in.

Oh, Jesus, Sam thought.

Jesus, Jesus, Jesus.

This is what it feels like.

He couldn't tell how many of them there were. There were two of them, jumping him from behind, getting him down right away, pushing his face into the dirt at the far end of the courts, between the fence and the woods, out of sight even if you were standing in centerfield of the baseball field.

Right away one of them had undone the buttons on his pants, and pulled them down around his ankles.

Then his shorts.

Nobody saying anything until now.

He had smelled something, like ammonium. Or maybe it was rubbing alcohol. One of them had spread him. Then the tip of something. Back there. Gently. Like they were teasing him.

Playing with him.

"You don't want to be an asshole, do you, Sam?"

The same raspy voice.

Sam couldn't tell whether it was young or old, black or white.

"Get it, Sam? *Asshole?*"

Sam didn't know what he was supposed to say to that, so he didn't say anything.

*"Answer me."*

Giving the stick or whatever it was a little push, making Sam groan. Or maybe start to cry. Just thinking about what could happen next.

"No," he said. "I don't want to be an asshole."

"Good."

Taking a little pressure off.

"Please don't," Sam said.

"You smell anything, Sam?"

"Yes."

"Know what that smell is?"

"No."

"Mineral ice, Sam. Makes even a broomstick slide in easier than you'd think."

"Please," Sam said. Whispering himself now, his own voice harsh, like he couldn't get it to work right, feeling the weight of whichever one of them was sitting on him.

It was somebody big.

He never should have come here. Never should have let them pick the place. He should have called Ben.

Too late.

He felt the cold ground on the side of his face, a hand on the back of his head holding it there.

The tip stayed where it was, Sam thinking of it like it was the tip of a knife.

"We want you to stop now, Sam. You and your friend Ben Mitchell. The two of you have got things all fucked up, Sam. Over nothin'. Over some bullshit thing like goes on all the time. Only now y'all won't let go."

Another little push.

Sam held his breath.

"But just because you are all fucked up, doesn't mean you can't fuck things up royally around here."

He felt the tip start to enter.

Sam thinking back now for some crazy reason.

Remembering the first time he was old enough for the doctor to stick a finger up him. Not knowing what was coming, even when the guy told him to roll over on his side, still thinking it was his normal physical. Then letting out a scream his mother said she could hear in the waiting room. . . .

"Hear me good, Sam. None of us had anything to do with Bobby getting himself killed."

Us.

"It's why you've got to leave that be now. Can you leave it be, Sam?"

Keeping the tip of the stick where it was. Not in, not out.

"Yes."

He pictured himself with his pants down.

Please let it be over.

"Yes," he said, "I can."

He wanted to ask about Drew. Wanting to know things even now, humiliated this way. More scared than he'd ever been in his life.

"All you can do is hurt people, and get yourself hurt. So I want you to tell me you're going to stop this shit now."

"I'll stop."

"People who poke around sometimes *get* poked, so to speak."

"Yes."

"Bobby was a team man. Drew's a team man. Now you've got to be a team man. Can you be a team man, Sam? Somebody wants to help instead of hurt?"

"I wasn't trying to hurt . . . "

The stick went in a little more and Sam cried out.

"I asked, are you a team man, Sam?"

"Yes!"

"Because if you're not, if you're lying to me, the next time I will shove this stick so far up you that it will come out your fucking ear."

Sam squeezed his eyes shut.

Don't cry, he told himself.

"We're going to be watching you. And we will know if you tell the police about this, or anybody else. You're not going to tell, are you?"

"No."

Something had registered now, in some outside part of his brain. Some part of his brain that was still working. He just couldn't think clearly enough to figure out what.

All he could do was pray for this to be over without them doing it.

It.

"Get your friend to stop. And we never have to meet again. All's you got to do is stop."

"What am I supposed to say to him?"

"You're the one with the words, Sam."

They must have put the mineral ice close to him now, so close, the smell so strong, Sam was afraid he might be sick.

"Neither one of us wants there to be a next time, do we?"

"No."

"We don't really want to hurt you, Sam. Or anybody close to you?"

"No!"

He must have sounded like a siren in the night.

"Shhhhh. I said, we don't *want* to hurt you or anybody close to you."

"You . . . wouldn't . . . "

"But we *could,* Sam." The whisperer got close to his ear now and said, "If we can get you down, we can get your mom down."

Then they put some kind of blindfold on him and tied his hands behind him, telling him it would only take him a few minutes to undo his hands once they were gone.

The last thing he heard:

"All the way next time, Broomstick Boy."

They left him there with his pants down.

Sam Perry, he thought.

Press Correspondent.

Now he cried.

# 14

Sam called Kate on her cell just when she and Mitchell were about to give up on him, and told her that he'd nearly gotten all the way there before remembering, like a complete dope, that he'd left his backpack at school, and that he'd meet her at home.

So Mitchell and Kate took one more walk down Main Street, had one more cup of Hiram's hot chocolate, and then Mitchell drove her home. When they got there, Sam's Volvo was in the driveway, and every light in the house was on.

"Kids," she said, sitting there in the front seat.

"I never know how I'm supposed to respond to that."

Kate said, "When you're single, you think there should be a manual about men. Then, when you become a mom, you want there to be a manual about babies."

Mitchell smiled. "Wait, you mean it's not the same book?"

Kate said, "You can have the rest of it, just give me something to help me understand teenaged boys. And mine is relatively normal."

Mitchell said he'd call Sam in the morning before school, fill him in about his conversation with Show. But when Mitchell did call, a little before eight, Kate said that Sam had been throwing up all night, and she was going to keep him home.

"I didn't hear a thing, I was dead to the world," she said. "But he said it was every hour on the hour."

"Tell him to feel better."

"I'm off to work," she said. "Why don't you give him a call around lunchtime, you can tell him yourself."

He called at noon and got Kate's voice on the machine. He drove over to the new Barnes & Noble in the Bays, found a copy of Studs Terkel's *Giants of Jazz* and a new Joshua Redman CD, came home, tried Sam again around two. Got the machine again. Maybe he'd gone back to bed, and had the answer-only deal going with the machine. Mitchell considered calling Kate again, but finally decided just to take a ride over to the house.

The Volvo was in the driveway, exactly where it had been the night before. Mitchell rang the doorbell and waited, then finally heard him coming down the front stairs.

When Sam opened the door, he was wearing a faded blue cap with "9" on the front, which Mitchell knew meant Ted Williams. White Lobster Roll t-shirt, from the lobster joint out toward Two Mile Harbor. Faded jeans with tears in both knees. Old-school Adidas Country II running shoes, white with the three green stripes, the ones Sam admitted he'd bought because he'd seen Mitchell wearing them. He didn't look sick to Mitchell as much as he looked like he hadn't slept in about a week.

His skin was the color of paste.

"Hey," Sam said, leaning on the door frame, making no move to ask Mitchell to come in.

Mitchell grinned. "You look as shitty as your mom says you feel."

"Yeah," he said. "Stomach. There's nothing worse in the world than throwing up."

"You feeling any better now? I tried calling a couple of times, to get you up to speed on some stuff that happened last night in town."

"I guess I was sleeping."

"All day?"

Sam said, "Listen, I'm still feeling kind of punk, maybe I could give you a holler later when my brain's working better."

Mitchell said, "Sure, no problem." But stayed where he was, studying this new Sam. There was something off with him.

"Hey," he said. "You okay, partner?"

"Like I said."

Sam took the Williams hat off, curved the visor a little more, put it back on, as if giving himself something to do with his hands. "You know," he said, "I've been thinking, maybe I'm not up for this anymore. The way you are. I mean, I got to thinking about it last night, being in the gym, seeing how good these guys are, how excited everybody was. How happy. I've got to go to school with these guys, hang with them if they'll still let me. Basically I want to do the best job covering the season I possibly can. And I don't think I can do that if they're all looking at me like I'm some kind of enemy of the state."

It sounded to Mitchell like a speech he'd been rehearsing.

"You just decided this last night, huh?"

"Well, like, no. Actually, it's been coming up on me for a while. And I've had plenty of time to think on it today, between puking my guts out."

"And sleeping," Mitchell said. "And not answering the phone. Been a full day for you all around."

"Excuse me for getting sick as a dog on you and slowing down our big investigation."

"Sam," Mitchell said. "Is there something you're not telling me?"

"Listen, I gotta go lay down, or I'm gonna get sick right here all over again. I'll call you tomorrow or something, okay?"

"Okay."

Sam said, "And promise you won't say anything to my mom. I want to tell her myself."

"Promise," Mitchell said. "But listen, kid, why don't you just think about this a little . . ."

"I've already thought about it."

Then he shut the door, and locked it.

**M**itchell was at the bar at O'Rourke's on Thursday night, pretending to watch hockey, when Kate Perry came through the front door. She was looking about as happy to see him as Art Daneko had been about half an hour before, when Daneko had finally left the place after having a few with two guys in DANEKO LANDSCAPING parkas.

Jimmy O'Rourke had been standing at the door when Daneko went through it. He saw Daneko slow down when he noticed Mitchell sitting at the bar, saw him glare at Mitchell, saw the smaller of the two guys in the parkas, a small black guy, practically push Daneko through the door.

"You two have issues, don't try to fool me," O'Rourke said.

"Your ability to read people, it's still like some kind of gift," Mitchell said.

"Thank you," O'Rourke said.

"I thought this was your date night with the missus."

"Just waiting for my cutie to finish with her bowling league."

"You married a bowler?"

"Two-ten average," O'Rourke said. "I'm pretty proud of her."

Now Kate Perry said to Mitchell, "I called your house. When you weren't there, I thought you might be here."

He hadn't heard from her, or Sam, since Sam had shut

the door in his face Wednesday afternoon. He had thought all day about calling Kate, wanting to ask her if Sam had told her what he'd told Mitchell before he shut the door in his face. But he'd promised the kid he wouldn't call. A promise was a promise, especially to a kid.

Especially with something this big.

"Was Sam well enough to go to school today?"

"No," she said.

"So, he's still not feeling any better?"

"No, as a matter of fact, he's not." She looked around to see if anybody was listening, lowered her voice. "They got to him."

"They?"

"They," she said. "Them. Whoever's behind all this insane bullshit."

"Sam talked to them? Like in person?"

"They got him to go to Mallozzi." She looked around again and said, "Could we possibly have this conversation somewhere else?"

"Sure." Mitchell grabbed the Syracuse jacket from the back of his barstool, threw a twenty on the bar, followed her out to the street. Other than the Christmas lights strung in the trees along Main Street, there was no sign anywhere that there had been a small-town carnival here a couple of nights before.

Mitchell had known for two days there was more bothering Sam Perry than an upset stomach. By now, Mitchell knew the way the kid looked at him, the way he acted in Mitchell's presence. He tried to be cool about it, especially now that he thought of them as a team, Mitchell treating him like an equal. But he knew he was still getting the same hero worship from Sam Perry he'd seen that first day at Hiram's. Sam tried to keep it under control, knowing that every time he didn't Mitchell would call him on it—make some kind of joke, or hit him with a put-down.

But it never really went away.

Until yesterday. He'd been a different kid. Mitchell went
through all the possibilities, thinking maybe something had
happened with Ken Glass the night before, between the end
of the game and when Sam was supposed to show up in
town. Or maybe one of the players had gotten up in his face.

Even one of the stars, which Mitchell knew would lay
the kid out.

Something, though.

Something big enough to have him talk about walking
away.

Now here was his mother saying *they* had gotten to him.

"I parked at the store," Kate said, and started walking in
that direction, hands jammed into the pockets of her leather
coat, a Red Sox cap of her own on her head. She had told him
at the street fair that she'd grown up outside of Boston, a town
called Lincoln, north of the Mass Pike, she said, on 128.

They walked past Mayer's, past the parking lot where
he'd talked to Show, past Starbucks.

"I knew there was something he wasn't telling me," Kate
said, not looking at Mitchell.

He wanted her to get on with it, but everything about her
manner, the clipped way she was talking, the way she was
so tightly wound, made him understand he couldn't push.

"He must have told you I stopped by yesterday."

"Of course you stopped by," Kate said. "You keep going
with this and he keeps going because he wants to be just
like you. And now the thing I *told* you I didn't want to happen happens."

She let a couple of kids, boy and girl, holding hands,
pass them. Still telling it her own way, at her own pace.

She stopped now in front of the antique store, Olde East
End, that had been here since Mitchell was in high school,
even though he couldn't remember a single time in his life
when he'd been inside.

She finally looked at Mitchell.

"He didn't want to talk yesterday, he didn't want to eat,

he just wanted to sleep, maybe he'd feel better in the morning. Only he didn't feel better this morning, so I kept him home again. He was still in his room when I got home from work tonight." She nodded, as if confirming her own version of things. "It was clear he'd been crying, his eyes were all red. I asked him what was the matter. He said nothing. I sat down on the end of his bed, like I did when he was little and he was afraid of the dark. Or couldn't sleep. Till he could sleep. It was then I noticed how quiet it was in there, even though it's never quiet in there. No music. No TV. No funny instant-message sound coming out of his computer. The impossible. A quiet bedroom for Sam Perry. I said, 'Honey, what's going on?' He said, Nothing, he was still just feeling like crud. His word. And that he was going to turn in early and hope he felt better in the morning. I got up, kissed him on the forehead, which is a move I usually have to sneak in on him, told him I loved him, turned off the light, and closed the door behind me."

There was a bench in front of Olde East End. She sat down. Mitchell sat down next to her. There had been a little shooting gallery set up here a few nights ago.

"I went downstairs to read. I don't know how long he was standing in the doorway when he said, 'Mom.' I nearly jumped out of my skin. He asked if I'd talked to you in the last twenty-four hours. I said I hadn't. That's when he told me he was quitting the story, he just wanted to go back to covering the team."

Mitchell wanted a cigarette.

Kate said, "I asked him why. And then he did something that really did make him look like a little boy. He started looking everywhere in the room except me. At the pictures on the walls. At his feet. At the ceiling, mostly. Like he did when he knew he'd done something wrong and knew he had to tell me about it."

She was nodding again.

Now her eyes, Mitchell saw, were red.

She said, "You know what you said the other day about secrets? I never had to worry about Sam having secrets. He could never keep the big things to himself." She turned and looked at Mitchell. "He couldn't tonight. That's when he told me they were going to hurt me."

"Who was going to hurt you?"

"He doesn't know," she said, and told what Sam had told her, that people—players?—he couldn't see had grabbed him from behind at Mallozzi and threatened him and threatened her.

"They didn't hurt him?"

"He said no, they just wanted to scare him. Though he started looking around again when he told me that."

"What was the threat?"

"That if they could get to him that easily, they could get to me. Something along those lines."

"I need to talk to him."

"*No.*"

"I need to know more about this, Kate. They must be getting worried if they set him up this way and grabbed him."

"You kept pushing," she said. "Now they've really pushed back, haven't they?"

Before he could say anything to that, her cell phone went off, as loud as a siren on the empty street.

"Sam? . . . Oh, sorry, I was expecting Sam, he was home sick today, and I just had to run into town. . . . Oh, my God, that's wonderful. . . . Oh, God, you must be so relieved. . . . Where? . . . Uh-huh. . . . I'll just tell Sam where I'm going and be over as soon as I can."

Kate Perry stuffed the phone back into her pocket.

"Drew Hudson woke up," she said.

**S**he said she was going to the hospital to be with Shelley Hudson. Mitchell said he had sort of figured that out for himself.

Then she asked Mitchell to stay away from Sam for the time being. No more visits to the house, no phone contact.

"Your call," he said in front of River Road.

"Nothing permanent," she said. "Just until he's himself again."

"I hate to have to keep pointing this out," he said. "But we're on the same side here."

"I'm just on Sam's side. And I didn't make him drop this. I didn't talk him into anything. This was all on his own."

Mitchell said, "Bite my head off if you want. But Drew Hudson tried to take one way out. Is this yours?"

"You want me to admit I'm scared out of my wits? Okay, I am. You got me. I'm scared, my kid's scared. We're officially out. You're on your own from now on."

"Can we talk about this tomorrow when you've calmed down?"

"I'm calm now," she said, and got into her car and left him standing there as she drove off, burning a little rubber as she did.

Mitchell walked back to O'Rourke's. Now there was an NBA game on the TV set, the Lakers against some team in retro jerseys he didn't recognize. He'd never been a Yankee fan, but at least they never fucked around with the pin-stripes. He looked on the restaurant side and there were only two tables occupied. Four people left at the bar. One of them was Jimmy O'Rourke, at the corner near the front door where Mitchell had been. Mitchell could see he had a Canadian Club and ginger ale in front of him. O'Rourke had always called it his prom drink. He had gray curly hair, shading toward white these days. He had a wide face that was beginning to show all the prom drinks he'd had in his life, especially around the nose, which was veiny and red and getting flatter by the year. But his blue eyes were as bright as they'd ever been, always scanning the room like searchlights, even as he was talking to you, trying to spot the table or the place at the bar where the most fun was.

Mitchell sat down next to him. "I thought you said this was date night?"

"She and the girls had a big win in the semis over Bruegger's Bagels and decided to stay at the alley and celebrate there."

"You seem to be bearing up pretty well without her."

O'Rourke said, "When was I not happy in my own joint, with a fresh one in front of me and a game to watch?"

"That," Mitchell said, "is as good a definition of America as I've ever heard."

He ordered a Dewar's on the rocks. He clicked his glass against O'Rourke's, like this was the old days in midtown Manhattan. He drank some Scotch, then he said to O'Rourke, "You say you know this town."

"It's my business to know. I want them to think I'm their friend."

"So let me ask you a crazy hypothetical," Mitchell said. "Who would the big loser be if there was no basketball season?"

"Now, that's a question out of the cheap seats."

"Humor me. You know you're not really watching this game, you always hated the Lakers."

"You mean who gets hurt besides old Jimmy on game nights?"

"Just who in town takes the biggest hit overall."

"The town probably takes the biggest hit in town," he said. "South Fork's going to be on ESPN at least four times this season. The way the kid from Cleveland was."

"LeBron."

"He went to private school. This is a public school. But it's run by the town, and the way the town charter is written, the town gets to keep all the television money. Some of which goes back into the school, some goes into the bank. I forget the dollars, but it's pure profit."

"Better than a new tax assessment."

"Bet your ass."

Mitchell said, "Okay, the town loses and the school loses. Who else?"

"Probably Show Watkins. I mean, okay, everybody and their aunt knows the kid's going straight to the pros and a sneaker contract faster'n shit through a goose. So he really doesn't *need* this season. But it wouldn't hurt him to get those television games, just as a way of driving his price up. Hyping his own hype, so to speak. Especially if Nike and Adidas decide to have a fight over him, which I hear they're going to."

O'Rourke lit a cigarette. Mitchell gave him a look. O'Rourke said, "I'll take the fine." He blew a perfect smoke ring at the ceiling, the way he used to at his joint in the city before the tobacco cops started running the world. "The other kid, Glenn, I think he's bulletproof. He's got any school he wants if he doesn't play another minute of high school ball, from Duke to UCLA. After that, he could even go a Bill Bradley if he wanted to, even though he won't."

"Rhodes scholar?" Mitchell said.

"There if he wants it, from what I hear."

"What about the townies like the Bender kid, and Eric Daneko? And the other big black kid, the one who's related to the cop?"

"Christian Bowdoin."

"What about them?"

O'Rourke said, "In a lot of ways, they need the season more than anybody. And put the coach in with them, just because he's looking to promote himself into a college job. But Hank Bender and Art Daneko were both in here the other night talking about how much their kids need a full ride for college. Good colleges, anyway."

"I know Hank Bender said something about that to me," Mitchell said. "But c'mon, could those scholarships possibly mean that much?"

"Guys like us, without kids, we've got no clue what college costs. And the other kid? Christian? His old man picked potatoes at Hurley's Farm until the day he dropped dead doing it. Your buddy Art? He's got two trucks, one crew. Believe me, he's not sitting here nights thinking about which beachfront property he wants to buy. And Hank Bender, your old buddy, has been drawing a policeman's salary his whole life. Which part of the south of France you think he's retiring to?"

"It might be more important to him that his kid gets out than anybody we're talking about."

"You go all the way back with him, right?"

"He thought sports would get *him* out. Then it didn't. He's been stuck here ever since."

"You make it sound like he's been doing time."

"No," Mitchell says. "But he does."

O'Rourke offered him a cigarette. Mitchell shook his head, saying he'd exceeded his daily limit about six hours ago. Then O'Rourke said, "Why are we talking about somebody canceling the season? People around here would rather have you burn down town hall."

"I'm just talking."

"You never just talk."

Mitchell finished his drink.

"This basketball team is important to these people," O'Rourke said.

"Hank Bender said the same thing to me," Mitchell said. "All I'm trying to do is figure out how important."

"Season starts in a couple of days."

"Yeah," Mitchell said. "Let the games begin."

# 15

Mitchell drove into town Friday morning, bought the papers, drove home, made himself a second pot of coffee and read them. He noticed a small box buried in the sports section of the *Press* about Drew, no byline, saying he'd come out of his coma. Maybe Sam had called it in. Or maybe he was too scared even to do that.

When you came right down to it, who could blame him?

Better question:

If Sam really was out, why was Mitchell still in?

Because he still had to know, that was why.

He had to know who'd gotten into his house. Who'd talked to Drew Hudson after Sam left that day. He had to know who'd smashed Kate's window and slashed Sam's tires and finally gotten to Sam and threatened him and threatened his mom. He had to know, once and for all, what had happened that night in Connecticut.

One kid dead and another one just now coming out of a

coma. Now Sam Perry, the best kid in the whole town, was afraid to open his front door.

Push hard enough, Kate said, they'll push back.

But *who* had Mitchell pushed too hard?

He thought about taking a walk to the beach when he was done with the papers. Instead he put on old gray sweatpants, an old Pepperdine sweatshirt, a knit cap, and his old Adidas Superstars—low cuts, white on white—grabbed his indoor/outdoor Spalding ball from the closet, and drove over to Mallozzi Park in the middle of the afternoon to shoot some hoops.

Maybe the basketball gods would inspire him.

The temperature gauge in the F-150 said it was forty-one degrees outside, but Mitchell didn't feel the chill once he got himself warmed up, mixing in driving layups with jumpers from the outside. He noticed that all the rims at Mallozzi had nets. It was always a big deal in public parks, he knew, even in small ocean towns like South Fork. In the old days, he'd gone to Jersey City to write a column about the growing-up years of Bobby Hurley Jr. when Hurley had been the star point guard, one of the great college point guards of all time, at Duke. Hurley had come out of St. Anthony's High School in Jersey City, where his father was one of the most famous high school coaches in America. Bob Hurley Sr. had given Mitchell a driving tour of all the Jersey City courts that day, showing him where all the best games had been when Bobby was a kid. It was all good, the old man telling stories about the courts and the neighborhoods until he'd come to a court where one of the nets was gone. Or both.

"In poor neighborhoods," Hurley Sr. said, "one rim without a net messes up a hundred kids." Mitchell had thought about it ever since, every time he saw a bare rim anywhere.

He wondered how many bare rims there had been for

Show Watkins, before all the AAU coaches and street agents and sneaker hustlers had started to come around.

Mitchell started to feel good now, stepping farther away from the basket in the fading afternoon sun, hearing school buses start to rumble toward town, feeling the breeze start to pick up a little and occasionally blow one of his shots away from the basket, even when he was sure he had put a sweet stroke on it.

It was when one of those shots clanked off the front of the rim and bounced away from him that he saw Glenn Moore watching him through the fence, grinning at him. He looked like he'd just come from school, with his open toggle coat, v-neck sweater, khakis. Backpack dangling from his right hand.

"You've got a little game," he said to Mitchell.

"Little being the operative word."

"For a guy your age, I meant."

"You better stop, the compliments are getting worse as you go."

"No, I meant that in a good way."

"Nothing that has 'a guy your age' in it is ever good for that guy."

"Did you play?"

"I wasn't quite good enough to make the cut. Baseball was my sport."

"It used to be mine," Glenn said, "until I sort of had to focus on basketball."

"Seems to be working out for you all right."

"I love playing, don't get me wrong," Glenn said. "But it's never going to be the be-all and end-all for me the way it is with somebody like Show. Or the ones on the team looking to score a full ride. They're more invested than I am."

"Invested?" Mitchell said.

"You know what I mean."

"Yeah, I do," Mitchell said, "but would they?"

Glenn ducked his head, grinning at Mitchell as he did. "I would have put it differently if I was hanging with my boys."

"Shouldn't you be invested right now in practice with your boys, by the way?"

"Tonight. Before our first game, we scrimmage at the same time the game will be starting the next night. Coach says it gets us into the rhythms of game day. Quote unquote."

"I'll bet he does."

Glenn said, "Coach doesn't believe there's any such thing as over-analysis."

"So what are you doing here?" Mitchell said.

"I was getting some cash at the Country Market, across the street," he said. "And then I got curious about who the lone shooter was over here."

"You're not supposed to be talking to me, by the way."

"That's just Coach being Coach," he said. "Actually, I've been *meaning* to talk to you."

Mitchell motioned toward the door. "Step into my office, then."

Glenn came around the fence, through the door open to the other court. The two of them sat down. Up close, Mitchell noticed that Glenn Moore's eyes were a couple of shades lighter than his skin. There was something about him that made him seem older than seventeen or eighteen, whatever he was. Something cool, self-possessed, as if the gods could never piss on him the way they did on other people. The big jock: the new American royalty, even as a senior in high school.

"I think you might have the wrong idea about our team," Glenn said.

"What idea is that?"

"C'mon, we're not going to play it that way, are we?" He smiled full now, showing him a full mouth of perfect teeth. Of course. "I'm the *captain* of the team, Mr. Mitchell, and I take the job seriously. Which means I keep the lines of communication open with my teammates. And my coach. I know you think there's some kind of big cover-up going on."

"But you're here to tell me there's not."

"Let me finish," Glenn said. "I know you've talked to

Eric, I know you've talked to Show, I know Sam Perry's got your ear. I *know*, okay? You think something got out of hand at camp and now we've closed ranks. You think it's got something to do with Bobby and Drew, and whatever."

"It's the whatever part I'm struggling with, frankly."

"I can't speak for everybody," he said. "But I don't think the good guys on this team would have anything to do with stuff like that. Do we fool around with each other? Yeah, we do. All teams do. I woke up one morning in Connecticut and they'd rigged this contraption that a bucket of ice-cold water fell on me. Drew had to find his way out of the woods with a blindfold on. Show's the soundest sleeper? They actually picked his bed up and carried it out of his cabin, so he woke up outside. Dopey high school hijinks. Like out of a summer-camp movie."

"You tell Hank Bender all that?"

"Of course."

Mitchell spun the ball on the tip of his right index finger like he was a Globetrotter.

"Pretty good," Glenn said

"All the guys on the team can't be good guys."

"On our team they pretty much are."

"Guess what? Even guys who look like good guys get accused of doing bad shit. You want a whole list from sports, or just a partial?"

"I'm just trying to give you our side of things."

"Forget about Bobby. Why do you think Drew Hudson tried to kill himself?"

"My father says you can't understand somebody until you walk a mile in his shoes."

"I don't need you to walk nearly that far."

Glenn said, "All I can tell you is that Drew hasn't been the same kid since his parents split up."

Now Mitchell smiled at Glenn Moore. "I've never heard of that causing rectal bleeding."

"You asked me about his suicide attempt."

"I tend to jump around."

"I'm just trying to give you an overall picture of Drew, is all."

Mitchell sat there. More school buses went by. Glenn Moore didn't seem uncomfortable with the silence. He didn't seem uncomfortable about anything, including the topic of conversation. Mitchell found himself thinking about how life's lottery worked. Glenn was black, but the kind of black that had obviously worked for him his whole life. Mitchell had seen it in sports *his* whole life: It was the kind of black that wasn't too black for white people. He was used to people liking him. It was part of the whole package. He clearly wanted Mitchell to like him. And like his teammates, too. Even though everything about him said that he was better than his teammates.

Mitchell said, "Anybody besides the coach give Drew a hard time?"

"You've been around sports," Glenn said. "You know there are guys on every team who are going to stick the needle in. Heck, I've seen it on every team I've played on my whole life, all the way back to Biddy League. And some guys getting needled take it better than others."

"Drew couldn't take it."

"Drew's too sensitive."

"That's the one they always go for first."

"On our team," Glenn said, "it's Show. He likes to get on people, that's just his nature. Even when we're playing, he can't stop talking. Coach doesn't usually like it, but with him he lets it go. He just looks at it as Show being Show."

"Great players," Mitchell said, "allow you to coach them. Even guys like Coach Glass know that, whether they want to admit it or not."

"The problem with Show," Glenn said, "is that sometimes he doesn't know when to stop. Like nobody ever made him stop, with the possible exception of his grandma. So somebody at practice, or on the bus, is always getting it.

Even me sometimes. It's *boy* this or *boy* that. I'm Golden Boy, always. Drew was Piano Boy, because Show found out he used to take piano lessons. Dave Bender is *Law & Order* Boy, because his father's a cop. Like that. Whenever one of us screws up, we hear it."

Mitchell said, "You and Show get along okay?"

"No problems."

Mitchell thinking: The fuck there aren't. Glenn Moore had been like the prettiest girl in class his whole life, and now Beyoncé had moved to town.

"You think Show is mean?"

Glenn paused. "I read somewhere once that Michael Jordan wasn't just the best player in the world, he was the meanest. I forget who wrote it. But the writer said that with the greatest athletes, it's not just ego and arrogance and talent, there's some cruelty there, too."

Mitchell nodded. "Larry Bird? King of the trash-talkers."

"So I think Show could be mean in that way."

"You think he's mean enough to hurt somebody?"

Another pause. "No," Glenn Moore said, but he didn't seem sure.

"Why'd you really want to talk to me?"

"We're a bunch of high school kids, Mr. Mitchell. We're just trying to have a season we'll all remember the rest of our lives. I don't think anybody would do anything to mess it up, I really don't."

"If you found out somebody did, what would you do?"

"I'd tell my parents, I'd tell the principal, I'd tell the coach," he said. "I'd even tell you." He looked down, almost shyly. "I've tried to do the right thing my whole life."

Mitchell said, "What's it like, having somebody like Show walk into a gym that's always belonged to you?"

"If it makes it easier for us to win, I'm cool with it. I'm like Jeter. Give me A-Rod next to me anytime." He played with the straps on his backpack. "This was actually supposed to happen a couple of years ago, we had this great kid named Kyle Sheppard. Not as great as Show, of course. Nobody is. He was this town kid, went away one summer to basketball camp, had this growth spurt. Nobody could believe it was him. We were going to be the dynamic duo."

"What happened to him?"

"We got tangled up going for a rebound, a couple of weeks before the season was supposed to start, and he wrecked up his knee." Glenn Moore looked at Mitchell, eyes big, filling up all of a sudden. "Show may call me Golden Boy, Mr. Mitchell, but I've been blaming myself ever since. It's why I'm bound and determined to make this thing with Show and me work."

"You're sure you're just eighteen?" Mitchell said.

Glenn Moore said, "My parents say I've always been big for my age, in all ways."

Mitchell slowly stood up, knees stiff by now. "Good luck with the game tomorrow," he said.

"A player we were just talking about once said that luck isn't something people need to wish on you, it's something you either got, or you don't got."

Clearly doing some kind of blacked-up impression.

"Michael or Larry?" Mitchell said.

"Show," Glenn said.


**W**hy hadn't he told his mom all of it?

Kate Perry had told Sam his whole life what a lousy liar he was. How she always knew when he was holding something back, or felt guilty about something.

But this time Sam had lied like a champ.

He had told her just enough about what had happened at Mallozzi Park, made it just frightening enough. Made it sound more like a mugging, with so much detail she didn't think he was leaving anything out. He told himself he was protecting her.

But as bad as Sam Perry was at lying to others, he was much worse at lying to himself.

The reason he hadn't told her was because he was too ashamed to tell her. Not just about how scared he was that night, but how scared he *still* was. How every time he closed his eyes, he could see the two shadow guys, big shadow guys, on top of him, and his pants around his ankles and his naked butt in the air, and one of them holding the broomstick there.

Whispering his name.

Almost like he was sweet-talking Sam.

Then Sam would open his eyes, sometimes keep them open all night long, because that's the only way he could get the fucking picture out of his head.

*If we can get you down, we can get her down.*

*All the way up next time, Broomstick Boy.*

Had it been like this with Drew? Sam kept thinking about that, too. Like maybe they were in the same club now. Maybe they could form a band: The Broomstick Boys. Except they must have gone all the way up with Drew, since he'd ended up in the hospital. Maybe they'd humiliated him enough that he finally tried to swallow a bottle of pills.

If Sam looked at it that way, he could consider himself lucky, like he'd dodged a bullet. Only he didn't feel lucky, he felt like that poor fat guy in *Deliverance,* a movie they'd watched recently for English when they were reading James Dickey. The fat guy they made squeal like a pig. . . .

He wanted to talk about this with Ben Mitchell in the worst way, explain why'd he been blowing him off, maybe even get him to buy his version of what had happened at Mallozzi. But Sam knew that was out of the question. This was Ben Mitchell, after all, who put things together, even when he didn't have all the right parts. Mitchell could put those eyes on you and not take them off, make you believe he had some kind of Superman X-ray vision.

Mitchell would know he was holding back, and Sam couldn't risk that, because eventually he'd break down and tell Mitchell all of it, and then Ben Mitchell, his hero, would see him the way Sam saw himself, every time he tried to close his eyes. . . .

He'd come home that night, after they'd left him there, and turned on every light in the house. When he'd heard his mother come in, he'd only shut the light off in his room, pretending to be asleep. After that, he hadn't thrown up, his stomach wasn't the problem, unless you were talking about his total lack of guts. Throwing up all night was just another lie he made up in the morning. He had just stared at the ceiling all night long, trying to imagine which of the players he'd watched that night in the Blue-White Game were capable of doing something like this.

Eric, his old bud?

Dave Bender, a cop's son?

Tommy Mayer, whose family had owned the hardware store in this town since World War I?

One of the big underclassmen, like Chuck or Ed Fusco? Glenn or Show?

Yeah, right.

Christian Bowdoin?

"You obviously went too far," his mother said when he told her his version in the morning. "That's what I told your friend Mr. Mitchell. The two of you took this too far and now they responded. And that, young man, is why you are making the right decision to get the hell out of this, and leave it to the professionals."

Like he was some helpless little boy.

A helpless little boy who felt betrayed on top of everything else, because somebody on the team had done this to him.

He knew he was a reporter, he knew this is what he wanted to do with his life. He'd heard enough the last couple of weeks from Mitchell about what he thought about some of the guys he'd written about in his life. But he wanted to like the guys on this team. A part of him wanted to feel as if they were all in this together. It wasn't hero worship. They weren't his heroes. Mitchell was. It didn't mean he didn't want them to do well.

*All the way next time, Broomstick Boy.*

It was the middle of Friday afternoon. In just over twenty-four hours, the season would start. He wasn't excited about that, just tired; he felt as if he'd been up for two days straight. He wasn't sick anymore, even if he'd convinced his mother he was. Just sick and tired of feeling like a helpless little boy.

He got up and turned off Norah Jones and turned on his computer and did what Mitchell had done.

Sam wrote.

He wrote what had really happened to him at Mallozzi until he got another call on his cell.

# 16

When Mitchell identified himself to Emmy Watkins over the phone, she informed him that she seemed to recall seeing him one time with Katie Couric. She said it was either the Ray Lewis trial or the start of the whole Kobe thing, she couldn't keep her cable TV cases straight sometimes. Mitchell said he was the exact same way, then asked if he might stop by to talk a little bit about her grandson, even on short notice like this. She said the coach had a rule about all interviews relating to the team going through him. Mitchell said that from what he knew about Emmy Watkins, it was hard for him to believe she was going to let some pushy coach tell her what to do, about DeShawn or anything else. Emmy Watkins giggled over the phone and said her late husband used to call men like DeShawn's Coach Glass roosters. Cock-a-doodle-do, she said. Then she told Mitchell to come on by, she'd make up her own mind about him.

Now they were in her neat-as-a-pin living room. Emmy Watkins, the one Show Watkins called his Two Mom, was in a long print dress, her feet covered by soft-looking slippers with sheepskin lining, no backs to them. She was wearing a big-faced watch on her slender wrist, the numbers so big Mitchell could make them out from where he sat across the coffee table from her. She had to be in her seventies at least, but her face was remarkably unlined, beautiful really, underneath white curly hair. There was intelligence in her eyes, he could see it right away. And some mischief.

"I see where your daughter kept your name," Mitchell said.

"She barely knew the name of DeShawn's father," Emmy Watkins said. "Which made him like all the ones that came after him."

She had the television set on, some news channel, sound off. It was just after eight. She said she'd let DeShawn take her Acura over to Coach Glass's nighttime basketball practice. Mostly, she said, she picked him up and dropped him off, she needed the car during the day to go from house to house, she had more families than she knew what to do with. Even after taking on more, she said, once her daughter passed, and she had to pay the rent on the apartment on Gerard Avenue. Explaining to Mitchell that she'd gotten a friend from the building, 825 Gerard, to live in the apartment with her DeShawn, just to get him through the school year.

She laughed at the end of all that, like she was embarrassed. "I'm sure that's more information than you need, Mr. Mitchell."

"No reporter I ever knew ever had too much information."

"It's the long way around of telling you I feel like I've got my hands full with these houses of mine," she said. "Even with people calling me all the time, telling me to call *them* if one of my slots opens up."

"I'm sure it's like every other job in the world," Mitchell said. "People know a professional when they see one."

She smiled at him. "Professional busybody, you listen to my grandson."

Mitchell asked about how hard it had been to get her grandson to come out here and live with her. Emmy Watkins had called it a battle royal, saying she didn't know until De-Shawn announced he was leaving Clinton how many coaches in what she called your metropolitan tri-state area were willing to take her grandson into their homes if he'd play his senior year for them. She said every time one of these coaches, recruiting him for high school at the same time all the other hustlers were already recruiting him for college, would leave the apartment on Gerard Avenue—this after his mother finally passed, she said, halfway through his junior year—De-Shawn would call and say he knew where he was spending his senior year, he'd made up his mind for sure this time.

Her dark eyes bright with fun now as she told him that part, and about how she'd put her foot down and told all the sneaker men to stay out of South Fork.

"In the end I decided that this boy needed a firm hand," she said. She held up a wrinkled hand, much older than her face. "Mine," she said.

"What about Antoine?"

She made a face. "Antoine's just got his hand *out,*" she said.

"I met him."

"I heard." Then she made a fluttery motion with her old hand, as if changing the subject. "Anyway," she said, "I told my grandson he wasn't going to live with his coach or some other coach, that he was going to come out here with me. And he went along."

Mitchell said, "He's better off, from everything I know about him. And you."

"All the listening he wouldn't do with his mother, he does with me."

Mitchell said, "He strikes me as being a good kid."

"Getting there," Emmy Watkins said. "Now that the two of us seem to have that temper of his under control."

"He doesn't strike me as a hothead," Mitchell said. "I've

only really talked to him one time, but I've watched him at practice. He seems to keep himself together pretty good."

"Now," she said. She narrowed the eyes a little, as if she was curious about something all of a sudden, tilted her head to the side. "Are we just talking here, Mr. Mitchell?"

"I'm going to tell you something you're just going to have to take on faith, Mrs. Watkins," he said. "If I tell you something stays between the two of us, it stays between the two of us."

She hadn't asked who he was working for, or even what kind of story he was doing. Maybe she just assumed. Or maybe, Mitchell thought, she was the one interviewing him. Getting things out of him. It had only been a few minutes. Mitchell had already figured out it was probably a mistake to underestimate Emmy Watkins.

"He came out here after he gave the beating to Mr. Harm," she said. "That made up my mind as much as anything."

Mitchell said, "I've read back on your grandson pretty thoroughly. I don't remember anything about an assault on somebody named Harm. Or anybody."

"That's because we buried it," she said. "No pun intended, of course."

"Who's Mr. Harm? One of his teachers at DeWitt Clinton?"

"Mr. Harmon Levitt. He ran DeShawn's AAU team, the Kings. Out of the King Church. Up on Frederick Douglass."

The King Church Kings were like the Yankees of New York City amateur basketball. They had been formed by a rich downtown money manager named Harmon Levitt, and had ruled AAU ball in most age divisions until a few years ago, when Levitt had been accused of child molestation by several of his former players. As much as he'd read back on Show Watkins's career, he still hadn't read enough, apparently.

"I'm sorry," Mitchell said. "I should have made the connection. I remember DeShawn played for the Kings."

"Even if he'd like to forget."

"This trouble he had with Harmon Levitt—was it before or after those players came forward?"

She made a sniffing noise. "Right before." She narrowed her eyes, pursed her lips together so hard they seemed to disappear. "Trouble," she said. "That's a polite way of referring to a rich fat old single man making advances on young boys in his program. Even if the situation is still being adjudicated, as they say. But they can adjudicate until the cows come home. He did what they said he did. Did it to all those other boys the way he finally tried to do it to DeShawn."

"And DeShawn didn't take kindly to that, I gather."

"No, sir."

"Was it the first time?"

"DeShawn says."

"And you believe him?"

"He had no reason to lie, Mr. Mitchell. He said that he and the other boys had heard things, you know, *before.* But he himself didn't want to believe that about kindly old Mr. Harm, who'd been giving him things since he was twelve years old."

"But then he found out firsthand."

"It was after practice one day, the two of them in the office Mr. Harm kept downstairs at King. He said that he knew how hard things were for DeShawn, what with his family situation and all, and that if DeShawn would just keep quiet, there could be some money coming his way. A real nice chunk of money, he said. And then he casually put his hand on DeShawn and left it there."

"What did DeShawn do?"

"He backhanded him halfway across the room, that's what he did. Then he picked him up, again according to DeShawn, like some little Raggedy Andy, and put him up against the wall hard and slapped him a couple of more times upside his head and didn't stop until Mr. Harm started blubbering. Then he walked out the door and never went back to King."

"Just the one time, you said. So nothing had been building up, then?"

"Oh, now that's a different matter entirely, Mr. Mitchell. I think something had been building up in DeShawn his whole life. For all that talent the Lord gave the boy, that smile, all that charm he can put on when he wants, he always had that anger in him. Even worse than his brother Antoine, who I always thought gave you that temper of his mostly for show, like he had to play the cop all the time, leastways before his fall. DeShawn, though, his anger came from the *soul*, Mr. Mitchell. Anger about what his mother became right in front of the boy's eyes. Anger about the way Antoine turned out. It's why he's always telling me he's in such a hurry to get to the good damn parts of his life. His words, not mine."

She sat with her old hands clasped tightly on her knees while she told Mitchell all this. When she stopped, Mitchell became aware of jazz music playing softly from another room in the apartment. Mitchell asked if that was Miles Davis and she said, "Clark Terry." Saying she could play her own music for a change before she picked up her boy at practice and he came home and started playing his Outkast or whatever it all was, boom boom boom, bam bam bam.

"Ma'am," Mitchell said, "I want to ask you a question you might not like very much: Can you ever see DeShawn losing his temper and behaving inappropriately with another kid?"

"You mean in the ways you've been asking all over town about?"

He smiled. "Yes."

"No," she said. "Not in a million years. Do something to another boy like maybe Mr. Harm wanted to do with him? My grandson? Never. I can understand you asking the question, Mr. Mitchell. But not my boy, no sir."

"Would he go along if the others were doing something like that?"

"DeShawn doesn't go along with others, Mr. Mitchell. They go along with him. Like he's always telling his grandma, he's the one *leads* the break." She shook her head. "He's got that temper on him, as I told you. And I'm always making him watch his mouth. But if DeShawn's got an issue with you, he won't come on you from the blind side. He will be right up there in your face."

"I appreciate your honesty."

"Remember something: He's a boy yet, even if he's in a man's body." She smoothed out what had to be an imaginary wrinkle on her dress, right above the knees. "These are all big boys. I'm not saying they don't do dumb things some-times. These ath-e-letes, they do dumb things their whole lives, don't they? I watch the TV. I see what happens to them over a woman, or what was supposed to be a night of fun at some club, or when they get behind the wheel of one of their fast cars when they shouldn't. DeShawn's made his share of mistakes, and he's going to make more. But I can't *ever* see him make the kind you're alluding to, sir."

"I've been doing a lot more around town than just allud-ing." He smiled at her again.

"And I do more than watch TV and clean houses," she said. "I can *hear*, Mr. Mitchell. More than people in this town think."

"I believe you."

She looked at him, her face looking young all of a sud-den, like a child looking at you, clear-eyed, wide-open, and telling you the truth.

"You're not the only one thinks he knows this town's se-crets," Emmy Watkins said.

**A**s far as Mitchell could tell, there was no official closing time for Hiram's. In the summer, you could walk down Main Street at ten o'clock and still see people at the counter, lined up to buy homemade ice cream. It all seemed to depend on the traffic. Gus, the owner, liked to say that he didn't go home every night with his pockets stuffed with money by closing the door when there were still paying customers wanting to come inside.

Tonight Hiram's was still open a few minutes after nine o'clock. Mitchell pulled up in his truck on his way back from Emmy Watkins's apartment, deciding on the fly to get a cheeseburger deluxe, and fries, and a chocolate milk shake, to go.

Hang around with these kids, eat like them.

There was one booth full of high school kids, two people at the counter, one at each end. The customer at the far end was Hank Bender, a bowl of soup in front of him, a cup of coffee, a newspaper opened to a crossword puzzle.

Mitchell placed his order with the high school girl behind the counter, then walked down to where Bender was. "This seat taken?" he said.

Bender looked up, no change of expression. "Free country."

Mitchell got the high school girl's attention, pointed at Bender's coffee cup. "How goes it?" he said.

"How goes what?"

"Life in general."

"You don't care about life in general, Mitch. Or my life in particular."

Bender sighed now, put his spoon down in his bowl, turned around on his swivel chair so he was facing Mitchell. "It's late, Mitch. I'm having a delicious bowl of Gus's reheated Manhattan chowder before I have to go pick up my kid, whose car is in the shop with a carburetor that looks like he dropped it off a fucking roof. But now I am not minding my own business anymore, am I? Because I am lucky enough to run into you."

"You were happier to see me when I showed up at your office that day."

"That was before you went out of your way to piss off me and everybody else in this town."

"It's a gift."

"Why don't we just get to whatever it is that's on your mind."

"You make any progress on Bobby Ferraro?"

"No. You want the longer answer?"

"Sure."

"Fuck no."

"So this was done to him by persons unknown, end of story?"

Bender said, "Would you like a discourse on how many people in this country, every single goddamn day, end up dead because they were in the wrong place at the wrong time? And how many of those murders end up unsolved?"

Mitchell didn't say anything to that.

Bender said, "I've talked to every kid I could think of that knew him well, even though it's a pretty goddamn short list. I've talked to his teachers and his guidance counselor and his father and his surrogate father, Ken Glass. I've put everything I found out with what I knew about him going in. He was a good kid. He was lonely. Getting to be manager of the team was about the biggest thing that ever happened to him. He wanted to coach someday. Maybe even be an assistant to his hero the coach, if the coach hadn't moved on to bigger and better things by then. Then something bad happened to this kid and he died. It sucks. But he died."

"And my theories that this all might have started with some hazing incident?"

Bender took in a lot of air, let it out slowly, as if afraid he might get the bends if he didn't. "Dead end," he said.

"You're telling me nothing went on over there."

Bender picked up his pencil and drew a big X across the crossword. Put the pencil back down. "Plenty went on over there, Mitch. They were kids on a fucking basketball field trip, going through the motions of bonding for their coach. Did they screw around a little? Yeah, they did. One of the nights I heard they rigged a Rube Goldberg thing so water fell on Glenn Moore, as a way of showing everybody was fair play. They somehow got Show Watkins's bed outside with him in it, which must have been some trick. They played Blind Man's Bluff with Drew one night. That's it. And if there was more than that and nobody's telling, including my own kid, who knows better than to hold things back on me, then they've done a hell of a goddamn job of getting their stories straight. I even took the ferry over one day and checked the place out myself. Imagine that. A cop with an agenda like me."

"I never said that . . ."

Bender held up a hand. "I've talked to every kid on that team twice. My own kid more than that. And do I believe that something criminal went on over there? No, sir, I do not."

Mitchell took a sip of his coffee, not looking at Bender, said, "Would your kid cover for somebody else?"

"My kid doesn't lie."

"Hank, don't take this the wrong way. But all kids his age lie. They lie about why they were late, or why they flunked the quiz, or whether anybody was drinking at the party, or smoking weed or Marlboro Lights. You did, I did, your boy does, maybe even Glenn Moore does. Kids lie."

"Now you're a parent."

"They lie, Hank. And sometimes they get clumsy when they're trying to cover up a lie. Clumsy or scared or both. So they throw a rock through somebody's window. Or slash somebody's car. Or get a kid alone in the park and try to scare the shit out of him."

"What kid in the park?"

"Which one do you think."

"Sam Perry?"

"Maybe."

"We're playing games here?"

"Hell no. I know the only game that matters in this town. And that's the one that gets played tomorrow night at seven-thirty." Mitchell turned then and saw the girl holding up the bag with his dinner in it.

He threw a couple of dollars on the counter. "You talk to Drew Hudson yet?" he said to Bender.

"As soon as his mother lets me near him."

"Hank?" Mitchell said. "I'm not giving up on this."

"There's a bombshell."

"You know what hazing is really all about, Hank? All these bullshit notions of loyalty to the group. At the start, anyway. Belonging to the group. Building cohesion. The stronger ones decide to impose order, everybody else feeling like they've got no choice but to go along."

"Your point being?"

"That doesn't just sound like the basketball team. It sounds like this whole town."

He ate half his burger, hardly touched his fries. The conversation with Hank Bender had made him hot. But then everything in South Fork was making him hot these days. If Mitchell could see on these kids' faces that they were lying, even a half-assed cop ought to be able to see it. Unless he didn't fucking want to, too worried that his own kid might be involved.

Unless he really was a cop with an agenda, the biggest of all, covering for his son.

Mitchell tossed the milk shake in the garbage without even opening it, deciding he would go down to Jimmy O'Rourke's and wash down Gus's burger with a cold beer instead.

He walked up the opposite side of the street from O'Rourke's, past St. Ann's, past DeMoulas's Liquor Store, which was directly across from O'Rourke's.

Parked in front of DeMoulas's was Art Daneko's truck. The store was closed, which meant Daneko had to be across the street at O'Rourke's.

Hail, hail, Mitchell thought, the gang's all here.

Bender said he'd pissed off the whole town? Well, jump ball. He was pissed off right back. He sat down on a bench in front of DeMoulas's and smoked cigarettes and waited for Daneko to come out, which he did about forty-five minutes later. Alone tonight, none of the guys from his crew with him. Mitchell saw him get halfway across Main, wait for a couple of cars coming from the west to pass, then continue toward his truck.

Mitchell stepped around the front of the truck, leaned against the hood.

"Hey, Art," he said.

"Jesus." Daneko shook his head. "You again?"

"Me."

"I got nothing more to say to you, except for this here: If you're still standing in front of this truck when I get inside and turn the key, you're going to get run over."

The parking lot next to DeMoulas's, always full of cars on summer nights, was empty. Mitchell jerked his head in that direction, knowing Daneko would follow.

Hang around with kids, start to act like them.

He took about ten steps, looked over his shoulder, saw Daneko coming around the front of the truck, stuffing his car keys into the side pocket of his vest.

Daneko said, "You been waiting for me out here all night?"

"It was more of a spur-of-the-moment thing."

They were in the middle of the parking lot now, lit only by an outside floodlight over the side door of DeMoulas's.

"You're fucking serious," Daneko said, like he still couldn't believe it. "You really want some of me."

Mitchell put his arms out. "Yeah, I do."

"This is stupid."

"You're stupid, Art, if you thought I was afraid of a slob like you."

With that, he put his hands up, took two long steps to close the distance between them, and hit Art Daneko with a straight right hand. He couldn't remember the last time he'd hit anything except his fast bag. So he felt the sting in his knuckles even as he knew he'd caught Daneko flush on the left cheek. Daneko didn't go down. Mitchell hadn't expected him to. Daneko said, "Okay, asshole," and got his own hands up now and circled away, moving cautiously to Mitchell's right. But Mitchell could see already that Art Daneko wasn't nearly as formidable an opponent when he didn't have the element of surprise going for him. Mitchell took a slide step of his own to his right, planted, and hit Daneko with a left hook underneath his rib cage. Daneko made a sound like air coming out of a balloon. Still didn't go down. Mitchell had needed to hit somebody for a while. Hit *back*. Now Art Daneko was handy. Mitchell said to him, "See *this*, this is a fair fight, Art." When Daneko got some breath back in him, straightened himself up, Mitchell put a jab in his face, felt the sting of that, too, ducked under the wild right that Daneko tried to throw, hooked him with a right this time, under the ribs on the other side, then hit him as hard as he could with a left hand that caught Art Daneko flush near his left ear. Now he went down.

Mitchell looked down and saw blood on Art Daneko's left cheekbone, from the cut next to his eye.

Mitchell knelt down next to him.

Art Daneko covered up with both hands. "No more," he said.

Mitchell said, "That night you came to my house—did you touch my computer?"

Daneko said, "The fuck are you talking about?"

"Did you write anything on my computer?"

"No." He licked some blood from the corner of his mouth. "I can barely turn on the one at the office."

"I just had to make sure," Mitchell said.

"This is only over for now," Daneko said.

"You're right," Mitchell said. "Just not the way you think."

# 17

South Fork easily won its opener from Oceanside, 83–53. Show Watkins had twenty-two points, fourteen rebounds, twelve assists, five blocked shots. Glenn Moore had twenty points, Dave Bender hit four three-pointers, Eric Daneko ended up with ten rebounds. Everyone who saw the game agreed that South Fork would have beaten Oceanside by fifty points if Coach Ken Glass hadn't cleared his bench with ten minutes left in the game.

However, it wasn't the big story out of South Fork in Sunday's edition of the *Long Island Press,* even if the game did get pretty good play in the sports section.

The big story was Sam Perry's, on the front page, based on his exclusive interview with Drew Hudson.

In it, Drew Hudson told in graphic detail about what was supposed to have been a night of harmless high school hazing at the team's preseason camp in Connecticut that had turned into the equivalent of a sexual assault.

The headline on Page 1 came from one of Drew's quotes:

### "A NIGHT IN HELL"

It started innocently enough, he told Sam, the whole team seated around a campfire after a touch football game, Coach Glass giving them some time to themselves. Bonding time, he called it. Drew said it was at the campfire that he was told by the senior veterans on the team—Glenn and Dave, Eric and Christian Bowdoin—that he was the underclassman who'd been selected for initiation.

The senior veterans told him they were resuming a South Fork tradition.

"You're the unlucky loser," he remembered Dave Bender telling him.

Glenn Moore laughed and told Drew Hudson not to worry, they were going easy on him, this wasn't going to turn into *Lord of the Flies*. Drew remembered Glenn laughing again and then asking for a show of hands for how many guys on the team had even read *Lord of the Flies*.

The deal, Glenn said, was this: They were going to tie his hands behind him, blindfold him, take him out in the woods, and simply ask him to find his way back to the cabins.

And to make it more interesting, they all had different kinds of noisemakers with them: kazoos, harmonicas, whistles, clickers, even bags that made farting noises. The rest of the players were supposed to scatter in the woods, try to confuse him, send him in all different directions, and Drew would have to figure out which one of them was really trying to lead him into the clearing.

So the seniors took him out into the woods, turned him around a few times, wished him good luck.

Left him there.

It wasn't long before he heard all the noises. Like in that pool game you played when you were a kid, Marco Polo, the one where you closed your eyes and people called out to you and you tried to dive toward them and tag them, Drew told Sam.

Mostly he remembered the stinking kazoos.

The sound effects didn't last long, though.

Soon, the only sounds around him were the crickets and wind rustle and bird noises of empty woods in the night.

In the distance, he could hear music coming from what he assumed was one of the cabins.

What he didn't know: By then, his teammates had all just gone back to their individual cabins. That was supposed to be part of the joke, nobody coming for him, at least not right away.

"Some joke, huh?" Drew said in the *Press*.

Somehow, after what felt like an eternity of bumping into trees and bushes and tripping over God-knows-what-else he was tripping over and hearing whatever animals he heard running around in the night, Drew made it to a clearing. He was pretty sure it was the clearing between the last cabin, the one closest to the woods, empty that week, the one that belonged to counselors when the place was a summer camp.

"Hey, guys," he called out. "I made it."

The music had stopped playing.

"Hey, guys, c'mon, come untie me."

That was the last thing he said before he felt a hand go over his mouth. Then there was a raspy voice next to his ear, impossible for him to recognize, saying, "What's a cute boy like you doing out here all by yourself in the woods?"

Drew thought it was part of the joke.

Because everything was supposed to be, that's what they'd told him.

Then two of them, at least two of them, maybe more, had him inside one of the cabins. By then, they'd tied a rag into his mouth, much too tight, the knot biting into the back of his head. He thought it might be the empty counselors' cabin, the one set off by itself, but he wasn't sure.

Still thinking this was just part of it, that at the very end, some of his teammates had decided to scare the crap out of him.

Then they had him down.

They were taking off his pants, and his underwear.

The only one doing any talking was the whispery voice.

"You like to get close to nature, right?" the raspy voice said.

He felt what he thought might be a pinecone pressed up against him.

"If you can handle this, we figure you can handle anything," the voice said.

Drew waited, not believing this could be happening to him. Not with his own team. Not after a night sitting around a campfire.

Not after all the laughs that had started everything.

Finally a voice Drew recognized yelled out, "I can't!"

"Shut your fucking mouth. *Now.*"

"I can't do it!"

"Shut up and do it, you little girl, or you're next."

"Don't make me."

That voice, Drew was sure, belonged to Bobby Ferraro.


**S**am had gotten the story this way:

Drew called on his cell phone.

"I heard what happened to you," Drew said. "Your mom told my mom."

Sam thought: Only instant-messaging works faster than moms.

Sam told Drew he was doing all right, even though he wasn't, even though he felt like he was still afraid of his own shadow.

"More important," Sam said, "how are you doing?"

Drew said, "I'm ready to talk."

Just like that.

Sam felt like the phone had given off some kind of electric shock.

"Drew . . . you sure about this?"

"I'm sure."

They ended up speaking for over an hour in Drew's room, just the two of them. Sam was paranoid the whole time that his tape recorder wasn't working; he kept checking it every few minutes to make sure he could hear the whirr of the heads turning. To back it up, he took notes as best he could, especially on stuff he thought was key.

But then, just about everything coming out of Drew's mouth was key.

When they got to the day he took the pills, Drew said he didn't want to talk about that for the newspaper. Sam almost said: After everything you've *already* talked about? But knew enough to keep his mouth shut, he didn't want to do anything that would slam Drew into some kind of shutdown mode. So he nodded, like he was cool with everything, when Drew said he'd tell Sam what happened that morning, but didn't want to say anything else in the paper except that he just couldn't take it anymore.

Which, he said, was the truth anyway.

Sam shut off the tape recorder.

Drew said that a few minutes after Sam left that day, his cell rang, almost like whoever was calling knew Sam had just left.

It was the whispery voice.

"Your cell doesn't have caller I.D.?" Sam said.

"The number came up 'unknown.'"

"What did the guy say?"

"Basically, that I better keep quiet about what happened, or it would happen again. And keep happening. 'It won't end,' he said. Said that if I ever got the urge to tell, I better move out of South Fork that day. Because every day after that, for as long as I was in school everybody'd know I got buddied that way." Drew frowned. "You ever heard that word? Buddied?"

Sam said no.

"Then," Drew said, "he said I didn't want to end up like Bobby, did I? And hung up."

Sam didn't know how much weight Drew had lost, just that he looked too skinny, too pale, his eyes too big for his face. Like some kind of faded picture of the kid he used to be. Or the *after* shot in one of those before-and-after weight-loss ads you saw in magazines. "That's when I snapped," he said.

He said he got crazy then, cleaning up his room, making sure everything was organized, went downstairs, saw the typed pages from Mitchell he'd left on the coffee table. Had the presence of mind to make sure the fireplace flue was open and burned Mitchell's story. Like it was some record of everything he didn't want people ever to know.

"Even though I could tell that you and Mr. Mitchell know," Drew said. "Crazy, huh?"

He thought about leaving a note, had no idea what he wanted to say. Or what he should apologize for. "In books and movies," he said, "the note is always about being sorry, right? But I wasn't sorry. I just wanted to get that night out of my head once and for all, how they weren't done after the pinecone, how they had that broomstick . . . Do you get that?"

Sam said, yeah, he did.

"I wasn't even sure what I should take," Drew said. "My mom's pills were out on the counter, so I grabbed them. She calls them her happy pills, I told you that, didn't I?" He swallowed hard. "I remember thinking, Well, what the fuck, Drew, at least you can die happy."

He looked at Sam, eyes starting to fill up. "Funny, huh?"

Sam said, "It's over."

Drew said, "Is it over for you?"

Sam had told Drew the truth about Mallozzi, working it out in his own head that he owed him that much. "No," he said, "it's not over for me."

Sam went home and transcribed the tape over the next couple of hours. When he was done he called Mitchell, who was out. He thought about riding around town looking for him, finally decided to just go over to Mitchell's house and wait. When Mitchell got out of his pickup, Sam was on the front steps waiting, underneath one of the new flood-lights Mitchell had put in. He handed him the folder with Drew Hudson's interview in it. Mitchell read the first page before he even opened the front door, then said, "We've got work to do."

Sam said, "I don't know how to write this."

"I'll help you," Mitchell said.

**S**am finished the first draft about two in the morning. He kept asking Mitchell if he should have asked a better question here or there. Mitchell said he'd done fine. Sam said, yeah, but there's big holes, he hadn't been smart enough to ask about after the attack, where he spent the rest of the night, stuff like that. Drew had just jumped ahead to the next morning, going home, being afraid to tell. Mitchell said there were always holes, this wasn't a lawyer show on television where they tied up everything with a ribbon after the last commercial break. And Mitchell said he had a feeling that no matter what tough questions Sam might have asked, Drew's story wasn't going to change very much.

Sam had asked why Drew didn't tell somebody that first night, the coach or one of the players. Drew had closed his eyes, like he was exhausted all of a sudden.

"You've got enough story," he said.

One last question, Sam said: How come you never said anything to Bobby?

Drew said the Friday Bobby disappeared, it had been him and Bobby alone in the locker room before practice. And he had finally walked up to him and asked him why he'd done it. Not if. Just why. Just like that, matter-of-fact. *Why*? And Bobby had looked at him and said, "If I went along, they said they wouldn't do it to me. They lied." Then walked out of the locker room.

It was the last time he saw him, or talked to him.

"High school boys," Mitchell said to Sam, when he was finished writing.

"What about us?"

"Show Watkins's grandma said I should remember I was dealing with high school boys. She didn't put it this way, but she meant most don't know their ass from their elbows."

Sam said, "It's like they've been making this up as they went along."

"And still are," Mitchell said.

Sam went home to get some sleep, as jazzed as he was, came back the next morning. They worked on the piece a little more, cutting things, adding things, Mitchell still showing him how he could move stuff around to make it read better. When they were both happy, Sam called the sports editor at home, Saturday morning, told him what he had. The sports editor said to e-mail it to him on his AOL account, he didn't want it floating around the *Press*'s computer system for anybody to see.

The sports editor said, "Drew Hudson isn't going to back away from this, is he?"

Sam said it was all on tape. The sports editor said that as soon as he read it, he'd get one of the paper's lawyers in to look at it. Sam asked if he should still go to the South Fork–Oceanside game and write a sidebar. The sports editor said that Damon Wills could handle the game, that he was going to have Wills wait until afterward, when the other guys were writing their stories, and get Ken Glass alone for a reaction. Maybe Glenn Moore, too.

Then they were going to put it all in the paper.

"What happens after that?" Sam said to Mitchell when he got off the phone.

"After the shit hits the fan?" Mitchell said. "If you don't mind a mixed metaphor, that's when they'll want to shoot the messenger."

# 18

Show had the keys to the gym. Nobody else on the team knew he did. Not even Glenn. If Glenn had a set of keys of his own—to go along with the keys to the fucking city—him and Show had never talked about it. Not that him and Glenn talked about much more than what one of them wanted the other to do when he came off a screen, or was looking for a lob. Or when they were going to run whatever they wanted coming out of a timeout, no matter what Coach Glass had just told them to do.

Show knew you didn't have to be some kind of brain surgeon to know that whatever Glenn said to people, he didn't need somebody like Show showing up at his school, wanting to share his ball.

Show knew he was getting in the way of Glenn's personal damn spotlight, the one that had been following him around his whole damn life. Glenn didn't want people to know that, of course. Truth be told? He was like Show in that way: just letting people know shit about him he *wanted* them to know.

All's Show knew was that he had his keys and could pick his spots and have the gym to himself, like this here, on a Sunday afternoon. If one of his teammates happened to show up, Show would just tell them that Reggie, one of the janitors, had let him in. Just make something up on the fly, like he did. Let Two Mom worry about whether enough lies like that would get you sent straight to hell.

Show'd always thought of hell as anyplace he'd ever been in his life where he didn't have any control. Or where somebody was trying to do him wrong for no reason.

Like Mr. Harm.

He needed to be alone today.

A court of his own, that's where he was happiest. Always. Alone on some nice court. Even a street court used to be all right, as long as he had it to himself. But always outside, over at Rosedale Park, someplace like that where he'd go play sometimes, there'd be somebody coming along eventually, giving him that hey-y'all, you want some company? Or asking if he wanted to go one-on-one. Or some such. Not seeing that he just wanted to shoot around by himself. Just another way of people messing with him when he had everything set up nice. A clean nice gym like this, doors closed, was better. Someday he was going to have one at his own big-ass house. Get himself some converted barn, like he saw at Cal Ripken's house one time, they were doing a piece on him on ESPN. Full-court, indoors, out on his property someplace. A full exercise gym in the upstairs part. Even a scoreboard. Show *loved* that. Ate that shit *right* up. When Ripken would play pickup ball in the offseason, allowed to do that because he had it written up in his contract, he'd always make sure to invite ten other guys. Eleven in all. They'd sub in and out, everybody got to play. But the reason he invited eleven was that the guy sitting out could work the scoreboard.

Show could imagine himself with a setup like that, his own gym, have his boys on 24-call, go out there and practice any time of the day or night, green grass and trees all around, Two Mom maybe cooking something up if she felt like it. . . .

Show shook his head, to clear it out. Bring himself back. He knew he better enjoy the last of his quiet time while he had it. Knowing that Christian was coming over, all jammed up because of the story about Drew in the paper.

Christian waking him up and then pretty soon going back over that night, how nobody knew where anybody was after the campfire, after they took Drew out there. How nobody seemed to be in the cabin they were supposed to be in.

"You're saying I had something to do with this, Spud?" Show had said on the phone.

Not calling him Spud because of the old-time midget player, Spud Webb. No, Show called him that because Christian's father had worked one of the potato farms. Knowing Christian didn't like it, but would take it. The way they all took it when Show dished it out.

"I'm just sayin'."

"You're *always* just sayin'. You know I went for a walk down by the water, then went and talked with Coach. And when you tell me you were playing video with Golden Boy and Dave Bender, I don't go askin' them, Is it true?"

"People are going to believe Drew."

"A mommy boy like that? Don't be so sure." Then he said to Christian, "You going to start acting like a mommy boy now?"

Christian said, "You know me better."

"For how long? Two whole months?" Show had said on the phone.

He heard banging on the door at the other end of the court now. Meaning he must've forgot to unlock it. So he jogged down there, saw it was Christian, in his LeBron red headband, South Fork tee, Nike sweats that looked like they were store-bought on the way over. Like Christian his whole self just came out of a box.

"I talked to some of the other guys on the team after I talked to you," Christian said. "Some of them sound like they're half-afraid they're going to get arrested."

"If they didn't do nothin', they got nothin' to sweat themselves over."

Show passed him the ball, Christian passed it back, saying, "I'll play in a minute. Right now we got to talk on this a little more."

"You see me goin' anywhere?"

Christian said, "Lot of the guys said what I said, people are gonna believe Drew."

"'Cause he's such a reliable source? He just swallowed a bottle of meds. I'm telling you, what makes it so damn auto-matic the boy is telling the truth?"

"The paper," Christian said. "And I saw where they already picked it up on the ESPN dot com. Most likely it's on television, too."

Show stepped back, outside the three-point line, shot from the left elbow and made it.

"Money," he said.

Christian said, "Don't act like you're not sweatin' on this yourself."

"Let me ask you something," Show said, laying the ball on his hip. "What Drew said happened—were you one of the ones did it?"

"Are you freak? I don't even like to *think* about shit like that."

"Think I do?"

Christian said, "But if Drew's even close to telling the truth, then somebody on the team is lying."

Show said, "If they're lyin', they're dyin'." He gave a little roll to his shoulders. "Either way, it's not our problem now, is it?"

"You can't be this cool, nigger."

"Yeah," Show said, "yeah, I can."

Monday was reaction day in the newspaper, as Mitchell knew it would be, the other papers playing catch-up to the *Press*.

Pete Hamill, one of Mitchell's newspaper heroes, had once told Mitchell at some panel discussion at NYU, "You either set the debate or join the debate."

Sam Perry, Press Correspondent, a high school kid, had set the debate.

Everybody else wanted to talk to Drew Hudson, get a piece of him before the next news cycle began. But nobody could, because he and his mother had left South Fork Sunday night. Shelley Hudson had called Kate Perry to tell her. When Kate asked where they were going, Shelley Hudson said, "Away."

Kate asked about the police.

"They had their chance," Shelley said.

Kate said she asked, what about school, and Shelley said, "What about it?" Then Kate asked when they would be back and Shelley said when the police found out who did this. And if they didn't, she said, maybe never. Then she told Kate she'd be in touch and hung up.

Mitchell had seen Kate in the front window of River Road on Monday morning, right before she opened up the store, rearranging some of the clothes she had stacked on a big antique display table. She waved to him, told him about the Hudsons, then told him how many calls from television stations and radio stations she was getting for Sam.

"What do I do?" she said.

"Just say no."

"To everybody?"

"For now," he said. "He doesn't want to look like he's

grandstanding, like he's making it about him. Though if you watch a lot of television, that looks like the national pastime for newspaper guys every time they get the chance."

Kate had a big Starbucks on the counter. She sipped from it, turned around and said, "You were right, by the way."

"Said the judge to the defendant."

Kate Perry said, "Don't make this hard, I'm trying to apologize here."

"Sam was right," he said. "I've mostly just been along for the ride."

"Sure you have," she said, then paused and said, "Hey, how about the three of us have dinner at the Perry house tonight?"

Mitchell said he'd bring the wine.

He went home and turned on Channel 12, saw the "Live" graphic in the right-hand corner of the screen, saw Norman Brodie, the principal at South Fork High, talking about "troubling allegations made by a troubled young student of ours."

To the television set, Mitchell said, "And why do you think he's troubled, you dumb cocksucker?"

Then Norman Brodie, tall and skinny and somehow reminding Mitchell of a cartoon undertaker in his dark suit, said that the school would be working very closely with the fine South Fork Police Department to get to the bottom of this. And, he said, if it turned out that any members of the basketball team were involved in anything "unseemly," there would be "dire" consequences.

The money shot came at the end.

"I just caution everyone to remember something," Principal Norman Brodie said. "Allegations, no matter how serious, are not arrests. Arrests are not indictments. Indictments are not convictions. For now, all we have are charges made by one of our students. And reported in the newspaper by another student."

Brodie made it sound like it was something in the school paper.

He was still talking when Mitchell shut off the set.

The next game for South Fork was Wednesday night, in Hopeville, about an hour up-island. As far as Mitchell knew, Coach Ken Glass's practice was at its normal time, after school. He drove over there about four o'clock. The young black cop, Christian Bowdoin's cousin, Mitchell couldn't remember his first name, was posted at the only entrance to the school parking lot. He was holding a clipboard. When Mitchell rolled down the window, Officer Bowdoin said, "Name."

Mitchell said, "We met once before, the night somebody pitched that brick through Kate Perry's store window."

If he found the information fascinating, he managed to keep himself under control. "Name," he said.

"Mitchell. Ben Mitchell."

Bowdoin looked down his list and said, "Sorry."

"You're kidding?"

"I hardly ever kid around when I have to deal with this many reporters in one afternoon, trust me. Your name isn't on the list, I can't let you in. Orders from the chief, and from the principal."

"I didn't know I had to call ahead to go to basketball practice."

"Today you do. It's closed to the public."

"I'm not the public."

"You're not on my list, you are," Bowdoin said.

Mitchell made a U-turn and drove back down Farm Road, deciding how much he really wanted to see for himself how an arrogant little peckerhead like Glass would play this. Enough to back-door his way into practice, he decided, then drove all the way around to the entrance to Waverly Park, the biggest public park in South Fork, the one with about ten soccer fields and the old Waverly mansion in the middle of it, now used for weddings and graduation parties and holiday bazaars. Mitchell hadn't been over to Waverly since he'd been back in town, but if his memory was right, the running and walking trail that snaked its way all around the property took you right past the back end of the high school's property, behind the football field. Mitchell parked in the lot in front of the Waverly mansion, made his way along the path made muddy by rain the night before, finally came to the opening in the woods that brought him out behind the end zone bleachers. On the other side of the football field was the service entrance to South Fork High. There was a janitor sitting on top of the loading dock, legs dangling, smoking a cigarette, grinning at Mitchell.

"From the ESPN," the guy said. "You're on the ESPN regular at all, I never forget the face."

"You got me."

All those years in newspapers, now all anybody cared about was television. A beautiful thing.

"Got you tryin' to sneak into practice is where I got you."

"What's your name?"

"Reggie. And just 'cause you got me on a first-name situation now doesn't mean I'm gonna let you in."

Mitchell had stopped at the ATM on his way over to the high school. He pulled a crisp fifty out of his wallet, showed it to Reggie, then handed it to him. Reggie took it, slipped it into the pocket of what looked like a bowling shirt, said, "Enjoy practice."

Mitchell had originally thought Glass might close practice today. But he had decided to make it business as usual, with the exception of Officer Bowdoin. So there were a couple of dozen media people in the bleachers, across from the bench side of the gym. Mitchell spotted Sam up near the top, where they'd first watched practice together.

When Mitchell got up there, he said, "How'd it go today?"

"Like you said. I'm the bad guy."

"With the players, you mean? Or everybody?"

"Everybody except the teachers, and I can't say for sure about them."

"Drew's gone," Mitchell said, "and you're here, kid."

"Oh yeah. I'm here."

"Any of the players say anything to you?"

"Dave Bender and Eric and Christian Bowdoin were at this table at lunch. When they saw me just walking in their direction with my tray, they got up and walked out, eye-balling me *real* hard before they did."

"This is hardball now," Mitchell said. "Wear a helmet."

"Or a suit of armor," Sam said.

On the court, Coach Ken Glass blew his whistle a couple of times, like he wasn't just trying to get the attention of his players, but his media audience as well. He even positioned the players so their backs faced the side of the court where Mitchell and Sam and the other reporters and TV people were. So he was addressing everybody at the same time.

"I am going to remind you of something we talked about the first day we were together" is the way he began. "The strong don't just survive. Hell, anybody can survive. The truly strong aren't ever satisfied with surviving. They want to *triumph.*"

"Jesus Christ," Mitchell said to Sam.

"The strong group," Glass said, "cannot be ripped apart, no matter how much the weak try to do that."

He was walking up and down in front of his players, hands behind his back.

The old Patton dodge, Mitchell thought.

"The *strong,*" he said, voice rising a little bit now, "never have to explain what makes them strong, and keeps them strong. They just have to know, in a way the weak never will."

He stopped.

Now he was talking to the players.

"If we stay together and stay strong, can anybody defeat us?"

"No!" the South Fork players yelled.

"I didn't catch that!"

*"No!"*

Now he stared past them, up into the bleachers. Defiantly, Mitchell thought.

"You people want your sound bite for today? My response? There it is." He stuck his whistle back in his mouth, blew it again, and said to the players, "Two lines for layups."

"What did you think?" Sam said to Mitchell, keeping his voice low, even way up here, as though Glass might hear him, bring him down and make him do push-ups.

Mitchell said, "I think he's crazy."

Mitchell told Sam to stay with the rest of the reporters after practice in case Glass decided to give them some kind of limited access to the players.

"If you do get in that locker room," Mitchell said, "don't put yourself in a situation where one of these dinks might try to call you out in front of everybody. 'Cause no matter how much of an asshole they'd be, it's still their turf. There hasn't been a media guy ever who came out a winner in one of those scenes."

"Got it," Sam said.

Mitchell said, "You know the deal. They're strong, you're weak."

"How could I forget?"

"And don't stop for a secret rendezvous between now and dinner."

Sam said the normal practice was two hours, depending on how pissed off the coach was when they got near the end. So they were only about halfway through when Mitchell left. He had plenty of time to walk back through Waverly to where he'd parked his car, drive back around to Farm Road, park about a hundred yards away from where

Officer Bowdoin was still on guard duty, wait for practice
to end and Eric Daneko to pull out of the lot in his second-
hand Explorer, one badly in need of a paint job, Mitchell
had noticed on his way back to Waverly.

Eric is where I came in, Mitchell thought.

Eric had gotten drunk and said something to Sam. Sam
had asked him about it when he sobered up. Eric had been
scared enough about that to run to somebody.

Once and for all, Mitchell wanted to ask Eric how he
knew so much about that night in Connecticut if he hadn't
been in on it.

For now, he sat in the car and listened to Joshua Redman, wondering how he would have sounded with Miles.
Mitchell wished he had something to read now. But then he
hadn't known he was going to be on his own little stakeout
until he got to thinking about Eric again while he and Sam
watched him practice. So Mitchell tried to answer the kind
of silly questions Jimmy O'Rourke used to ask him late at
night. Who were the only two guys in baseball history to hit
home runs before their twentieth birthdays and after their
fortieth birthdays? O'Rourke would give you one clue:
their names rhymed.

Ty Cobb and Rusty Staub.

And which basketball player had won an NCAA championship, an ABA championship, and an NBA championship?

Tom Thacker, out of the University of Cincinnati.

Which NBA coaches had won titles with two different
teams?

Alex Hannum, Phil Jackson.

There was a time when his head was filled right to the
top with trivial shit like that.

He got off sports finally and sat there thinking about
how happy he was to be having dinner with Kate Perry.

He saw Glenn Moore leave the parking lot in his Mercedes. He saw Dave Bender drive out, then Sam in the red

Volvo. There was just enough daylight left for Mitchell to see Emmy Watkins pull up in her Acura, drive off with her grandson.

At six-thirty, Eric Daneko's Explorer came out of the lot, took a right on Farm. Mitchell pulled out behind him. When Daneko made a left on Ocean, going toward town, so did he. Did Eric know Mitchell drove an F-150? He couldn't remember, so even in early evening, dusk easing into night in South Fork like a page being turned, he kept a good distance between them.

When Eric got to Main Street, he pulled up in front of Zhivago's Deli, kept the engine running, went inside, came back out a minute later with a quart-sized bottle of Mountain Dew, a soft drink kids loved because it had enough caffeine in it to fuel a Mars mission. Mitchell hung back in front of O'Rourke's, just up the block. Daneko must have been drinking Mountain Dew, probably listening to his own music. Probably not Joshua Redman or Miles. Or Coltrane. Or Art Pepper. Finally he put the Explorer back into drive, turned around in Mayer's parking lot, where Mitchell had talked to Show the night of the street fair. Then he took a right at the monument and headed back up Ocean.

Was he going back to school?

Sam had said that the Danekos lived over on the north side somewhere, near Shore Haven. So the kid wasn't going home. But where? Maybe a girlfriend's house. Maybe to sit and look at the water at the end of Ocean and drink Mountain Dew and forget about Drew Hudson and Bobby Ferraro, and think about what was really important:

Ball, beer, girls, instant messaging, video games, sleep. ESPN.

Mitchell checked his watch. Not even seven o'clock yet, which meant he still had plenty of time to get to Kate Perry's dinner on time, all he had to do was swing by the house, get out of his dirty sneaks, maybe change out of his jeans and into a pair of khakis.

He'd stay with the kid for a few more minutes, give up on this plan and come up with a new one that wasn't worth a shit in the morning.

He was still keeping his distance from the Explorer, focusing on that, not letting his mind wander too much, starting to wonder if the kid was just riding around for the hell of it, the way kids did, when he noticed that the Explorer had taken a left off Ocean, gone down three houses, stopped in front of 55 Jobs Lane.

Mitchell's house.

Mitchell hung a left of his own on Silver, the small deadend street right before Jobs, a few hundred yards down Ocean, waited to see if Eric Daneko was dumb enough to leave his car parked right out front and try to get into the house. But then, why the hell not? His old man had parked in front, walked up the front steps, and popped him.

Had he remembered to leave the alarm on?

If the kid did try to get into the house, Mitchell didn't want him to get spooked by the alarm and run away, he wanted to walk in on his ass.

Mitchell sat in his car and waited. Eric Daneko did the same. Mitchell laughed out loud in the front seat of his truck. Picturing himself in his car like this, this close to his own house, hoping the kid in the other car would try to break into the house.

Eric got out of the Explorer now.

Mitchell got out of the truck, shutting the driver's-side door quietly behind him, jogged along the privet line at Dr. Arnie Korval's house. When he got to the end of the Korval property, Mitchell noted that the floodlight on the big tree near the road hadn't come on at seven o'clock, the way the electrician who'd wired the thing had promised it would. It meant the timer was probably off again.

Eric Daneko walked up the front steps, pressed his nose

against the window next to the door, looked inside. There was one light coming from the front living room, one Mitchell must have left on when he left to go to practice.

Mitchell felt like he and Eric Daneko were a couple of ten-year-olds playing cops and robbers.

The kid came down the steps, walked around the left side of the house, stayed back there a few minutes, came back around to the front again, stopping between the house and his car. It was then that Mitchell stepped away from Dr. Korval's privet and said in a loud voice, "You doing a site survey for your old man?"

As big as he was, as tough as he thought he was, Eric Daneko couldn't help it, he made a sound like a small dog yelping.

"Jesus Christ, you scared the *piss* outta me!" he said.

"Sorry, I usually try to be more of a sport when people are sneaking around my house at night."

"I wasn't sneaking."

"You sure looked like you were casing the joint to me."

"Wait a second: You think I was, like, trying to break into your house, dude? For what?"

"You tell me."

Daneko gave a frustrated shake to his head. Mitchell took a good look at him, saw he had the suburban-homey look going for him: Old Navy hoodie. Baggy jeans, probably the Hilfigers Sam said that white kids favored because black kids did, hanging so low on his ass Mitchell was waiting for them to go. His replica Brooklyn Dodgers cap turned just so to the side, homey style.

"I was looking for you, is all," Eric said.

"You were looking for me."

"Yeah."

"You mind telling me why?"

"My father says when you've got important business, you don't talk to some guy who just reads the book, you talk to the guy who wrote the book."

Mitchell said, "What the hell are you talking about?"

"Sam Perry's not doing all this himself, that's what I'm talking about. My dad says you're the one calling the shots."

"Your dad's wrong."

"He doesn't think so."

"I don't imagine he would."

The kid made a sound that was like a groan.

"I love my dad," Eric said, "but he can be a total bucket sometimes."

"We had a fight, you know that, right?"

"He said you had a couple."

"Only one's going to make it into the *Ring* record books."

The kid looked at him. "What?"

Mitchell said, "What did he tell you?"

"He said you jumped him from behind the other night, sucker-punched him. But I didn't think that was your style, you like to come straight-on at somebody."

Mitchell jerked a thumb at the house. "You want to have this conversation inside?"

Eric shook his head. "Shouldn't be here at all. Coach would brick me if he ever found out."

"But you're here."

Mitchell didn't see anything in telling him he'd been following him since practice. The two of them stood in the front yard, maybe six feet apart, waiting for somebody to make the next move.

"I didn't do it," Eric said, blurting it out. "I know you think I did."

"We talking about Drew or Bobby? Or both?"

"I don't know what-all happened with Bobby, I swear."

"So when you were drunk that night and talking about bad shit happening, you meant Drew?"

"Yeah." He stared down at his basketball shoes. "I meant him getting buddied that way."

"Buddied."

"It's an expression the guys use. For what happened."

"If you didn't do it, how did you know he got buddied, Eric?"

Eric Daneko stared past the house, in the direction of the ocean, or maybe the other side of the world. "'Cause Drew came to me for help that night. Like, after it happened."

Son of a bitch.

"To your cabin?"

The kid nodded, still not making eye contact with Mitchell.

Mitchell said, "Who was your roommate?"

"Christian. It was me and Christian. Dave and Glenn, of course. Show was supposed to have Tommy Mayer with him, but Tommy came down with something right before we were supposed to leave."

"Were you with Christian the whole time?"

He shook his head. "He had smuggled in his laptop, even though Coach said it wasn't allowed. I think Glenn told him to. It was Glenn being bad without really being bad. He said he was over playing the new James Bond game with Dave and Glenn."

"You ever ask them if Christian was with them that night?"

"He said he was. Why should I?"

"Because he could have been lying."

"These guys are my teammates, dude. You can't trust your teammates, who can you?"

Mitchell said, "Good question."

"Coach says this is the time when you got to stay strong."

"I forgot." Mitchell made a motion like he was showing him to a table. "Sit down and tell me about Drew."

They sat on the front steps, in some kind of weird alliance, at least for the time being. Eric told about him and

Christian having the last cabin before the big one the counselors used in the summer, the one closest to the woods.
Said he thought he heard somebody crying and went outside and there was Drew, sitting under a tree. Hands still
tied. Still blindfolded. Shaking like a leaf, Eric said.

At first, Eric thought he was just afraid of something
that might have happened out in the woods.

Then Drew told him.

"I said, like, no way. He looked at me with these sad
eyes, like the saddest eyes I ever saw, and said, 'They did it.'
I said that if they did it, we had to go tell Coach right now.
Then he grabs my arm hard and says, 'No way, you can't
tell anybody!' I say, Come on, man, this is like some shit
you read about, we gotta tell Coach. And he makes me
promise not to. Then I offer to take him back to his cabin
and he says he can't go back there, no way."

"Who was Drew rooming with?"

"Bobby."

"He tell you Bobby had been one of them?"

"No. Just could he sleep on our floor tonight? I said, like,
whatever. By the time Christian got back, Drew was asleep,
though I think maybe he was just pretending. Christian
asked me what he was doing there and I just made up some
shit about him and Bobby having some kind of beef. Christian let it go, even though he probably wondered, since
Bobby never had any kind of beef with anybody."

"You didn't tell."

"I told you, dude. I promised. Drew and me promised
each other. It was, like, we never had the conversation."

"So why are you and me having this conversation?"

"I just know you've been pissed at me since I gave Sam
that hard time and whatnot. And I don't want you to think
that because I did that, I could've done the other."

Mitchell was looking at his quiet street, his quiet little
town. "And I'm supposed to believe you."

"You think I came here to lie?"

"Who'd you think you were protecting by not telling, exactly?"

"I didn't look at it that way, I just looked at it that I promised, is all."

"You think some dipshit code of jock honor applied to something like this? Jesus Christ."

Eric Daneko put his face in his big hands. "I didn't know what to do."

"And you didn't look at the guys on your team crooked after that?"

"Yeah. And sometimes I'd say to one of the guys, like, whatever happened with Drew that night, I didn't go back out to look for him? But nobody'd say anything, just that he musta made it back on his own."

Mitchell turned. "Hey," he said. "Look at me now."

The kid turned. Big scared eyes on him now.

"Is there anything else?"

"No. I told you what I know. Drew told and now I'm telling."

"Who did this?"

"You think I haven't asked myself that? Goddamn, dude. What he said they did. I have no idea." He stopped, bopped his head from side to side. "Unless."

"What?"

"You're asking me my opinion? And it doesn't go any further than you and me?"

Mitchell said, "You got my word."

Eric gave the look-off again.

"The only one I could see losing it enough, going off and doing something like that, would be Show."

Mitchell blew some air out of himself. Looked up at the sky. Clear sky. Covered with stars. Big moon. Even the night sky somehow told him where he was.

"You know him well enough by now to say something like that?"

Eric said, "No, see, that's the thing. I just see how he *is*. You understand? I'm just sayin'. I see how he works people over. There's a side of him I wouldn't want to fuck with, is all."

"Go home now," Mitchell said. "But before you do, answer me one more question: When Sam came to you, asked you about the night you got drunk, who did you tell?"

"Who said I told anybody?"

Mitchell said, "Eric, let's not start fucking around now."

"I told the seniors," he said. "In the locker room. Not exactly what I said. Shit, I couldn't remember what-all I said. Just, like, that Sam thought he was onto something."

"Which seniors?" Mitchell said.

"All of them."

# 19

After dinner, Kate Perry said, "Have you noticed that we never talk about anything except South Fork basketball?"

Mitchell smiled at her. At the way she sounded. "Are you saying all I talk about is my work, dear?"

"Oh my God," she said, "did I sound like a wife?"

Mitchell raised his eyebrows as an answer.

"Kill me now," she said.

They had cleared the dishes together, Mitchell insisting that he help out, telling her that he cleaned up after himself every night at home. Sam was upstairs doing homework. Or more likely, Kate said, instant-messaging his friend Maggie Chaplin, who'd moved up-island to Syosset this year. Mitchell asked if Maggie was a girlfriend-type friend, he'd noticed that Sam didn't talk about girls much. Kate said they'd been an item junior year, broken up when she moved, were trying to work it out now that Maggie was thinking about going to Syracuse as well.

Kate said that for the time being, most of the patch-up work was being done via instant messaging.

"A modern form of counseling," she said. "I'm waiting for them to find a way to start families over the Internet."

"All I talk about with him is South Fork basketball," Mitchell said, "and newspapers."

"Of course," Kate said. "You're guys. I used to ask my husband what he talked about on the golf course with his pals and he'd look at me and say, 'Golf.'"

They were in the living room now with their coffee. She said she was going to put on some music if he didn't mind. "Do you like jazz?" she said. Mitchell told her he was a big jazz guy, heavy on the sax guys. "Don't get me wrong," he said. "I still like old-time rock and roll. But it just seems like I've got jazz on in the house, and in the car, more and more." She put on Ornette Coleman, telling him she'd decided to start playing jazz in the store, she thought it set the proper mood. Kate was wearing some kind of retro stonewashed jeans that seemed dark on one side, faded on the other. A white turtleneck. When he told her the sweater looked nice, she said that ever since the movie with Diane Keaton and Jack Nicholson, a lot of women her age had fallen in love with white turtlenecks. She was barefoot, legs tucked underneath at her end of the sofa.

"I'm not going to be afraid of this anymore," she said.

"I'm not sure I know that one," he said, "but maybe if you hum a few bars."

"Seriously," Kate said, "I've been thinking the last couple of days about how I've reacted to things. And it's not the way I react to things."

"You're worried about your kid."

"He's not a kid, even though I still want him to be." She looked past Mitchell, as if checking to see if Sam had come downstairs without either of them hearing him. "And what he's done by staying with this, writing the story, putting himself out there, shows the kind of nerve I want him to have."

He let that sit there. She told him that she'd finally got her nerve up and opened the store after her husband died. "We had stores for teenaged girls around here and stores for women between fifty and dead," she said. "I took the rest of the field." That had always been her dream, she said, even though it took the nightmare of her husband dying young to get her there. Mitchell said his dream was maybe to find a small college someday, teach writing and journalism. "Not the junk journalism you see now," he said. "The kind for kids who still think they can change the world." He looked at her. "Like your kid," he said.

Then it was quiet, neither one of them saying anything. And not feeling as if they had to. After Ornette Coleman, he heard Carol Sloane singing along with old Clark Terry. Mitchell tried to remember the last time he had been this comfortable just sitting and talking with someone, not wanting to be somewhere else, alone. Remembering at the same time that he was feeling this way with Sam Perry's mother.

"I want him to fight this all the way," she said. "You can't let these monsters get away with it."

"Is that what you want, or what he wants?"

"What we want."

Mitchell had told her and Sam at dinner how popular he was getting with South Fork players all of a sudden, even though they were supposed to be avoiding him like some kind of plague. First Glenn, now Eric. Now, Sam out of the room, he and Kate went back to talking about Eric's stop-by, how hard that must have been for him, whatever you thought about him. Or his father. She asked if someone like Show Watkins, who had so much going for him and so much on the line, would risk his future doing the kind of things Drew Hudson said were done to him.

"Could he be that much of a bully at heart?" she said.

"What if he's more than a bully?"

"Now, what's that supposed to mean?"

"Nobody in this world ever thought Kobe was anything more than the All-American kid until he got accused of rape. I'm not talking about the merits of the case, whether you really think he did it or not, how they finally called it off. The fact is, we only know what these guys want us to know. I interviewed Kobe plenty of times, got along fine with him. But I knew I was seeing the Kobe he wanted me to present to the public. I didn't know what he did after he went home and shut the doors. And ever since he got clipped, I've wondered how many more of these big sports stars, ones I covered for years, had a dark side. Could turn into some kind of sicko as soon as we weren't watching."

Kate said, "Are you talking about Kobe here, or O.J.?"

"I'm just saying," Mitchell said. "Show's grandma told me about his temper. Glenn told me how he likes to work the guys on the team over with his mouth. Eric tells me the same thing, not in so many words, how much of a prick he can be."

"So how do you find out?"

Mitchell finished his coffee. "That again."

"You'll think of something."

"You think?"

They sat talking about music for a while. When they got on soul music, she said Aretha, he said Otis Redding. She said Led Zeppelin, he said Stones. She said R.E.M. He said Aerosmith. Then they were talking about all the groups that sounded like garage bands, all the way to White Stripes. It went like that. She asked about newer groups. He said he loved anything by Counting Crows, even that song from *Shrek 2*. She asked if he'd heard a new guy named Jack Johnson and Mitchell said the only Jack Johnson he knew was the black fighter James Earl Jones played in the movies. They kept going back and forth, like it was tennis, laughing a lot.

Finally, Mitchell looked at his watch. "I should go."

Kate said, "Well, at least we got off business at the very end."

"Sometimes I feel like I'm back in the business."

"You should be."

"Let's see how this comes out."

He yelled up to Sam to stay where he is, they'd talk tomorrow. "Cool," he heard, over some loud music that didn't sound much like homework-doing music. On the way to the car, Kate asked Mitchell if he'd mind checking up on Sam tomorrow night, she had to spend the day and night in the city, looking at a few more late-entry shows for her spring clothes. She said at this time of year, she went in every couple of weeks, just to stay on top of things. Anyway, she said, there were two shows in the afternoon, downtown, and one first thing the next morning in some showroom in midtown, so she was staying over, treating herself to a night at the Sherry-Netherland.

Mitchell told her he could stay over with Sam if she was really worried. She laughed and said, "On what planet do you think he'd let you babysit?"

"Then I'll have to find creative ways to check in on him," Mitchell said, "without him knowing I'm checking in on him."

It was the same big clear sky from before, when he'd been on his front porch with Eric Daneko. He just liked it better now, standing here with Kate Perry. He told her that, trying not to make himself sound like some sort of frail.

"I had a good time," she said.

"Same."

The truck was between them and the house. She gave a quick look up at the second-floor window of Sam's room, as if making sure he wasn't watching them. Then she leaned up suddenly, gave Mitchell a quick kiss, ran back toward the house.

He watched her go. Then stayed in the driveway after she

shut the front door, looking across Bridge Lane suddenly. Looking all around him in the night, a winter wind on his face, the sound of a train in the distance, wondering why he was on his guard even after a sweet time like this, why he couldn't shake the feeling, all the time these days, that he wasn't the only one doing the watching in South Fork.

**D**etective Hank Bender was near the front door of the school the next morning when Sam showed up. Sam asked right away if there was some kind of new trouble he hadn't heard about yet. Dave Bender's dad said that, no, he was just back for another round of interviewing the players and Coach Glass, wanting to see if he could come up with some timeline about where everybody was when Drew said he was attacked.

"*Said* he was attacked?" Sam said.

"I still got no witnesses," Bender said. "And no corroborating testimony. Until I do, it's an alleged attack, son. I'm just here to come at everybody a little harder today."

"Why would Drew lie?"

"Your friend Mitchell says that kids lie all the time."

He gave a lean-back stretch to his back, as if it had stiffened up on him. "Listen, I don't know how much help I'm going to get," Bender said. "My own kid is so scatterbrained he can barely remember his class schedule. I have to beg him to wear the Nike watch I bought him for Christmas."

Trying to be his friendly neighborhood cop, Sam knew.

"Well, yeah, I can be the same way sometimes."

"Did Drew mention what time it was when he thought this happened?" Bender said.

Sam almost said that Drew probably didn't get the chance to check his watch, but didn't.

"Like I said in the piece," Sam said. "He just guessed it was between eleven and twelve, he didn't look at his watch until later."

Bender put a hand on Sam's shoulder. "Is there anything
you *didn't* put in your story, son? Anything else I need to
know? About any of this?"

Sam flashed on what had happened to him that night in
Mallozzi, wondering if Bender knew somehow and was
just testing him.

"No," he said. "It's all in there."

"Because I could sure use any help I can get," Bender
said. "Like I said, I'm gonna need more than Drew's version to move this thing forward."

Now he patted Sam on the back. "You think of anything,
you call me."

"Sure."

"We're on the same side, you know," Dave Bender's dad
said.

"No disrespect, sir," Sam said, unable to keep this one
in, "but what side is that?"

And walked into school without looking back.


**A**fter practice, Sam went into the locker room with Damon
Wills and the other sportswriters. Jeremy Schaap of ESPN
was there with his crew to do a piece on South Fork basketball, everything that had been going on since Bobby Ferraro, for their *Nightline*-like show, *Outside the Lines*.
Schaap introduced himself and said he might want to sit
down with him at some point. Sam said he was sure that
would be fine, not wanting to admit he really couldn't say
yes or no without asking his mom.

When they got into the locker room, none of the players
would talk to him.

Most didn't even look at him.

Sam tried Glenn Moore first.

Glenn looked up, like he was embarrassed, said in a
voice that sounded like it came from the bottom of his
locker, "Not today, okay?" Then nodded in the direction of

Coach Glass's office, as if that explained everything. Sam went across the room to Show Watkins. Show smiled at him, his big Show smile, and said, "You shittin', right?" Then got up and walked toward the shower room.

Dave Bender, in a quiet voice, said, "Go fuck yourself."

As soon as Tommy Mayer saw Sam coming across the room, he disappeared into the bathroom.

Give it up, Sam thought. When he turned to leave, Coach Ken Glass was leaning against the door frame.

"Got everything you need?" Glass said, making no attempt to move out of the way.

Sam didn't say anything.

"Fun being a shit-stirrer, isn't it?" Glass said, and gave Sam just enough room to pass, whispering, "I'm watching you."


**B**en Mitchell offered to stay at the house. There was a big part of Sam that wanted him to, but he said, no. Are you kidding? he said. He was fine, he'd spent plenty of nights alone, stop treating him like some kind of baby.

After he hung up the phone, he remembered what Mitchell had said the other night about all the dumb codes that jocks had and thought:

It's not only jocks.

He just knew that if he needed a babysitter, then he was still afraid, and he'd sworn to his mother that he wasn't going to be afraid anymore. It meant he had to start somewhere.

He wondered if Drew was still afraid at night. . . .

He'd gone through the whole house once he got home from practice, locked all the doors, even the ones to the back deck outside his mother's bedroom upstairs, turned on all the lights in the front and back of the house even though it wasn't completely dark yet, wanting them to be already on when it *was* dark. Hit the alarm code and then the STAY button. Stay home. Alone. Shit, he could handle that for one night. If he needed anything, Mitchell was five minutes away. Ten, tops.

He sat at the kitchen table and did his homework there, somehow feeling the house was more secure if he was downstairs. Still trying to decide what was worse, Show's smile in the locker room or the dead-eyed stare he got from Dave Bender. Or the sarcastic chop-busting from the coach.

My guys, Sam thought, my team.

Go, team.

He put on *The Diary of Alicia Keys* and backed it with Norah Jones, not wanting anything too loud tonight. Even thought about playing some of the jazz that his mother and Mitchell liked so much. He didn't want to rock the house tonight, the way he usually did when his mother was away. She had already called twice from the city, making up lame-o excuses both times. Get her a number she'd left on her pad on the counter. Oh, and remember to put out the re-cycling, Wednesday was pickup day. Mom stuff. He told her he'd see her tomorrow, he was fine.

He started an English paper on modern crime writers, got a few pages into it, couldn't concentrate. He shut off Norah, tried to get into a college basketball game, thinking he could hang in there until the eleven o'clock *SportsCenter*.

He tried to read the papers he hadn't had time to read in the morning.

He thought about Bobby and Drew instead.

What else?

He'd read up on hazing, because Mitchell had told him he should. Read about how it was about power, mainly. By now, he knew you had to factor in raging testosterone any time you were talking about high school and college guys, especially when they were jocks. And there was the huge element of peer pressure, being afraid to break away from the crowd, afraid *not* to run with the crowd, the security kids always seemed to feel in what one of the articles

called the "ruling group." Everybody talked about mean-
ness, and an underlying level of sadism. But they all said it
started with power, the way rape did.

Being in control.

Control freaks, he thought, in every way.

Sometimes, he'd read, the perpetrators hurt a teammate
because they couldn't get at the ones they really wanted to
hurt: abusive parents, abusive coaches.

Like that.

Somehow they had gotten Bobby to go along, telling
him that he was next if he didn't. Then doing it to him, anyway. Maybe that was the ultimate power for them, making
him part of the group and then screwing him over the very
next thing.

Drew said it had almost been like love talk, the guy
whispering in his ear.

The first call, and hangup, came a few minutes before
eleven.

He picked up on the second ring.

"Hello."

Click.

Sam checked the caller I.D.

Unknown caller.

No thing, as the dudes on the basketball team liked to
say. All the dudes except Glenn Moore, who didn't seem
like a black dude at all, who spoke better than any English
teacher in school.

Ten minutes later, another call.

Sam got it on the first ring this time.

"Hey."

Click.

Unknown caller.

One time, he and Mitchell had been bullshitting at
Mitchell's house, and Sam had asked about life on the road,
what that was like, how he couldn't wait. Mitchell told him
what it was like to go from hotel to hotel, sometimes for

two or three weeks in a row if he was covering something like the baseball playoffs and World Series. How there was a lot to be said for living in hotels, good ones anyway. But that the worst part of it, for him, was when he'd get sick. Every couple of years he'd get sick as a dog in the middle of the night, at some Westin or Marriott or Hyatt in Phoenix or Miami or Dallas, and eventually he'd have to ask himself the question:

How sick was he?

Sick enough to call the desk, or a doctor?

Or just ride it out?

How scared am I? Sam wondered.

He went and looked out of one of the front windows, facing the driveway. Right. So he could catch this asshole calling from his front yard, right there in plain sight. He closed the drapes and went back through the house again, doing a total anal-retentive check of all the doors and windows, closing more drapes, pulling down more shades. Yeah. Block the bogeyman's view.

How scared am I?

Scared enough to call Mitchell?

Come *on*.

He sat and tried to focus on *SportsCenter.* Dan Patrick and some new black guy he didn't recognize. NBA highlights. Hockey highlights. Bill Parcells talking about what it was like to be facing Joe Gibbs again, now that Gibbs was back with the Redskins.

Eleven-thirty.

It could have been a mistake. Somebody punching out the wrong number in haste, then doing it again. Sam did it all the time. *Everybody* did it all the time.

The phong rang again.

"Hey," Sam said, "c'mon, who is this?"

"Somebody just having a nice time watching you."

The whispery voice from Mallozzi. Or one just like it.

Sam felt dizzy now, remembering Coach Glass whispering to him in the locker room that he was watching him.

The hell?

"Hey, asshole, is this all you got? Crank calls? Fuck you."

But he didn't hang up.

The raspy voice said, "You got a lot of lights on in that house, for a tough guy."

He was somewhere close by. Sam felt himself get one of those full-body shivers, running right up his back to the back of his neck.

"You know that pay phone outside the little school 'cross your little street?"

Pause.

"I know you're alone, Sam."

Click.

Sam hung up, called Mitchell, told him in a sprint what was going on, what the guy had just said, where he said he was.

Mitchell said, "Don't open the door for anybody but me, I'm on my way. If the bastards call back, tell them that."

"I think they're done calling."

Mitchell said, "Remember my Mattingly?"

"Yeah."

"Get one of your own."

And hung up.

Sam wasn't crazy about the idea of going into the basement. But that's where his father's golf clubs were. He turned on the lights at the top of the stairs, went to where his mom kept the clubs, with the other stuff she couldn't bring herself to throw away. He grabbed an old Titleist seven-iron out of the bag.

He was at the top of the steps when he heard a window breaking somewhere in the back of the house and the alarm going off like an air-raid siren.

Sam froze.

Keep going, or wait for Mitchell?

He decided he wasn't going to hide in the basement. Pushed the door to the dining room open, the noise of the alarm insanely loud now. On the other side of the dining room was the kitchen, and his mother's den, and a guest bedroom. His mother's bedroom above that. He didn't know why he was so sure it was the kitchen window being smashed, but he was. If not the big window over the sink, then the window part of the kitchen door.

Maybe they had broken it to get inside.

Sam put a baseball grip on his father's seven-iron, moved into the dining room. Wanting to shut off the racket of the alarm, the wail of it making it hard for him to think. But the alarm pad was near the front door and the crash had come from the other direction.

Somehow he heard the phone ringing again. Was it them? Or the alarm company? His mind going a hundred miles an hour now as he made his way slowly across the dining room, not sure what he was going to find when he got around the corner.

Now, in addition to everything else, he heard the ding-dong of the doorbell.

Mitchell.

Sam backed away from the kitchen, then turned and ran for the front door, opened it for Ben Mitchell. Who'd brought his Mattingly with him.

"You all right?" Mitchell said.

"Yeah."

Sam put a trembling hand up to the alarm pad, punched out their code, shut the thing up finally.

"Are they in the house?"

"I don't know," Sam said. "I'm pretty sure I heard a window breaking."

"Let's go," Mitchell said.

The phone stopped ringing finally. It had to be the alarm company. They'd call back, Sam knew, they always did one more time before they called the police. The house was quiet again, except for the sound of the television. They came around the corner of the dining room, saw that it was the window over the sink that had been broken.

In the middle of all the shattered glass was the broomstick, one end of it painted red, obviously to simulate blood.

"Subtle," Mitchell said.

Then he went to call the police, saying that couldn't hurt, even in South Fork.

# 20

Mitchell knew that Christian Bowdoin worked at the South Fork YMCA on Saturday mornings, making some extra money officiating rec league basketball games. He stopped there first, talked to him between games. Christian wasn't too thrilled about that, but went along, not wanting all the parents and kids in the gym to see him blowing Mitchell off. After that, Mitchell drove over to the small Shore Haven shopping mall, where Sam said Dave Bender was working part-time at the new Tower Records.

It had been the same with Christian Bowdoin as with the others: Even though he knew he wasn't supposed to be talking, there was a part of him, a kid part, wanting to make sure Mitchell didn't think *he* was involved. Wanting Mitchell to like him, in some weird way. So he said more than he should have, even though he didn't think he was saying anything at all. It was as much of a plan as Mitchell had, isolating them one by one, getting them to start turning on each other without knowing that they were. Eventually, he'd have to figure out which ones were lying. Just not yet. As strong as they thought they were, as strong as their fuckwit coach was telling them they had to be, they had to be scared now. And looking around.

But then, Mitchell thought, they should have been looking around all along, the dumb shits.

It wasn't really much of a mall in Shore Haven. Gap, Gap Kids, King Corcoran supermarket, hair-and-nail place, toy store. There was a place called Bertram's Hot Yoga. Mitchell couldn't tell whether that was a new style of yoga or a form of self-congratulation. Tower Records was between Gap and Gap Kids, a smaller one than Mitchell expected, even out here, maybe because he was used to the Tower Records up on Sunset in L.A., which was big and loud and busy as a freeway, and Mitchell's favorite music-buying place in the whole world.

Dave, wearing a blue zippered shirt, was helping a stringy-haired, nose-ringed kid in the rap section when Mitchell came in. Mitchell noticed that the right sleeve on Dave's shirt covered the upper half of the huge dragon tattoo on his upper arm.

He went to the jazz section at the other end of the store, put on some headphones, busied himself listening to the first few cuts of an old Coleman Hawkins. It was noon, straight up. Mitchell was wondering what kind of shift Dave Bender worked, whether or not he got any kind of lunch break. He kept his back to the store, listened to Coleman work through a version of "Body and Soul" as unique to him as his handwriting.

At a quarter past twelve, he heard Dave Bender tell his manager he was going to run across to the other side of the mall, to a Subway Mitchell hadn't noticed when he'd driven through the parking lot, and ask if the manager wanted him to bring something back. The manager said, yeah, one of those new Southwest chicken barbecue deals, with cheese.

"Peace out," Dave said, then said he'd be back in twenty, if things got crazy the manager should call him on his cell.

Mitchell watched him walk out of Tower. But instead of heading straight across the parking lot, Dave hung a right, walked past the Gap, took a right there. Mitchell followed him, thinking the kid had left something in his car, maybe he'd parked by the Gap. But when Mitchell got to the far end of the Gap's big front window, he looked around the corner, saw Dave Bender keep going, all the way around the back of the store, into the back parking lot. Mitchell jogged to keep up. His new career: tailing high school kids. There was a row of green trash Dumpsters. Dave walked past them, toward the woods behind the parking lot. He turned around once, to see if anyone was watching. Mitchell pressed himself against one of the Dumpsters, feeling like an asshole, the way he had when he'd snuck up on his own house, checking out Eric Daneko.

Where the hell was this kid going?

Mitchell found out soon enough.

Dave Bender, the cop's son, walked into the woods, sure he was alone now, unwatched, reached into the pockets of his cargo jeans, and went through the process of lighting up a big old-fashioned American joint.

The kid leaned back against a tree, sucked in the dope in small stages, eyes closed, blew the smoke out almost as a last resort. He looked so happy, Mitchell felt guilty about crashing the party.

"Good shit?" he said.

The kid didn't panic, or act startled. Maybe it only took one hit to get his bliss. He turned around, smiled, dropped the joint into some leaves, rubbed it out with the toe of the Timbies he was wearing.

"Shame to waste it," Mitchell said.

"Waste what?"

"Hope it wasn't on my account," Mitchell said.

"Man, you don't give up," Dave Bender said. "Do you?"

"Your father know you're a pothead?"

Dave said, "Pothead? Wow. How fucking old are you?"

He had a deep voice, deeper than his father's. Other than that, looking at him really was like looking at Hank Bender twenty-five years ago. He didn't have the crewcut, he'd shaved his head closer than that, like one of the dudes.

"That's it? 'Wow'?"

"You say you caught me smoking a joint. I say I came out to take a piss. The main thing, dude, least the way I see it, is that you followed me out into the woods, like some sort of stalker deal. What do you think'll fry my old man's ass more?"

Mitchell said, "Tell you what: Answer a couple of questions for me, and your old man doesn't even have to know we talked."

"Dude," he said, shaking his head as if Mitchell was the saddest thing he'd ever set eyes on. "I'm gonna tell you what I told your boy, Sam. Fuck off."

Mitchell said, "How come you lied to Eric about where you were that night when Drew Hudson got assaulted?"

He didn't change his expression. Stayed in his street-corner slouch. But Mitchell saw something happen with his eyes.

"Who said I lied?"

"We talking about whether you did now, or whether somebody said you did?"

"Don't give me any of your bullshit."

Mitchell said, "You and Glenn and Christian were all supposed to be together when Drew says he got dragged into that cabin."

"That's right. Playing video. James Bond. Bam bam."

"Only Christian says he left you guys before."

"Before what?"

"Before Drew got put down."

"First of all, Christian wouldn't say that, on account of it's not true," he said. "Secondly, if you don't believe me, ask Glenn."

"I'm asking you. Trying to get things straight in my own mind, once and for all," Mitchell said. "When did Christian leave?"

"I don't remember what fucking time it was," Dave said. "My old man's always on my ass to wear a watch. You're just trying to mess with my head like you must've messed with Christian's."

"Who said I talked to Christian?"

"You said . . . "

"No, I just told you what Christian's *saying.*" Mitchell crossed his arms in front of him, grinned. "Could've been one of your other teammates told me what he's saying."

Dave closed his eyes, shook his head. "Is this all you do, go around pissing people off?"

"Let's change the subject for a second," Mitchell said. "You happen to know where Show was while all this male bonding was going on?"

"The hell should I know, why don't you ask him, it seems to be the way you get your ya-ya's, at least when you're not sniffing around Sam Perry's old lady."

Mitchell gave him a long look, keeping himself still. "It would be a mistake to piss *me* off, son."

Dave Bender just stood there, hands in his pockets, jangling some loose change he had in there, not saying anything back, rocking back and forth on the balls of his feet, whatever glow he thought he had working for him already gone.

"One more thing," Mitchell said. "Show had his own cabin, right?"

"What if he did?"

"I'm just wondering where he was while you and Christian and Glenn were piling up video kills."

"Like I said," Dave said. "Ask him. Or ask his nosy fucking brother."

"Antoine?"

"Another guy thinks he's some kind of cop. Or's still a cop. He got me outside Hiram's the other day, trying to be like my bud, asking me all kinds of shit. Asking me all about the team. About how far back everybody goes. About Glenn and Show. Did I have Show's back the way I did Glenn's?" Dave shook his head. "You guys need to get a life, no shit."

"What did you tell him about Show?"

"That he was my teammate, of course I had his back. And now," he said, "I got to get back to the store."

He took two steps. Mitchell stepped in front of him.

"One more thing," he said.

"We did one more thing."

"I lied," Mitchell said. "I just want you to remember that it took two guys to hold Drew down. All I need is for one to give the other one up."

"Fuck off," Dave said.

Mitchell slapped him hard across the face.

The kid's head snapped to the side, then snapped right back so he was full-face with Mitchell again, eyes wide, the red from Mitchell's hand clear on his right cheek. Dave Bender took a step toward Mitchell, hands starting to come up. Mitchell got himself ready.

Then the kid stopped himself, putting the brakes on at the last second.

"I'm not fighting you, man," he said. "Break my hand on your stupid face, fuck up my season. But my old man's going to hear about this."

"Good," Mitchell said.

He walked away, leaving him there. He'd lied a little bit about Christian. Let the two of them work it out. See who had whose back when it came right down to it.

He was making it up as he went along now.

———

Practice, Monday afternoon.

Mitchell was wearing his official laminated press card, the one with his photo on it, around his neck. The sports editor had sent a photographer over to Mitchell's house on Sunday afternoon, the guy had taken his picture, an intern had dropped the card off in the morning. More than anything, it was like wearing a sign that he had the backing of the biggest paper around here. And it was a sign to Coach Glass, the Napoleon of South Fork basketball, that he couldn't keep Mitchell out of practices or even the locker room without getting himself sideways with the paper that devoted more space to his team than all the others combined.

Mitchell even had a parking pass.

Now here he was, in his perch at the top of the gym, a few rows from the back wall, the only reporter there. Normally Sam would have been here with him, but both women who worked at River Road had called in sick that morning, so he'd been pressed into emergency service once school was out. Not helping women shop, he said, sitting at the antique table at the back of the store and writing out sales slips once they were done shopping. Hoping against hope, he said, that no girls he knew from school would come walking through the door.

Mitchell told him not to worry, sometimes real men had to do retail.

He also told him he had him covered if something happened at practice.

Something was happening now.

Show Watkins and Glenn Moore had been banging the shit out of each other, all the livelong day. Doing it for keeps. They had been together for the first half hour of the scrimmage, first unit against the second. But this was one of the days when the second unit had even less of a chance than usual—Mitchell couldn't remember them getting a single basket, just a couple of free throws when Glass would

blow the whistle—so finally Glass had tried to even things
out, Show on one team, Glenn on the other, have at it.

The first time down the court, Show had hip-checked
Glenn into the wall when the two of them were going for a
rebound. Glenn came back and hard-fouled him at the other
end, the kind that might have been called a flagrant in a real
game. They just went at each other after that, gloves off.
Sometimes Glass reacted to what they were doing, blowing
his whistle, telling them to cool it, they were going to be
teammates again once practice was over. Haw haw. Sometimes the nastier stuff happened off the ball.

Mitchell saw it all.

There would be one extra elbow from one or the other
underneath the basket, even after the ball was going the
other way. If it was Show who'd caught the last elbow, he'd
made sure to get in the first shove next time. All day. Like
this was a playground on a summer night with no refs, no
whistles, one of those no-blood, no-foul games. Fuck me?
No, fuck *you*. When they weren't leaning on each other,
they were giving each other the playground stare after one
would make a shot, or a pass, or a play. Every once in a
while, Mitchell would see them talking to each other. Then
would come the next body blow, usually in the subway-car
jostle for rebounds. Twice already they had gotten up on
each other, chest-to-chest, let's-do-this, forcing Glass to
blow his whistle again. It had all the charm of one of those
steel-cage wrestling matches Mitchell sometimes used to
watch when he was a kid, back in the days before pro
wrestling had turned into cross-dressing.

Ken Glass's regular practices ended at five-thirty on the
nose, unless he was punishing them for something. Or making them run some suicide sprints, just to show the media
what a hard guy he was.

Mitchell had just checked the clock above the basket
closest to him. Five-twenty. Show lost Glenn in a switch,

out to the right of the foul line, what the announcers insisted on calling The Elbow. Once Show had the step, it was clear he was on his way to the basket. Glenn spun around, apparently thinking he could still beat him there. Dave Bender, on defense with Glenn, tried to jump out on Show, but then Show was past him then, like he was nothing more than a speed bump. He took off about ten feet from the rim, ball in his right hand, held high. The old Jordan pose.

Somehow, Glenn Moore was there, setting himself like he was going to take the hit and the charge. There was no reason to do it, not with ten minutes to go at practice. Unless Glenn had decided in that moment that, fuck Show, he wasn't going to let him get off one of his sneaker-commercial dunks.

Somehow Show, even in midair, seemed to alter his flight plan, the way the great ones could, avoiding Glenn's block.

Glenn moved at the last second, to his left, clipped Show with his shoulder, spinning him out of the air now like a helicopter that had lost its rotor blades, the ball flying out of his hand, Show Watkins landing hard, with that bad crack you heard in basketball sometimes, on his right side.

He wasn't down for long.

He jack-in-the-boxed up, went right at Glenn before Dave Bender could stop him, screaming at Glenn now.

"What, you're gonna fuck *me* up now? Knock me out the air this time? Let's do this, you Golden Boy motherfucker."

Eric stepped between them. Dave got back in there. Glenn stood his ground. Mitchell knew he had to, that he couldn't take a single step back, or it would be official that the other guy was the man now. Another man-off in sports. Sometimes Mitchell thought he had been watching variations of it his whole life.

"Try that shit on me," Show said, voice still at full pitch. High-pitched. Not even sounding like him.

Glenn must have said something back, because now Show said, "They all might buy all your bullshit. Y'all are a team man only so long as it's your fucking team. You think I don't see through that shit?"

Trying to get through Dave and Eric. Glass trying to get his arms around Show's waist from behind, looking like some little cartoon Keystone Kop, blowing his whistle as he did.

Still loud enough for Mitchell to hear, Show said, "Think you can cut me and get away with it?"

Finally they got Show away. Show started to say something else, glaring at Glenn, but Glass blew his whistle again, telling them both to knock it off right now, that everybody should go get a drink.

When they all came back, Mitchell thought Glass would call off practice. Or at least sit one of them down. He didn't. Mitchell moved down closer to the court.

The two sides went up and down a couple of times after Glass started them back up. Tommy Mayer hit a three-point jumper for Show's team. Dave Bender did the same for Glenn's team.

Glass called out, "Next basket."

Tommy Mayer brought the ball up. Show set up in the low post, to the left of the basket, right arm up, calling for the ball, obviously wanting to take it right at Glenn one more time. Glenn tried to keep a long arm in front of him, fronting him the way you're supposed to, trying to move him off his spot, away from the basket. Leaning on him. Beating on him a little more. It was then that Show stuck his left elbow in Glenn's ribs, and Glenn folded up like a jackknife.

Show still waving for the ball as he did, almost like somebody else had thrown the elbow.

Glass blew his whistle.

Show turned around, saw Glenn doubled over, gave a couple of head nods like, That's right. When he did, Glenn came at him like a boxer coming out of a crouch, and threw a hard, neat elbow to Show's face.

Ed Fusco was on Show before he had a chance to react, putting a bear hug on him from behind.

Dave Bender tried to do the same with his man, Glenn. But as he did, Glenn wheeled around, swinging wildly, backhanding Dave so hard he sat down at the free-throw line, staring up at Glenn with this dumb look on his dumb face, mouth open.

Mitchell then heard Glenn Moore, captain of the team, scream at Bender the way Show Watkins had screamed at him a few minutes before.

"Don't you *ever* touch me," he said, then walked past his coach and his teammates and out of the gym.

Glass seemed to notice Mitchell then, for the first time. He walked over to the bottom of the bleachers, looked like he wanted to blow the whistle at him.

"Not one word about this," he said. "Not a fucking word. Or this whole team will shut your boy down."

Mitchell waited in the parking lot afterward, to see if it was all over. It was. He watched Tommy Mayer come out, Ed Fusco. Christian Bowdoin got into Dave Bender's car. Eric Daneko drove off in his Explorer. Ken Glass came out after Eric, got into his Lexus, slowed as he saw Mitchell standing next to the F-150, rolled down the window. "Not a fucking word," he said, rolled the window up, pulled away.

Emmy Watkins's Acura was coming in the other direction. Only Emmy Watkins wasn't behind the wheel today. Her grandson Antoine was. He stopped in front of the main entrance, picked up Show. They slowly made their way around the circle as Glenn Moore came through the front doors, alone, backpack in his hand. He pointed his keys at his Mercedes, parked about thirty yards down from where

Mitchell was. As he made his way across the grass median, he saw Mitchell.

Glenn Moore walked over to him. "You were there?"

"I was."

"I'm tired of playing captain with that guy," he said. "I'm tired of giving him the benefit of the doubt."

"You seemed to give as good as you got today."

"That's what he wanted," Glenn said. "He says I try to make him look bad and it's the other way around."

"But why?" Mitchell said. "The two of you are supposed to have the world by the balls."

"Because he's a bad guy," Glenn said.

He went and opened the back door to his car, threw the backpack in there like he was spiking it, drove too fast out of the lot. It wasn't until he was gone and the lot was empty that Mitchell noticed that Emmy Watkins's car was still parked at the corner of the gym, the driver's-side window down, Antoine Watkins staring at him, nodding the way his brother had when he put his elbow on Glenn Moore.

Then pointing at him with his finger like he was firing a gun.

# 21

The next night, Mitchell tried another way to make something happen. After South Fork beat Gannon 74–50, he wrote a guest column for the *Long Island Press,* one that started on Page 1, above the fold. They even gave him his own column logo, using the same picture the guy had taken for his press card.

Mitchell wrote the column at the small press table they'd set up for the overflow crowd of reporters at one end of the gym in Gannon, which was a short car ride and then ferry ride away from South Fork, over on the North Fork of Long Island. He wrote on the loaner laptop the sports editor of the *Press* had personally delivered to his house, wrote using the instructions for creating a story and saving it and sending it that the sports editor had taped near the screen.

For the first time since Tom Robards had killed himself, Mitchell wrote for a newspaper.

Once he got past the first couple of paragraphs, he wrote the way he used to, which means fast.

You know their names, because everybody around here who follows basketball knows their names. Glenn Moore, the golden child. Show Watkins, who's supposed to be the next LeBron. And Eric Daneko and Dave Bender, a cop's son. You know their names and all the others on Coach Ken Glass's team, which might turn out to be the best high school basketball team anybody's ever seen. It doesn't change that at least a couple of them are punk felons, and might have been involved in murdering the kid who was manager of the team.

As you watch them run up and down the court, run up the score the way they did on poor Gannon High last night, remember that two of them and maybe more than that held down one of their teammates and violated him in unspeakable ways, the same as some punks on the Mepham High football team did once to one of their own.

Then left their teammate blindfolded and tied up in a cabin in the woods.

His teammates did that.

They know who they are.

Don't you want to know?

Because until we do know, this glorious basketball season at South Fork High School is nothing more than the scene of a crime.

Are all of them punks? Some are. Only the police can't, or won't, find out who they are. The halfwit principal of the school, the great Norman Brodie, acts as if Drew Hudson somehow made the whole thing up. Or perhaps did these things to himself. Shame on him, and anybody else who doesn't want to know the truth.

Shame on a town that worries more and cares more

about winning basketball games than the victim of the
kind of crime Drew Hudson described to Sam Perry in
this newspaper not long ago. . . .

Mitchell finished at nine-thirty, a half hour before the
ten o'clock deadline, the sports editor telling him they
needed more time if they were going to run it out front.
Then he went through the process of sending it, confirming
with the desk that they had it in the house, saying he'd call
back after they'd given it a first read.

When he called back, they switched him to the copy editor Sam had told him about, Bill Price, who said, "It's a
pleasure to meet you, Mr. Mitchell, even over the phone."

"Ben."

"Okay, then. Ben."

"Everything okay?"

"*Yeah,*" Price said, the way kids said it, making it into
two syllables, almost in a singsong way.

"Then I can go get on the ferry."

He heard Price call out, asking if anybody needed to
talk to Ben Mitchell, then came back on and said, "The
sports editor would like a word with you."

Price switched him over. The sports editor got on and
said, "Well, this is gonna singe everybody's fucking eyebrows." There was a pause and then he said, "You're good
with all of it?"

"I wrote it."

"Even the parts at the end where you talk about how
none of the seniors on the team seem to be able to get their
stories straight about where they were when it happened to
Drew Hudson?"

"They said what they said. Nobody said it was off the
record."

"I wanted to ask you about one other line. Near the bottom? About the police?"

"Where I say that if I know these things, the police must know, too," Mitchell said. "Unless they don't want to?"

"That's the one."

"Put it in the paper," he said.

"By the way," the sports editor said, "it just occurred to me that we didn't talk about a fee."

Mitchell told him it was on the house.

What he didn't tell the sports editor: Feeling this way again, even for a night, he should have paid them.

The column ended this way:

**Where was Show Watkins when it happened to Drew Hudson? Where was Glenn Moore, the captain of the team? And Eric Daneko? And Dave Bender, whose father is running the investigation for the South Fork Police Department?**

**You know the old line from the news?**

**It's 10 o'clock, do you know where your children are?**

**You should want to know where these kids were around 11 o'clock, one night in October.**

**Or don't you want to know?**

Mitchell was listed in the South Fork phone book. The calls started coming about eight the next morning. The first voice, male, told him to leave town if this was such a terrible place to live. He checked caller I.D. Blocked. Then another male voice. "Somebody should do to you what they did to the Hudson kid." Unknown caller.

Then a woman's voice. "You should be ashamed of yourself, making it seem as though these boys are guilty until proven innocent."

That one came from the main number at South Fork High School.

He decided to let the machine pick up after that, putting

it on answer-only. Put on some Ray Charles and cranked up
the speakers for "Night Time Is the Right Time." Went upstairs, took a shower, got dressed in a sweater and jeans and
old Rockports.

His first visitor rang the doorbell at nine o'clock, sharp.


**M**att Ferraro said he should have called first, but he was already in the car and decided he wanted to have the conversation in person, anyway.

"I had an early meeting with the real estate woman," he
said. "I'm putting the house on the market."

"Not the same pond," Mitchell said, "not the same
house."

"Something like that."

Mitchell asked if he had time for a cup of coffee and
Ferraro said, no, if he left in the next few minutes he'd have
timed his trip into the city perfectly, barring an overturned
tractor trailer on the Expressway.

The two of them stood there awkwardly on the porch,
waiting for somebody to make the first move. Matt Ferraro
in his blue shirt with the white collar like the anchormen
wore. Maroon tie with faint white stripes. Suspenders. All
put together and on his way to the big city to make more big
deals. Maybe selling the house was another way of trying
to make everything seem normal, come back toward some
kind of normal life a little more. Even though Mitchell
knew there was no way for him ever to come all the way
back, put himself all the way back together.

"I know you probably expected to hear from me after the
story came out about Drew," he said. "You know, him saying Bobby was one of them."

"The story was what it was," Mitchell said. "You read it.
Drew wasn't blaming Bobby. It's clear he thought they
made him do it."

Matt Ferraro cleared his throat a couple of times. "Anyway, there's something you ought to know. I couldn't decide whether to come to you with this, or Hank Bender." He worked his mouth into a smile that looked more like a grimace. "You won. You seem to care more. If I didn't know it before, I sure as hell knew it after reading that piece you wrote today."

Mitchell said, "You said there's something I should know."

"My gun's missing," Matt Ferraro said.

"Your gun."

Ferraro said, "I keep a gun in the house. Not much of a gun. A twenty-two I felt I could handle and use if I ever had to. Bobby called it a glorified cap pistol. I picked it up a couple of years ago, after a couple of winter break-ins near the pond. Smash-and-grab deals, television sets, DVD players, like that." He shook his head, embarrassed. "My wife said it helped her sleep, though I thought the Temazepans she was taking by the fistful were already doing a pretty good job of that. Anyway, I got the gun and kept it in a locked drawer next to my bed. Key in the drawer above it. I hadn't even thought about the thing in weeks. Then, the other night, I'm watching an NRA guy and some gun-control woman scream at each other on television. O'Reilly's show. He looked happier than a pig in shit watching them go at it. And the NRA guy hacks me off so much I decided I'm going to take my glorified pistol and throw it in the pond."

"But it was already gone."

"Gone. And the only person who knew where it was, could have taken it, was Bobby."

"But why would he?"

"Sometime that weekend," Ferraro said, "he must have thought he needed it."

"Which means he was scared of somebody."

The father said, "Or looking to protect himself from somebody."

"The cops really want to believe he was killed by persons unknown," Mitchell said. "But if that was the case, why would he go and get the gun?"

"I went to bed thinking that and woke up thinking that."

"He had to know who did it."

"They were coming for him or he was going for them," Ferraro said. "That sound right to you?"

"Yeah," Mitchell said, "it sure does."

Matt Ferraro put out his hand and Mitchell shook it. "You handle this any way you want to," he said. "But now you know everything I know."

Mitchell watched him walk down the front walk, thinking: Just not everything your kid knew.

The other car pulled up in the driveway about the time Mitchell was going to drive to Hiram's for a late breakfast. He heard it before he saw it. When he looked out one of the front windows, he saw the blue Taurus come to a loud rough stop, gravel flying everywhere, then watched Hank Bender get out with the engine still running, take a few steps toward the house, then go back and shut the car off and slam the door shut behind him.

He had the newspaper in his right hand. Mitchell was still listening to Ray Charles. He shut off the music and opened the front door. When Bender saw him, he threw the newspaper in Mitchell's direction, pages flying everywhere. Because of the crewcut, Mitchell could see veins popping on both sides of his forehead, so blue they looked like somebody had painted them on.

"It's a goddamn good thing I'm a cop," he said.

Mitchell said, "Good for whom?"

"You must want to catch a beating," Bender said.

"You think we're going to settle this by *fighting?*" Mitchell said.

Mitchell remembered Hank Bender like this when they

were kids. He'd get brushed back by some high school pitcher, or get hit, and everybody on both teams knew that as soon as he got up, he was on his way to the mound.

Bender made a gesture that took in the newspaper scattered around him. "You started it," he said.

Not even caring what a dumb-ass he sounded like. But then nobody in town seemed to care lately. It was all jock stare-downs and high-test testosterone.

Mitchell included.

"I said what needed to be said."

"What? That I don't want to find out what happened with those kids?"

"Maybe just not the ones related to you," Mitchell said.

Bender was on Mitchell then before he knew it, grabbing two fists of the old gray sweater Mitchell was wearing, driving him across the porch and hard into the doorjamb, Mitchell's head hitting it so hard he felt like somebody had popped him from behind with the Mattingly. Bender was close enough to him that he could smell the coffee on his breath, knew that if he leaned in any closer they would be nose to nose.

"Now you listen to me," Bender said, pushing his hands up and into Mitchell's chin, the sweater halfway up Mitchell's belly. "I am working this case the best I can. I know more than you know. I know more than you think *I* know. But unlike guys like you"—another shove against the wall—"I don't convict a bunch of kids in some piece-of-shit newspaper until I have all the facts I need."

Mitchell thought about getting his arms up and pushing back, but was pretty sure that if he did, Hank Bender was going to have all the excuse he wanted or needed to bounce him from one end of his front porch to the other.

He relaxed himself instead, let his body sag, and said, "I didn't make anything up and you know it."

"You're a cute bastard, you really are. You made everything sound the way you wanted to. The kids did it, they're covering for each other, I'm helping them. You even bring the principal into it."

"He's a dickwad. The allegations of a troubled young man. Fuck him."

"You think you helped me by writing what you wrote today?"

"That's not my job, helping you do your job."

"What is your job, I forget? Being some kind of asshole troublemaker?"

Bender gave him another shove. Mitchell hit his head again. He said, "It got me out of South Fork."

"Now you're back, and you're gonna step all over whoever you have to step on to feel big again."

"I don't want them to get away with it."

Bender let go of him.

"You're on your own from now on," he said. "You get no more help from me."

"Yeah, you've been a great comfort to me so far, Hank, no shit."

They were still only a couple of feet apart. Mitchell casually slid himself past the front door to create more space, give himself room if Bender came at him again. "And, by the way, if you ever put your hands on me again I'll file assault charges. Before I write your ass up in the paper."

"Tough guy," Bender said. "Tough enough to slap kids." He chin-cocked at Mitchell. "Right?"

"*Your* kid had it coming."

"So he says something you don't like, you slap him. You say this shit about me in the paper, though, and I'm supposed to let it go. How's that work?"

"Is that what this is all about? Jesus Christ." Mitchell spread out his arms. "Then let's go."

"You're not worth my job."

"Your kid said I wasn't worth breaking a hand on."

Bender started to say something else, bit down on his lower lip instead. Mitchell could see the sweat on him, feel the heat still coming off him. "You watch your back from now on, Mitch, that's all I'm gonna tell you."

"Now I'm gonna tell you something: Nobody has to talk to the police if they don't want to. So get the hell off my property."

Hank Bender gave Mitchell the same sad look his kid had, out behind Tower Records.

"Let me ask you something before I go, and you don't have to answer if you don't want to: What if Drew Hudson made it up? What if there've been a couple of times in high school where he said teachers came at him, only nobody ever could prove it, it was his word against theirs?"

"And how does that explain how he ended up in the hospital that first time?"

Bender said, "You think a broomstick is the only thing that causes what happened to him?"

"What is that supposed to mean?"

"Use your imagination."

"Right, Hank," Mitchell said. "Drew made it all up. And Bobby Ferraro killed himself. And that brick threw itself through Kate Perry's window. And Sam Perry got himself down in Mallozzi that night. And it was the neighbors' kids who threw a broomstick with red paint on it through the Perrys' kitchen window."

"You know it all, Mitch. You always did. Who knows? Maybe if you get real lucky this time, you can have somebody else kill themselves."

There was nothing for Mitchell to say to that, now or ever, not to Hank Bender or anybody else. When Bender was gone in his town cop car, he went around the front yard and picked up that morning's copy of the *Press*, hunted down every single page of it, even the wrinkled-up ones, until he found his name and his column on the front page.

Saved him the trip into town.

# 22

She loved being the last one out of the store.

Kate loved being *alone* in the store, really, because it was in those quiet times, with the CLOSED sign in the front door, that River Road felt most like her own little world.

Kate loved sitting at the antique desk where she wrote out the sales slips, not wanting the last part of someone's shopping to feel like some supermarket checkout stand. She wanted a more low-key feel to River Road, a more elegant feel, more of a classy goodbye than the *ka-ching* of a register. So they wrote everything out by hand, even the credit card slips. It took longer, but just felt right to her.

Sometimes, when Karen and Linda, the two women who worked for her, were gone, when it was just Kate, she would go around and try on some of the new clothes herself. Or move displays around, just a couple of feet this way or that. As a way of putting her hands on the whole business.

And sometimes she would just do what she was doing now, make herself a cup of tea, some nice English breakfast tea even in the early evening, put on some music while she totaled up how much money they'd made for the day. Now she was playing the CD that Ben Mitchell had given her. Miles Davis's *Kind of Blue*. He'd dropped by in the late morning, taking her outside to tell her about his visit from Matt Ferraro and then one from Hank Bender right after that.

Then he'd reached into the bag he was holding and came out with the CD, gift-wrapped.

"If you're going to play jazz in the store," he said, "play the best. Of course, once it gets inside your head, you won't be able to get it out."

She couldn't get Mitchell out of her head.

Sam would kid her about it, his way of trying to get at her feelings for Mitchell, and she'd laugh and wave the whole thing off and tell him he was being plain silly.

But her boy was smart. And didn't miss very much, even with this story about the basketball team on his mind constantly, dominating his life. Dominating *their* shared life. It was what was going to make him a great reporter someday, she was sure.

If they all survived this.

So before she'd change the subject, she'd tell him he was imagining things anyway, that Mitchell had just managed to go, in fairly short order, from annoyance to acquaintance to somebody who might possibly actually end up a good friend one of these days.

Her boy would say, "You two seem to have an awful lot in common."

And she'd say, "We have you in common."

He'd walk out of the room then, grinning at her, saying, "Whatever you say, Mom."

She'd go back to thinking about Mitchell a little more.

She felt as if she'd been watching him get up the last few weeks. Get up after being knocked down. And watching him come alive, a little bit at a time, come out of himself, from that still place where he watched things himself.

Sam had gone on and on about what a great columnist he'd been, he'd shown her the piece that Mitchell had written about the whole case, the one Drew Hudson had burned the day he swallowed the pills. But she had to admit, she didn't really see it for herself until today, his column on the front page of the *Press*. It got her to feel what he wanted her to feel about everything that was going on, almost like she wasn't involved, and it was happening to someone else, in some other town.

He got her mad all over again.

He was smart and tough and had a passion for his work, even though he wanted to act as if he was just tagging along with Sam, as if Sam was the one all on fire with it.

And she had kissed him.

Where had *that* come from?

Kate Perry was a lot of things. Impulsive was not one of them. Not with men. *Especially* not with men, and especially not in all the years since Steven had died. But there she was in the driveway, jumping up to kiss him like some teenager, then running into the house without looking back. And sitting right back down in the living room and listening to Louis Armstrong and Ella on the same couch where the two of them had been sitting. *Still* acting like a high school girl, replaying a date.

Even now, in the quiet store, past closing time, she could actually feel herself coloring, hearing something Sam always said to her inside her head, something he said he'd picked up hanging around Coach Glass:

Where we goin' with this?

Home, she thought. We are most definitely going home.

Sam was at an early movie with a couple of kids from the school paper. She had thought about giving Mitchell a call, seeing if he wanted to meet her at O'Rourke's for a burger. She knew he was at home, he said he had a ton of calls to make, going through all the South Fork kids who'd played for Ken Glass over the eight years he'd been on the job, trying to find out if there'd been any hazing incidents in the past that South Fork players of the past had been too scared or too intimidated to talk about. You never know what might turn up, he'd said in front of the store, looking at her with those steady, dark eyes.

Down, girl.

Go home after she did some quick food shopping, have a nice civilized glass of wine, read the new *Vogue*. Or rent a movie of your own. Just don't get stupid here. The way Ben Mitchell was talking about South Fork, he was going to be out of here as soon as this was all over, whenever that was, back to L.A. probably. Or New York. Or Chicago. Writing his column all over again. She could see it in him, even today when she talked about what he'd written, the excitement in him. He was like a drinker who thought he'd quit for good, then took that first drink, and away he went.

And when he was gone, where would she be?

Where she'd been since Steven died. Alone. With Sam. Telling herself that Sam and the store were enough for her, at least for now, maybe she'd have a change in attitude once Sam was off in college somewhere, and she was completely alone.

She shut off every light except the one near the back door. Checked one last time to make sure the front door was locked. Looked around in the light that came through her new front window from the old-fashioned streetlight in front of the store. God, she really did love this time of night, the first darkness of Main Street feeling as fresh to her as the first morning light out her bedroom window at home. She put her Mont Blanc pen into the stand on the desk, next to her to-do list for tomorrow. Rinsed out the mug that Sam had given her on her last birthday—no reason to dwell on which one—the one with "Boss Mom" on the side.

Time now for her guilty pleasure: one Marlboro Light on the bench near the woods beyond the parking lot, where she knew she could sit by herself and not worry about somebody she knew, starting with her kid, coming up from behind and saying, "God, I didn't know *you* smoked."

She set the alarm code, turned off the back light, locked the back door, felt the chill of the night come rushing up to meet her, pulled up the collar of her black leather coat, and checked to see that the cigarettes were in the hidden side pocket in her satchel. Looked up, as she always did when she got outside. A lot of stars tonight. She loved the night sky out here as much as Ben Mitchell said he did.

Him again.

She had parked at the back end of the small municipal lot, the one behind the stores at her end of Main Street and the duck pond that somehow the city fathers had preserved, along with the playground for small children on the left side of it and a pretty wooded area on the right. This wasn't something big and sprawling like Mallozzi Park. This was South Fork's Central Park—actually called that—a vest-pocket park, something you could wrap around you like a blanket.

Her quiet end-of-day spot. A bench tucked in near the woods, one you could barely see from the edge of the water, one she pretended belonged to her.

She sat down, lit her cigarette, happy with how bright the water looked tonight, lit by a full moon. Told herself to sit here and relax and think any kind of end-of-day thought except one more about Ben Mitchell.

Then she felt something that felt like ice against her right cheek, cold and sharp, making her jump. She started to turn, but then felt a big hand on her shoulder, a hoarse-whisper voice say, "If you turn around I will use the knife y'all are feelin' on your pretty face to cut your throat."

Then the voice told her to get up and not make a sound, they were going to take a little walk.

_____

They were back into the woods now. He still had his hand on Kate, her left arm. She was able to glance down enough to see he was wearing gloves, so she couldn't see whether he was white or black. The knife stayed against her face.

"Can I ask you what you want?"

Her voice sounding to her as if it were coming from across the water.

"Due time."

"Because if it's money . . ."

"Shut up, Mrs. Sam's Mom."

They had most of the trees behind them now, making the night darker now, the lights of town almost completely gone.

"Get down on the ground now. Face down."

Kate stiffened. "Please don't do this."

"I'm not here to rape you, Mrs. Sam's Mom. Though I got to say you do have a nice ass on you." A low chuckle come out of him. "Man, y'all don't get none of this."

"Then what . . ."

"Just shut up and do what you're told. *Now get that sweet ass a yours down.*"

She dropped to her knees, feeling him move with her. Then she was stretched out on the cold ground, feeling leaves against her face, feeling how hard the dirt was. The knife stayed with her the way he stayed with her, like they were dance partners.

"The men in your life aren't getting the message here. So maybe you will. I was always taught women are smarter'n men. Most of 'em, anyways."

She waited, afraid to move or breathe. Somehow the whispery voice seemed to fit the muted night sounds around her.

"See here, this is all messed up now, 'cause of your boys. Don't you hate when shit gets messed up? Bobby Ferraro got his own self killed, it had nothing to do with the boys on the team. And Drew Hudson, that girl? He made most of it up to make everybody feel sorry for his sorry ass."

Kate said, "But what about the threats, what you did to my store, Sam's tires . . . " She couldn't make herself remember the whole sequence of things.

"We was just playin', don't you get it? Thinking we'd scare you off and this and that, and that would be the end of the whole damn thing. But no, they had to stay with it, turn every damn boy on the team into a suspect."

Kate felt a tear roll down her right cheek, on the same side as the knife.

"Now they're tryin' to ruin everything. For everybody. And for what? For nothin', that's what for."

Another pause.

"You hearin' me, Mrs. Sam's Mom?"

"Yes."

"You make them stop now."

"I . . . I can't."

The voice was right next to her ear, close enough for her to feel his breath. "Sure you can."

He pressed the knife hard enough that she worried that he had broken her skin.

"You tell them that they let this here go now, or the next time I will cut you."

She was crying now, she couldn't stop it.

"Tell them they got it all wrong and tell them to leave the boys alone."

She didn't know what she was supposed to say to that, just felt whatever words she might have used die on their way to her throat. She started to sob now, her chest going up and down so hard she was afraid she was going to be the one to make the knife cut her.

"If they don't stop pushing," the voice said, "it will be you first. Then I will go do your boy."

From the sky, she heard the call of a night bird, and then another, and another.

"Tell your boyfriend all that there."

Another pause.

"Can you do that for me, Mrs. Sam's Mom?"

"Yes."

"Don't make me come back. We don't neither one of us want that, do we?"

"No."

He told her he was going to get up now, to keep her face in the ground and count slowly to a hundred.

"If you look up before that," he said, "I'll come back and do you now."

I was starting to worry," Two Mom said when he came through the front door. "You said you were just going out for one of your short walks. What your grandfather used to call a constitutional, back when we were just a couple of blocks from Prospect Park . . . "

"Back in the day," Show said, finishing her own thought for her.

"Back in the day." She was already in her pink bathrobe, watching one of her *Law & Order* reruns, he wasn't sure which one without seeing the cop faces. And not even sure he could keep them straight then, whether it was one of the old regular shows or the SVU or the victims one, some nights there seemed to be more *Law & Order* shows on regular and cable TV than there were games.

She kept her eyes on the set and said, "Where'd you go?"

"Just *kept* on goin' tonight, all the way into town. There was some trouble today at practice. Glenn took a cheap shot on me, then tried to come at me. Tried to make me look bad, like I told you he does."

Now she muted the set, all alert, nearly flipped herself out of her recline-back.

"You didn't fight the boy, did you? All along, you've been saying that's what he wants."

"He took me down out of the air, but I bounced right back up on him, Two Mom." He put his hands out, like he was telling her not to work herself up.

"All I give him was a piece of my mind. Let him know *I* know what time it is."

"What did the little coach do about it?"

"With Glenn? Nothin'. Acted like it was no thing. Told us he hoped it was all out of our system."

"Is it?"

"On that? Pretty much."

"Anything else you're not telling me, DeShawn?"

Leaning hard on his birth name.

He said, "Oh, I saw Glenn out there with Ben Mitchell, before Antoine and I pulled out the lot. Probably givin' him an earful about this and that and the other. But I let him go, took Antoine to the train, like I told you I was going to, came home and walked until it was time to turn around and come home."

She stared at him, like she did, like trying to see all the way down into his soul, finally turned and went back to the set, putting the sound back on. Nodding. "Now they're getting to it," she said. "I *knew* the restaurant owner was lying to them ten minutes ago."

"Two Mom," he said, "I don't mean to interrupt on your show, but there is something I've been thinkin' on. Not to do with Glenn. Something I've been thinkin' on for a while."

She pointed the remote at the set again, where the old cop was saying something to the big black cop, the younger one who reminded Show of the Mailman, back when the Mailman still had his hair.

Two Mom gave him another good look now, up and down, Show still standing next to the coffee table. She kidded on him sometimes, saying he was so big, he was like a magician when he walked in, turning her nice living room into something that felt small as a storage closet.

"Didn't I clean those jeans?" she said, giving him her raised eyebrow.

Show looked down himself now, at the grass stains on the knees. "Now, stop yankin' on me," he said. "There's some old stains even *you* can't get out." Smiling at her with the last, not wanting to get into it again any more than she did.

"If I were bigger or you were smaller," Two Mom said, "I would've been yanking on your ear the way I did when you were a little boy, and you and Antoine would get after each other like a couple of alley dogs."

Show saw her stop herself now, frowning on herself, the way she did when she'd lose her train, something that was starting to happen more often, even if it wasn't anything the two of them talked about.

"Where was I, before I got onto you and Antoine?"

"Askin' on my jeans."

"I'll have to run 'em through again, try out that new Tide."

He sat down on the couch she'd just had new-slipcovered, across from her TV watching chair, her little slippered feet, in her Uggs her grandboy got for her, on the flip-up part of the chair, nearly pointing to the ceiling.

Show sighed, impatient to get to it, but knowing he couldn't rush her from one thing to the next. So he said, "Jeans can wait until tomorrow, Two Mom."

She shook her head. "After my show. You can throw them into the dryer when they're done, I'll be sleeping by then."

He felt himself rocking a little on the couch, back and forth, making it squeak the way it always did when he was on it.

Show said, "You always say we should talk about things, not keep them all hidden or locked up."

"Only because it's the smart thing, whatever kind of relationship you have."

Show surprised himself then, coming out with something

he hadn't rehearsed inside his head, on the way back from town.

"You're the smartest person I know, you know that, right?"

"Ooh," she said, waving her little veiny hand in front of her. "Air's getting mighty thick in here all of a sudden." Twinkle in her eyes for him now. "You must want something, DeShawn Watkins."

"I want to leave," he said.

Two Mom didn't say anything now. He saw her eyes change, the fun come right out of them as if he'd reached across the room and took it out himself. She clasped her hands together, like she was setting herself to pray for something.

Patience, most likely.

"I'm not sure I want to live in this town no more," he said.

# 23

When Mitchell opened the door, Kate came into his arms as if that's the way they always greeted each other.

He didn't say anything to her at first, even though he'd noticed the dirt on one side of her face. Neither did she. They just stood there in his open doorway, his fire still going behind him, Ornette Coleman coming out of his speakers, Kate Perry with a fierce hold on him.

Finally he pushed back a little and said, "What happened?"

He could see how red her eyes were, noticed what looked like a tiny paper cut on her right cheekbone, an inch below her eye. A few dried leaves on the shoulder of her coat.

"He had a knife," Kate said.

That was as far as she got before she leaned into him again and started to cry.

They were on the couch. Kate had gone into the downstairs bathroom, cleaned herself off, put a small Band-Aid from

Mitchell's medicine cabinet on her cheek, even put a brush to her hair. He asked if she wanted a glass of wine. She said something stronger. He said her choices were Scotch or Scotch. She managed a smile and said she'd love a Scotch, please, on the rocks. He went and poured her a big shot of J&B into a tumbler, came back and handed it to her. She drank half of it down, made a face like a kid taking medicine. He sat close to her on the couch and she told him all of it from the time she closed up the store, Mitchell stopping her every once in a while to ask a question. She even tried to do a bad impression of the kid's whispery voice, using the same words he'd used. Ornette Coleman blew his way through "Chronology." The fire kept going, Kate even jumping one time when the logs shifted and one of them fell. Mitchell thought about fussing with it, putting on another log. The guy thing to do. But he was here on the couch, with her, his arm still around her. He wasn't going anywhere.

"You think it was a black voice?" he said.

He had his chin resting on top of her hair.

"Or someone trying awfully hard to sound black," she said.

"Just about all of them do," he said. "The white kids, I mean. And the black kids? They want to sound even blacker, more gangsta, than the other black kids. I wanted to give Dave Bender a good shake the other day, remind him he was white and tell him to get over it."

"I just know he was strong."

"You couldn't tell how big?"

"No."

Mitchell said, "It has to be one of the players. Or the coach."

Kate shifted slightly, dropped her head a little, looked up at him. "Ken Glass?"

"I'm not ruling out anybody anymore," he said. "The other day he told Sam he was watching him, and that night the voice on the phone used almost the exact same words, right before the broomstick came through the window."

She put her head back down. Mitchell noticed a few strands of hair spilling out on her forehead, and brushed them away gently with his free hand. She looked up again, not smiling, just looking at him. Mitchell said, "You're sure Sam will check his phone for messages when he's out of the movies?"

"If he had the phone on vibrate instead of turned off," she said, "he might be on his way here already. He's a kid. You don't know how obsessive they are with their phones. It's like if they don't keep checking them, they're like hand grenades that could go off in their pockets at any moment."

"You guys can stay here tonight," Mitchell said. "Or I can stay at your place."

"Yes," she said.

He didn't press her on which one, just reached over now and got her glass off the coffee table. She took a smaller sip of Scotch this time, handed the glass back to him. "That's enough."

"The guy," Mitchell said, as a way of gently bringing her back. "He kept calling you Mrs. Sam's Mom?"

"Yes."

"Show Watkins calls his grandma Two Mom, for whatever it's worth."

"You think . . . ?"

"I think I'd like to know where all the members of the South Fork basketball team were the last couple of hours, though I'm not likely to find out."

Kate said, "Could the police help?"

"The South Fork Police? Is that a rhetorical question?"

"Sam said your father was a policeman."

"By the time he got out here, he was mostly just a drunk. He was a great cop in the city. Or so I was told. After he left there, he was just hanging on." He sipped some of his drink.

"I've always thought I must have a lot of him in me, though. The cop part, not the drunk part. Just the way I go after things."

She sat back from him now, turned so she was facing him.

"This person tonight. Could he have been telling the truth in some weird way? That you and Sam have got this wrong somehow. That mostly they've just been trying to scare you off so you'd leave them alone."

"And the guys who've been trying to scare you really don't know how Bobby Ferraro died?"

Kate nodded.

Mitchell shook his head. "That doesn't mean no. It means I don't know. What I do know is they're acting scared now. Taking chances they shouldn't be taking."

He got up, walked into the kitchen and came back with a couple of cigarettes. Kate looked at the door. "I don't want Sam to see me smoke." Back to being a mom.

"If he shows up in the next five minutes, I'll take the hit," he said.

She took a drag, holding it, telling him that her one smoke of the day came a little later than she'd planned.

"Will they stop now?" Kate said.

"You mean if I don't?"

"Something like that."

"Maybe," Mitchell said.

"But you won't stop?"

"No," he said. "I figure one of these days they're going to come at me with more than some stupid message on my computer screen."

"They did something they felt like doing at the time, and even after that, they still thought they could get their way," Kate said.

"And just make it go away."

They both heard the car in the driveway then. Kate Perry got up off the couch, tossed her cigarette into the fire, came back and took one more quick sip of Scotch. Then she leaned down and put her arms around him and kissed him full this time, both of them all the way into it right away, as if they'd done this sort of work before.

"Thank you," she said.

"You are welcome."

"To be continued," she said, then asked if he had any good mints as they heard the ring of the doorbell, saw Sam's face pressed to the window next to it.


**M**itchell slept in Kate Perry's guest bedroom, upstairs in the front of the house. He said that he couldn't see the creeps coming back at either Kate or Sam, but from now on they weren't going to take any chances. New rules. Kate left the store when everybody else did. Sam did his work with the team after practice, came straight home. Mitchell would go to all the games with him, Kate could come, too. Sam would never be the last one out of the writing room after a game, even if he had to come home and finish his story.

Everybody had everybody else's cell phone number.

"When *does* this end?" Kate said before she went to bed.

"Soon."

"You lie about as well as my kid," she said. "No wonder the two of you get along so well."

When she was gone, Mitchell told Sam about his conversation with Hank Bender, Bender saying there were other ways for somebody to get the kind of injury Drew had sustained.

"Does Drew have a girlfriend?" Mitchell said. "Just for the record."

"I told you, we weren't that kind of friends anymore."

"But kids around school know things whether they're friends or not, just from other kids."

"If you care about stuff like that," Sam said, "and I didn't."

He gave Mitchell a slit-eye look. "Are *you* starting to think Drew made it up?"

"No," Mitchell said. "But that doesn't mean he couldn't have made up some of it."

"Why?"

"I'll know that when I know which parts he didn't make up."

Mitchell was wide awake at six-thirty. Kate was already gone, on her way to the first of three ferry rides that would finally deposit her in New London, Connecticut. From there she would drive a couple of hours to Boston for her annual dinner date there with her two college roommates from Boston U. There had been an oh-shit moment for her the night before, when she remembered the trip. Then she had started for the phone, saying Oh my God, there was no way in the world she could still go to Boston at a time like this, before Mitchell and Sam double-teamed her, telling her this might be a perfect time for her to get out of South Fork, even for one day and night. But I'm not up for something like this, she protested. Mitchell said, You should be up for something like this. She said two against one wasn't fair, but she was too tired to fight them. She'd go, spend her one night a year at the old Ritz, but be back early enough the next morning to open the store.

She said to Mitchell, Are you sure I'm not running away? To do that, he said, takes more than one night at the old Ritz. Watch my kid, she'd said. He said he'd be back in the guest room that night, maybe he and Sam would even have a boys' dinner at O'Rourke's.

He went home, showered, tried to come up with a plan for the day. He wanted to talk to Drew Hudson again, but Kate said she hadn't heard from Shelley, which meant she still didn't know where they were. He wanted to find a way to make another run at Christian Bowdoin, just because he thought that out of all of them, Christian was the weakest. He wanted to find an innocent way to ask Emmy Watkins where Show had been during the time when Kate Perry had a knife to her face, just because he knew he didn't need a court order to get Show's grandma to talk to him.

*Mrs. Sam's Mom.*

The part he couldn't get out of his brain.

There was a street sound to it.

He went upstairs, wrote out more index cards, started all over again on his corkboard, still waiting, after all this time, for everything to come into focus.

Whatever had happened that weekend, Bobby had decided he needed his father's gun. Nobody had seen him, according to the cops. Mitchell asked Matt Ferraro at the house, that first Saturday, about Bobby's cell. He said it was usually his favorite toy, he'd sometimes put the phone on himself like a camera, send him messages at work. But the police had confiscated it after they found the body, thinking they could use it to track his calls, or even whereabouts, using new technology with cell towers, the last weekend of his life.

But Hank Bender had told him that other than a couple of calls to school, they'd found nothing of interest.

Sometimes Mitchell got so fixed on Drew Hudson that he forgot Bobby was the main event, just because his life in newspapers told him that murder always was.

*Now you know everything I know.* That's what Bobby Ferraro's father said.

What secrets *did* the kid have?

All kids had secrets.

He didn't know what Hank Bender knew about the kid's phone calls leading up to the weekend he'd disappeared. Bender had made a sweep of the kid's laptop. You had to these days, a computer being the modern form of background check. What was the slogan: Where do you want to go today? The computer told you where, and what you'd seen along the way. What if Hank Bender hadn't checked closely enough? Or had missed something?

He went into his wallet and found the card Matt Ferraro had given him and called him on his cell even though it was seven in the morning, got him right away, asked if the police had returned Bobby's computer. He said they had, last week. Mitchell asked if anybody besides them had access to the computer. Ferraro said no. Mitchell asked if anybody had been in the house before Hank Bender hauled the computer off to the South Fork police station.

"Well, the team," Ferraro said. "They were all there after the funeral. Them and Ken Glass. They stopped by to pay their respects before practice that day. Is that important?"

"I'll let you know," Mitchell said, then asked if he had Bobby's screen name and password. Ferraro said he did, just give him a second. He must have been at his desk already, Mitchell could hear the *tap-tap-tap* of his own computer keys. Ferraro then read off the screen name, **BF1987**, and the password, **TeamMgr**, explaining that he and Bobby had a deal, as long as the old man always had the current password, Bobby could get unlimited everything that wasn't rated Triple-X.

"It was another way of pretending I was involved," he said. "But the truth is, I'm still not involved enough. After Hank Bender dropped off the computer and I hooked it back up, I realized I hadn't even closed out Bobby's accounts. So I'm about as on top of everything as I always was."

"It's a good thing," Mitchell said.

"Why?"

"Because it makes it easier to get some questions answered," Mitchell said, "even if it's only online."

Matt Ferraro then told him where the spare key was hidden near the front door and told him to have at it.

**B**obby Ferraro wanted to be a basketball coach a lot more than his father knew.

If his father, by his own admission, hadn't been much of

a father figure, there sure seemed to be enough of those to go around in the back bedroom facing Fogg Pond. There were books by and about Red Auerbach, Pat Riley, Bob Knight, Phil Jackson, Dean Smith, Rick Pitino.

On the kid's desk was a framed photograph of him and Coach Ken Glass, Glass's arm around his shoulders, both of them wearing T-shirts that read SOUTH FORK SPORTS CAMP. The two of them about the same size. Bobby Ferraro with long, curly hair, a good-looking kid with sad eyes.

The inscription from Glass:

"To Bobby, a future coach. Best always, Coach Ken."

Here Mitchell was now, alone in the dead boy's room in the quiet house, feeling as if he were in The Coach's Corner of some bookstore.

He sat down at the desk, turned on Bobby's computer.

Mitchell was decent with computers, even if he'd never achieved true nerd status. He clicked on Internet Explorer, went to AOL, then AOL Mail. Lots of junk mail still coming in. Apparently unlimited everything for Bobby Ferraro didn't include spam control. There was a lot of information about summer basketball camps that were called Five-Star this or All-Star that, up and down the East Coast.

Mitchell clicked on Sent Mail, just to see how far back it went. There were about two hundred and fifty sent messages, the last one the Thursday night before he disappeared. So he hadn't sent out any mail the weekend he disappeared. Or somebody had cleaned it out. Why not? If somebody had gotten to Mitchell's computer, somebody could have gotten to Bobby's.

Everybody on the team, the father said, had stopped by to pay their respects when the computer was still in Bobby's bedroom. . . .

He went to Old Mail. More junk. But junk that didn't start up again that Monday.

So there were three missing days of mail.

Or no mail at all.

Except junk mail never stopped, it was stronger and more regular than the fucking tide.

He could ask Hank Bender about it, but that would be a waste of time. He called Matt Ferraro back. "Call Bender later," Mitchell said, "ask him if he somehow copied Bobby's incoming and outgoing e-mails just for the weekend he died. Make it sound casual, that you're a complete computer dope . . . "

" . . . which I am."

" . . . and that you were just wondering."

"You don't think he'll tell you."

Mitchell laughed. "Fuck, no."

"Talk to you after I talk to him."

"I'll try not to call you anymore today."

"Call me all you want," Ferraro said.

Mitchell went back to the computer, realized there was no icon for instant messaging. Didn't all kids instant-message? Wasn't it some kind of law somebody passed? Not Bobby Ferraro, lonely kid, now dead, survived by the sweethearts on the South Fork High School basketball team.

Trying to stay strong in the face of adversity.

Mitchell went back to Sent Mail, clicked around, found a way to get the fifty messages before the ones in Bobby Ferraro's files, saw there were several messages sent to "KGlass" at the South Fork High School Web site in the days leading up to the Connecticut trip. Most of them were just peppering Glass with basketball questions. More were about how Bobby could do the best job he could this season, telling him more than once how much he looked up to him, how much he wanted to learn.

"Coach," one said, "I know you weren't a great player or even a good one. That INSPIRES me as much as anything. Bobby."

"Coach," another one said, "you know I will do anything to help us get to where we need to go this season. Bobby."

Another: "Don't worry, I'm watching Dave like a hawk."

What the hell did that mean?

Why did Dave Bender need watching like a hawk?

The last one, from the day before the trip, read this way:

"Coach: I know you asked me to be your eyes and ears this season. And you KNOW I will. I was in the gym today, and I just think you should keep an eye on Show with Glenn. Could be some jealousy issues there, like you said. Tell you about it Over There. Assistant Coach Ferraro (ha ha)."

But nothing to Ken Glass after the team got back.

Which made no sense to Mitchell.

Any e-mails that Bobby sent out to the team were sent out in bulk. Straightforward stuff about what time to be at practice, the day they were all supposed to take their physicals. What time the bus would take them over to the ferry for the trip across the Sound to Connecticut. Requests for jacket sizes and sweatshirt sizes and even hat sizes.

He sat back down and went to Bobby's Folders files. Schoolwork there mostly. Old term papers. No personal stuff. But then the only personal stuff Mitchell had found was directed at the head basketball coach at South Fork High. Bobby Ferraro's only computer buddy seemed to be him.

Buddy list of one.

Other than the e-mail about Dave Bender, who needed watching, the most interesting one was about Show and Glenn. It was as if Glass somehow saw the trouble between Show and Glenn coming, long before the season started. Mitchell went back to it, printed it out on the small Hewlett-Packard printer on Bobby's desk. It meant something. Or nothing. Two star players who weren't in love with each other. Welcome to the world. Shaq never loved Kobe. Kobe never loved Shaq.

If Mitchell knew anything about sports, it was this:

They all wanted to be the fucking man.

And there could only be one on any team.

# 24

Sam called Mitchell on his cell just as he was finishing up with Bobby's computer, telling him Show Watkins hadn't shown up for school. First period had just ended, Sam said in a voice Mitchell could barely hear, explaining that he was calling from a stall in the men's room, and that if he got caught he was a dead man.

"He could just be sick, of course," Sam said.

"On a game day?" Mitchell said.

Mitchell told Sam to go back to class, they'd talk later, tried Emmy Watkins's number. Got the machine, left a message that he needed to talk to her. She was probably off cleaning her houses already. And maybe the kid was too sick to answer the phone. Only one way to find out. He'd drive over to Emmy Watkins's redbrick building with the quaint white shutters on Earl Avenue and sit out front until somebody showed up, either her or her grandson. And keep calling the apartment. If the kid was inside, he'd either have to shut off the phone or pick it up eventually.

When he got to 426 Earl, he saw Emmy Watkins's Acura parked right in front.

Mitchell walked up the stairs, rang the doorbell for 2C, heard her voice say, "Come on in, it's open."

Emmy Watkins was in the comfortable chair he'd left her in the last time he'd been here, as if she hadn't moved since then, wearing gray slacks and a gray sweater and white Reeboks that reminded Mitchell of nurses' shoes. Regis and Kelly were on her television set.

"I tried to call before I came," Mitchell said.

"I heard."

Mitchell was standing just inside the door. She was looking at the television as she talked to him, the sound down low. Kelly was laughing herself hysterical at something Regis had just said.

Mitchell said, "Would you mind if I sat down for a minute?"

Emmy Watkins made a sweeping motion with her small, old, veiny hand, as if telling him he could sit wherever the hell he wanted.

She looks older today, Mitchell thought. Something off with her, even the way she was staring at the set, as if she couldn't focus herself on anything right now.

"Miz Watkins, are you feeling all right?"

She seemed to hear him after a delay, like she was on the other side of the world and his question had just gotten bounced off some satellite.

"Fine," she said, and pointed the remote at the set. Whatever Regis had said now, Kelly was looking pouty, or maybe frowning because he'd asked her a hard question.

Emmy Watkins said, "You have children, Mr. Mitchell?"

"No, ma'am. We were talking about it right before the only things we talked about were who got the high-def TV and who got the dog."

"I had just the one. My daughter. Who turned out to be all I could have, after birthing her nearly killed me. Maybe that was a sign from the Lord, about the pain to come." She gave her head a quick shake. "And no matter how much I loved that one and tried to take care of her and prayed on her every day of her life, I couldn't keep her off the corner, Mr. Mitchell, off the corner and out the bars and away from the wrong men, before she stopped caring what kind of men."

Mitchell waited, watched her face get older and sadder as she went, those eyes that were so bright the last time squinting now, as if trying to pick out another distant point in her own past, or her daughter's.

"Then she had her two. Her big boys. You know how Antoine turned out, at least on his first go-through at trying to be a man. But DeShawn? He was given this gift. He never let himself go down that road that Antoine went down. Even if DeShawn swears Antoine's picked himself up now, put himself back on the straight-and-narrow."

Mitchell thought about the scene with Antoine at the Blue-White Game, remembered him staring across the parking lot after Mitchell finished talking with Glenn Moore, staring at Mitchell and then pointing at him, like he was firing a gun. But Mitchell just nodded now, as if agreeing with her.

"I met Antoine," Mitchell said. "And I've seen him around town, kind of hanging in the background."

"DeShawn said."

"I'm not exactly sure what Antoine's deal is," Mitchell said, "but my deal is to stay on his good side."

"Sometimes I think DeShawn believes in Antoine's good side more than Antoine does."

"Kid brothers look up to older brothers, even when they shouldn't."

"All I know is that DeShawn is my heart, Mr. Mitchell. He's a good boy, even if you don't think so. But now he's got it in his head that things are going bad for him in this town and it's not worth trying to change them. And I can't say as I disagree with him entirely, no sir."

Mitchell waited.

"I've been hearing things lately, Mr. Mitchell," she said. "All kinds of things. I know you think my boy's the bad one, and all the others around him, they're good. But it's not true."

"What's not true, ma'am, is that I've made up my mind that your grandson is bad."

"I know about what happened at practice the other day, with Glenn and him," she said. "I know you probably think, there DeShawn goes again with that temper of his. But he's not the only boy in this town with a temper, believe me. Or with a past. Or bears watching. You keep such a close eye on DeShawn, come around asking about him and where he was and all this and that, but how come nobody looks into that trouble the Bender boy had a few years back, some tournament?"

Mitchell thought of the e-mail printouts in his car, one of which said that Bobby had been watching Dave Bender like a hawk.

"What trouble?" he asked her, keeping his voice gentle.

"You're asking me what tournament?" she said. "And you the reporter?"

"You can make me a better reporter if you'll help me, Miz Watkins," he said. "Do you remember when this tournament was, or where?"

She shook her head. "All I know, all I *heard,* is that he beat some boy somewhere within an inch of his life."

"Who told you that?"

"I work a lot of houses in this town, is all I'm going to say to you," she said. "And sometimes the walls in those houses, they talk." She nodded slowly, in this slow rhythm, her eyes on him again. She said, "Everybody's got their secrets in this town, Mr. Mitchell. Not that any of them are doing me any good today."

Without the sound from the television, the apartment was completely still in the middle of the day. Mitchell looked past her, down the hall to where Show Watkins's bedroom had to

be. If he was in there, he was part of the stillness, too, asleep
or on his bed with headphones on. Somehow, though, the
place seemed empty except for the two of them. She hadn't
asked why he was here. He hadn't asked where DeShawn was.
It was as if they were doing some kind of careful waltz, just
without music, neither one of them sure who was leading.

"I've been meaning to ask you something," Mitchell
said. "A couple of nights ago, did DeShawn go out at any
time during the evening?"

She turned now, eyes alert. "Something else happen you
think my grandson did?"

"No, no, no," Mitchell said. "I was just supposed to meet
up with him and he never showed up."

There was no point in telling her about what had happened to Kate in the park, at least not yet. He just wanted to
know if the kid had an alibi, just without his grandmother
knowing he was asking about his alibi.

"He went out for about an hour, around seven," she said.
"Said everything was crowding in on him lately, he needed
to get out, get some air, give himself some room. Maybe
it's all the small apartments he had in his growing-up years,
makes him need wide-open spaces." She smiled. "Maybe
that's why he talks about that big house he's going to build
for us, where you can't see the end of the property in any
direction, even with a telescope."

"How long was he gone?"

"Hour or so. I remember speaking sharp to him when he
came back, wearing dirty jeans out in public like that."

Mitchell took a deep breath, let it out, smiling at her, trying to sound happy.

Dirty jeans.

"Well," he said, "that explains it, then, doesn't it?"

"What?"

"Why we didn't meet up."

He sat back. Regis and Kelly were still mugging, cracking each other up. Even without any volume from the set, it was as if they were providing the only life in the apartment, the silence between Mitchell and Emmy Watkins suddenly thick and dense.

Finally, Mitchell, almost in a whisper, said, "Miz Watkins? Where's your grandson right now? I know he's not at school today."

She pointed down the hall and said, "See for yourself."

Mitchell passed her bedroom on his right, went past a bathroom, came to the door of what had to be Show Watkins's room. It was open. Mitchell stood in the doorway, thinking this was the neatest teenaged room that he'd ever seen. Trophies, all from basketball, lined up on the top three shelves of a cheap-looking bookcase. Posters on the walls. LeBron. Carmelo. Kevin Garnett.

His laptop, some brand Mitchell had never heard of, was on the desk, closed. Printer next to it. There were two big speakers in the corners. A wicker basket that had three in-door-outdoor basketballs in it.

Everything in its place.

Everything except Show Watkins.

The bed was made, but there were four or five hangers on it, one pair of jeans, folded neatly. And one pair of white hightop sneakers, all white, looking as if they'd barely been worn. Like he'd changed his mind about packing them, left them behind along with the small stack of CD cases next to them.

Mitchell walked back to the living room.

"Did DeShawn go somewhere?" he said, touching Emmy Watkins on one of her bony shoulders.

The sound was back up on the television, a commercial, men and women in work clothes jumping around an office as if their team had just scored a touchdown in the big game, before he saw "Viagra" on the screen.

"Gone is where he went," she said.

---

When Mitchell got outside, he ran across the street to his car, feeling things moving now, something happening, even if he wasn't sure what, not knowing why it was important that he find Show Watkins, and right now, just knowing that he had to.

He tried Sam's cell, thinking he might have the phone on vibrate. Got his voice: "This is Sam, you called my cell, leave a message." Mitchell did, telling him he was in the truck on the way to the city to look for Show, telling the kid as concisely as he could to find out anything he could about Dave Bender getting into some kind of trouble at some kind of tournament beating somebody up, even if Mitchell didn't happen to know when the tournament had been played, or where, or against who.

"Hey, you're the reporter," Mitchell said, and said he'd check with him late in the day.

He drove fast when the traffic heading west on the Long Island Expressway would let him, got into the HOV lane as soon as he could now that the morning rush was over, focused on Show for now, even with what Emmy Watkins had told him about Dave Bender. Mitchell remembering a conversation he'd had with a psychiatrist named Martha Cassidy. He'd called her at the State University at Stony Brook a few days ago, mostly because she was such an expert on hazing that her name kept coming up every time he read up on the subject a little more. He'd told her his story and some of his theories and finally she'd said, "What if it's not hazing, at least hazing as we understand it?"

"I couldn't keep up with professors as smart as you in college," Mitchell said. "Help me out here."

"It could just be acting out," she said. "One of them unable to act on the cause of his problem, taking it out on people around him."

"Would it have to be somebody with a violent temper?"

"Violence in him. The capacity for it. Some level of cruelty that exists, or is apparent, in more subtle ways."

"A person like that—if he felt threatened, he could lash out?"

"Oh yes."

"Not worrying about the consequences."

"It would be part of the pathology, if you want to call it that. They wouldn't focus on the reaction. Just the action itself, the relief they feel from it. And," Martha Cassidy said, "sometimes the more they do act out, the more they get to like it."

Mitchell not remembering the conversation he'd just had with Emmy Watkins as much as the first one he had with her, when she talked about the anger Show Watkins had carried around in him his whole life.

**E**mmy Watkins told Mitchell there had been two apartments on Gerard, both of them between 157th and 158th. And another apartment, she said, on the other side of 161st, the Bronx County Courthouse practically staring them in the face. Emmy Watkins told Mitchell that from any of those apartments, you could walk outside and see at least a part of Yankee Stadium, though neither Antoine nor Show had gotten inside of it, Emmy said, until Show became a star at Clinton his sophomore year and the whole team went as a group one time.

"The only address in the South Bronx worth anything was the one belonging to the Yankees," she said. "Or so my late husband used to say."

It was a sunny day, but not on the part of River Avenue that backed up against Yankee Stadium. Mitchell remembered from his sportswriting days: It was almost always dark here, like there was always a storm coming, the rumble of the 4 train over his head, the shake of it, like a constant thunder. He walked past Stadium Souvenirs and an Apple Bank and Billy's Sports Bar, then Stan's Sports World and Stan the Man's Baseball World and Stan's Sports Bar and Restaurant. As if it should be called Stan's Avenue.

He walked up to Gerard from River Avenue, couldn't get inside 825 Gerard, across from the Gerard Laundromat and Ray's Cleaners and a check-cashing place called Envios de Valores. Above Envios de Valores he saw laundry hanging from a fire escape, even on the chilly November afternoon.

It wasn't Stan's World up here, though you could see the Bleachers Entrance to Yankee Stadium straight down the hill.

It was Show's World.

Mitchell went outside. On a hunch, he called DeWitt Clinton, asked for Ron Cimoli, the head basketball coach, Cimoli's name having stuck inside Mitchell's head from all the clips he'd read about Show Watkins. The woman answering the phone said he was teaching, but that she'd try to get a message to him. Cimoli called back about twenty minutes later, saying he was between one of the five social studies classes he taught every day. Mitchell introduced himself. Cimoli said he knew who Ben Mitchell was, he'd read his book. Mitchell asked if he'd heard from Show lately and Cimoli said as a matter of fact, the kid had called the day before yesterday, saying he had something important he needed to talk about. But when Cimoli tried to call him back on the number he'd left, it was a cell phone that had been disconnected.

"Is he all right?" Cimoli said. "I would've hated losing this kid to any school, of course, but I never thought that moving out there was the best idea in the world for him, even playing with that other kid."

"You've heard about the trouble out there, right?"

Cimoli said, "Who hasn't?"

Mitchell said, "I've been hanging around the team, trying to figure out who the bad guys are."

There was a silence on the phone, Mitchell hearing the shout of kids in the background, like Cimoli was in the middle of a crowded hallway. "Where's the kid right now?" Cimoli said.

Mitchell said he wasn't sure, that's why he was calling.

"I'll tell you this, and you do whatever you want with it," Cimoli said. "This is a good kid we're talking about. He had every chance in this world to turn into a career punk like his brother. But he didn't."

Now Mitchell paused. "You think he could hurt somebody?"

Ron Cimoli said, "Only if somebody tried to hurt him first."

There was a McDonald's about two minutes from the press entrance at Yankee Stadium, at the corner of 161st and River, across from soccer fields at Joseph Yancy Track and Field. He stopped and watched kids play soccer for a minute, then started to call Kate, force of habit, before he remembered she was in Boston. Let her enjoy the day and night with her roommates, without Mitchell calling from the big city with a play-by-play of his day.

He'd call her in the hotel when he got back to South Fork.

Mitchell hailed a gypsy cab, took a longer ride than he expected over to Rosedale Park, the Bronx bigger than he thought, thinking he might get lucky at Rosedale, another growing-up place Show always talked about, a famous basketball address. There was an after-school game going on when Mitchell got to Rosedale. Show wasn't in it. Mitchell sat and watched them play anyway. Finally hailed another gypsy cab, telling the driver to take him back to 161st Street and River Ave.

Reviewing all his suspects as he did.

One more time, he thought.

Maybe it was Dave who'd done it, the cop's son who might turn out to have a rap sheet of his own. Or Eric Daneko, no matter how much Eric wanted Mitchell to be his buddy now. Maybe Christian had gone along, because he was the type to go along, the type of follower any truly lousy hazing incident needed. Maybe even Glenn Moore had been in on it somehow, Mitchell knew he had to at least consider the golden boy now that he'd gotten a look at his temper. As much as Glenn Moore had to lose, almost as much as Show.

Still.

Show was the one who had run. Show was the one who had Antoine for a brother. Antoine the Cop, who said he'd do anything to watch his brother's back. Show was the one who had grass stains all over his jeans when he came back the night somebody put Kate Perry down in the park . . .

It was starting to get dark now. He had spent the whole afternoon in the Bronx, come up with nothing. He had the gypsy cab drop him at 161st, by the soccer field. He looked up, noticed that the lights at the top of the stadium were on. He walked in that direction, took the left when he got to Macombs Dam Park, the ballpark on his left, the lights of Macombs in front of him, and when he looked down at the two basketball courts there, two full courts with all the lines drawn on it, including what looked like freshly painted three-point lines, the Yankee logo in blue on all the white backboards, he saw Show Watkins.

# 25

He was wearing a red headband, black Knicks sweatshirt, black sweatpants, and shiny new black sneakers, high-tops, that seemed to be made out of patent leather. Mitchell looked around. Show seemed to be alone, spotting up from the outside for three-point shots, making most of them, moving around the arc the way kids did when they were playing Around the World.

Back in his own little world.

Occasionally he would fake the outside shot, drive for the basket, get there in what looked to be two long strides, elevate effortlessly, throw down a dunk that would rattle the backboard at Macombs, the one with the Yankees "NY" logo on it, like the 4 train was running over the top of it.

Mitchell made his way down the hill.

"Hey," he said when he was at the other end of the court, closest to the ballpark.

Show turned around, not acting surprised to see Mitchell there, not acting pissed, his face blank, ball cocked on his hip.

One more pose, from one more of them.

"I got nothin' for y'all tonight," he said. "I talked to Two Mom. She told me now you got it inside your head I's the one behind everything out there in Hooptie Town."

He hadn't told it to Emmy Watkins that day, and couldn't believe she would have told it that way to Show.

"I was misquoted then," Mitchell said.

"Serves your ass right."

Show turned around, took a dribble, took one quick look at the basket, shot the ball from what had to be at least twenty-five feet, made it.

"I just want to know the same thing your grandma does," Mitchell said. "Why you bolted."

Show leaned against the basket support.

"Didn't bolt. I just needed a little time to get some shit checked out." He shuffled his feet a little, quick and graceful, reminding Mitchell of the old Ali shuffle. "Me and Antoine just needed to do a step-back, reassess my all-around situation."

"You decide to do all that before a game on TV? I don't think so."

Show said, "I'll be on TV soon enough, and it won't just be some bullshit ESPN Number *Two*."

"I still know a little bit about the business, kid. Guy quits his team senior year, quits school, gets people wondering just how high they should take him, no matter how good he is."

"Who says I quit anything?"

"Your grandma seemed pretty worried . . . "

Show cut him off.

"Two Mom knows a lot," he said. "Not just everything she thinks she knows."

"So you're going back?"

Show shrugged. "I *told* you. I needed to check some things and this and that. Not just go from one move to the next, the way I do when I got a ball in my hand."

"You look guilty when you run."

Show Watkins smiled now. "You got it all figured out, don't you? Bad boy from the Bronx. Bad, bad boy. Bad temper on him, yo, to go with a bad momma and a bad brother went off and did time. Now he can't keep himself under control for one season out to Long Island, even if that will fuck up his whole damn life." He bounced the ball hard now, twice, the noise as loud as firecrackers.

"You said it," Mitchell said. "Not me."

"You're like Two Mom sometimes. You think you know and you don't know shit, about me or anybody else on the damn team. Runnin' around, reporter who was big time once still tryin' to big-time everybody. And it turns out you don't know half of what Antoine knows."

"You mean about that trouble Dave Bender got in that time?"

Show Watkins laughed. "You think Dave Fuckin' Bender's behind all what's goin' on?"

"Two Mom was talking about his temper this mornin'."

"Boy may have the red ass," Show said, "but he wasn't the one beat that kid, one showed his ass up in Rhode Island that time."

"Rhode Island," Mitchell said, trying to make it sound as if he knew more than he really did.

"That AAU tournament," Show said, "two summers before last."

"That's where Dave got into it."

"That's where they *say* he did."

"I feel like I'm trying to guard you," Mitchell said, "but you keep losing me in the switches."

"That's because you been thinkin' you had one story, only it was another."

"If you had some shit on Dave," Mitchell said, "how come you never said anything before this?"

"Because Antoine didn't have it all."

"But now he does?"

"Fuck yeah," Show said. Like that was the most obvious

thing in the world. "It was only *supposed* to be Dave was the one did it up there. Dave takin' one for the team, lettin' them put it on him until they all figured out how much money had to change hands. But once Antoine did a little of what he likes to call his spade work, one of his little jokes, he found out it wasn't ever Dave cracked the kid cross the head with the pool cue and kept cracking him till he nearly busted his head wide open. Dave and the boy, from the Boston team, had got into a little dissdown after the game that night, once they got back to the dorms. Antoine checked it out with the po-lice up there. But Dave wasn't the one waited for him later."

Just go with him, Mitchell thought. "Who was that?" he said.

Show said, "The one that's never supposed to get shown up. By Show Watkins or anybody else." He shook his head, like he was disgusted about something. "The golden boy."

"Glenn."

Show said, "Two Mom thought she had a secret. Was just the wrong damn secret, about the wrong damn boy."

It was then that Antoine Walker stepped out from behind Mitchell, the sound of his voice, that growl of his, making Mitchell jump.

"I kept tellin' little brother, once I got the lay of the land out there," Antoine said. "No motherfucker's that nice."


**Y**our old man was a cop?" Antoine said to Mitchell.

"Yeah."

"Good one?"

"Until he got drunk at the end and stayed drunk."

"I was, too. Good cop. Till I got too damn smart for my own damn good. Drunk with all the power I thought I had, guess you could say."

Mitchell didn't know how to respond to that, so he lit a

cigarette. Antoine motioned that he wanted one. Mitchell lit them both.

"You said you were just around to watch your brother's back," Mitchell said. "Sounds as if you've expanded your duties somewhat."

"Old habits die hard, baby, you were a street cop once. Old habits die hard. I just started watching everybody, was all. And listening a little closer on what Two Mom was saying about all those good boys in South Fork."

"And that's how you found out Glenn Moore beat a kid to within an inch of his life in Rhode Island."

"Yeah," Antoine said. He took a deep drag of his cigarette. "Except that by the time the boy woked himself up, Glenny's folks had gotten themselves up there, and money started to change hands. 'Cause they couldn't have no assault rap on their golden boy's permanent record. I figure old Hank Bender, the South Fork detective, must have gotten greased, too, because when they sorted it out, it was Dave and Kenny Hudson, the boy from Boston, got into it and Glenny the hero broke it up. Even though it was Glenn that Kenny Hudson had woofed all over in the game they played that night."

"How'd you find all this out?"

"Cops up there. On account of cops everywhere get yanked off when they know they got played. But there wasn't nothin' they could do once Kenny said he couldn't rightly remember what happened, and the mother said she didn't want to rightly press charges."

"You went to Rhode Island?" Mitchell said.

"I got time on my hands, and I still got the moves," Antoine said. He smiled, and looked exactly like his brother when he did. "Don't I, little brother?"

Show nodded. He'd let Antoine tell it, the three of them sitting in a circle at halfcourt, the court closest to Yankee Stadium.

"The cops just figure that Glenny's folks are paying out to Kenny Hudson over time, as a way of keepin' him quiet forever."

He motioned for another smoke with his fingers. Mitchell just handed him the pack.

"It doesn't prove anything," Mitchell said, "even if Glenn had beaten the kid to death."

"Doesn't prove anything, 'cept for this here," Antoine said. "A pattern. I wasn't lookin' to take this to the grand jury. I got like you after a while, just wanted to know who put those boys down."

"Antoine says it's just like him helpin' me put together one of my big puzzles, when we were still over at 825 Gerard," Show said.

"Damn, I'm good," Antoine said, then said to Mitchell, "Let me tell you about it. It's like they tell you when you're tryin' to check shit out on the 'net. Sometimes you just gotta keep goin' sideways, one thing to another, one thing leads to another, till you end up where you need to be."

It all started with Two Mom," Antoine said. "Two Mom listening and telling herself it wasn't snooping. Her new big client, richest one she ever had, talking one day about the time Glenn and Dave nearly got kicked out of fifth grade, running some new boy right out of school, bullying him, getting him down and tying him up, scaring him half to death."

"Sometimes they start young," Mitchell said.

"Anyways, the woman tried to laugh it off, saying they sure learned a lesson, even if it was just boys being boys."

"Which woman?" Mitchell asked.

Antoine smiled like he was about to win a spelling bee.

"Mrs. Moore, that's what woman. Couple of weeks now, big house over on Lily Pond."

"Your grandmother never told me she'd gone to work for the Moores," Mitchell said.

"You never asked. God*damn*," Antoine said, "you *sure* your old man was a cop?" He lit another cigarette, chaining now. "Anyways, there was the day when Two Mom was talking about Show and me, talking on all her worries, and saying how lucky she was to have a boy like Glenn, who was perfect. And Mrs. Moore laughed and said, 'Not always,' and then told her about the story about what they'd done to this poor Donnie O'Brien."

Two Mom, he added, being good with names, even if she couldn't always tell you what she had for breakfast.

So Antoine did a little checking, here and there, and found out that even at twelve years old, Donnie O'Brien was a stud ballplayer, and had beat out Glenn for captain of the sixth-grade travel team.

Antoine said that it looked to him like Glenny didn't ever want nobody else being the big dog. So him and his number one Dave ran little Donnie O'Brien out of school, and then he was the big dog after that in South Fork, until that big old white boy come along a few years ago, like somebody ready to fight him for the title.

Mitchell felt like he heard an alarm go off inside his head.

"Kyle Sheppard," he said.

Antoine whooped loudly, leaned over and slapped Mitchell hard on the back.

"Well, hello, the boy does know something after all," he said.

"Glenn told me about him," Mitchell said.

"Well, he probably told you his version of him," Antoine said. "But the truth was, Kyle Sheppard, just between one year and the next, had turned into as much of a stud as Glenny the golden boy was. And everybody is saying, Whoo-ee, we got a dynamic duo all set to go in South Fork.

"Except for one little problem," Antoine said. "Glenn don't like the duo part. So he undercuts him one day at practice. Not knowing he's going to fuck up the boy for good, that just turns out to be the cherry on the whipped cream. But smiling down at him, before the rest of the team got there, 'fore he started to cry, boo hoo, at what he'd done."

"Kyle Sheppard told you that?" Mitchell said.

"Down in South Jersey, where him and his family live now," Antoine said, acting smug. "On his way to Georgetown. And get this: The boy's got religion now. Tells me I should let it go on Glenn, 'cause he has, that he's turned it over to the Lord."

Antoine cackled again. "You can't make this shit up," he said.

Mitchell told him Glenn had nearly cried when he told him the story about Kyle Sheppard.

"Academy Award acting," Antoine said. "Like he's been acting the part his whole damn life."

He flicked his cigarette away.

"Fucking reporters," he said. "Never met one yet was as smart as he thought he was."

"It's not exactly an airtight case," Mitchell said. "I'm sure young Glenn would tell us it's just a string of coincidences."

"You know what we used to say coincidences was, when I was still with the cops? *Bull*shit, that's what."

Mitchell heard the arrival of a subway train at the 161st Street station, off to his right, the steady noise of car traffic from the Deegan coming at them from the other direction, the lights of the cars still in a slow, steady stream heading north toward the George Washington Bridge.

Mitchell said, "So you're telling me this kid only snaps out when his image of himself, or whatever, is threatened by somebody better than him?"

"Somebody who comes along to show him up, so to speak," Antoine said. "Like we've been sayin'. Only now he comes up on little brother here, and little brother's too good to take out, and this time the boy snaps out on himself, starts taking shit out on everybody else."

"That's what you think this is all about?"

"That all is my *theory* on things," Antoine said. "Course, what do I know, I'm just this badass crooked cop ex-con."

Mitchell said to both of them, "Why didn't either one of you ever say anything about this before?"

"Didn't put it all together, get my ducks lined up so to speak, until the last couple of days," Antoine said. "And to tell you the truth, I didn't give a rat's ass about those other boys. Then the motherfucker tried to take my little brother's legs out." He waggled a finger at Mitchell. "At which point," he said, "this shit became intensely fuckin' personal."

Mitchell said, "And now he's going to get away with it."

"Don't be so sure."

"What does that mean?"

Antoine said, "It means I've been leanin' on the boy a little bit. Call him up on the phone, whisper that I know about him, hang up. That I'm comin' for his ass."

"Scaring him the way he tried to scare everybody else."

"Check him out when you get back," Antoine said. "I think you could push the boy right off the edge, no problem."

"Glenn," Mitchell said, as if he still couldn't believe it.

"All day, every day," Antoine said.

Mitchell said, "But why would a smart kid take so many dumb chances?"

Antoine whooped again, louder than before.

"Well, sonofabitch," he said, "the high school boy ain't as brilliant as Professor Fucking Moriarty in Sherlock Fucking Holmes."

**M**itchell was walking back to his car, turning it all over, when he remembered he had turned off his cell when he'd started talking to Show, not wanting anything to interrupt them, then forgotten to turn it back on. He did so now, and saw he had missed a call from the *Long Island Press*. Saw that he had one voice message.

He clicked on it.

The excited voice of Sam Perry.

"I did what you said," he said. "I spent all afternoon on it at the *Press*. There *was* a big fight at an AAU tournament a couple of years ago. A kid from Boston named Kenny Hudson ended up in the hospital with his head half caved in. Somehow it got buried almost as fast as it happened. That's what Miz Watkins had to be talking about. I'm running around and my cell's about to run out of batteries, so I'll try to call you later. But here's the deal: Glenn was on the team, too. I'm gonna go meet up with him, get to the bottom of this. Check you later."

# 26

He kept the phone on the console next to him. Kept trying Sam every couple of exits on the LIE. Still no answer. Trying to keep himself calm, not having any evidence that the kid was in danger.

But sure somehow that he was.

Antoine had said he thought Glenn was ready to snap.

There was no point in calling Kate, all she'd want to do is jump in her car, make a late ferry, come straight home. He called O'Rourke's instead, got Jimmy, told him that if he saw Sam Perry come through the door to tackle him and keep him there until Mitchell got there. Then he went back to trying Sam's number, about every five minutes, tried him as he got off the LIE at Exit 70, when he made the turn off Route 111 to get on the four-lane part of Route 27, tried him when it turned into a two-lane road at Ocean Bays. In between he called the Perry house, hoping the kid might have just walked in the front door, safer than if he'd walked into church.

Nothing.

Sam had called Glenn Moore wanting to ask about Kenny Hudson.

Antoine had been making anonymous calls to Glenn, telling him he knew all about him, that he was coming for him.

Antoine thought Glenn was ready to snap.

Mitchell drove home. The front door was unlocked. No beep from the alarm code when he opened it. He tried to remember if he'd locked the door and set the alarm before he left. He probably hadn't, he remembered having to run back inside after he had the engine running in the truck, he'd forgotten his wallet. It seemed like a week ago.

Mitchell walked through his kitchen, to the stairs at the back of the house leading up to his study. He saw a faint light coming from there, like the night-light glow his computer gave off when all the other lights upstairs were shut off.

He walked up the stairs. The computer was on. No message this time, like the one he found the night Art Daneko popped him, the one Glenn Moore must have left for him. Nothing on the screen now except for Kirk Gibson, his new screen saver, rounding first after hitting that home run off Dennis Eckersley in Game 1 of the 1988 World Series, pulling his arm back like he was pulling a chain.

Mitchell couldn't remember what he'd had for breakfast sometimes, or where he'd left the reading glasses he found himself using more and more often, or the keys to the Lariat when he was in a hurry. But he was sure in this moment that he'd shut the computer off when he'd used it to check for messages the night before and hadn't turned it back on since.

He stood in the middle of the room, staring at Kirk Gibson, until he heard the quiet voice from across the room, almost as if the speaker didn't want to scare him.

"We need to take a ride," Glenn Moore said.

Mitchell wheeled around, saw the outline of him in the big leather chair on the other side of the room.

"Where we going?" he said.

"We've got your boy," Glenn said.

They took the truck. Mitchell asked where Glenn's car was and he said, "Where we're going." Mitchell asked where they were going and Glenn, talking to him without looking at him, said just to follow the directions he was giving him, he'd find out soon enough. After a few minutes, it started to rain. Mitchell put the wipers on, the slow back-and-forth of them the only sound in the front seat now.

Finally, Glenn said, "Why'd you start calling me like that, and then hanging up on me?"

"I didn't."

Mitchell didn't know whether he should bring Antoine into it or not. For now he needed to see where they were going with this, in all ways, wondering as they drove through the rain how much Glenn Moore would tell.

Wondering at the same time just how far off the rails the kid was.

"Of course you didn't," Glenn said. "It must have been somebody else obsessed with finding out about Bobby and Drew, somebody else who wouldn't let this go."

Glenn turned to him. "You have to understand that enough was enough, right? That when Sam came around asking about Kenny Hudson that the two of you had finally gone too far."

"Who's Kenny Hudson?" Mitchell said.

"Oh, right." Glenn bobbed his head up and down. "Now I'm supposed to believe you didn't send him around to ask about the tournament in Rhode Island. Right. The way you didn't make the phone calls. Take this next turn."

They were heading west on back roads south of the highway, the ocean off to their left, the rain starting to come down harder. Mitchell made the windshield wipers go faster.

"Take another left up ahead, on Sandy," Glenn Moore said.

The Lariat was the only car on Sandy Road, either direction. Mitchell drove toward the beach. He had the wipers going faster. Somewhere in the back of his mind, he remembered a big storm had been forecast for tonight, he'd heard it on the radio when he'd gotten a traffic report leaving the Bronx.

He was afraid to ask if they'd done anything to Sam.

Glenn said, "You got Kyle Sheppard to call me the other day, too, didn't you?"

"No," Mitchell said. "I've never talked to Kyle Sheppard. Even if I should have."

"*Don't lie to me!*" Glenn's voice sounded like a siren. "All of a sudden, out of the blue, he calls and tells me he *forgives* me? I asked him what brought this on, did somebody come around asking questions about his injury? Figuring it was you. But he says, no, that's not important here, what's important is that he'd gotten religion or whatever and decided to let all the feelings he had for me go. Turn it over to the Lord."

Mitchell could see there was no point in trying to change his mind.

"Right on Parish," Glenn said.

Mitchell took the right, said to him, "I don't know what you think I know. Or what you think I can do with it. But none of the stuff you're talking about would stand up in court. Or even in the newspaper. You're the smartest guy in school, you have to know that."

Mitchell could see the kid's smile, lit only by the bright dashboard lights. "You'll never stop," Glenn said. "That's why we have to stop this now."

"Meaning you and Dave."

"Who else?" Glenn said.

"You want this to stop?" Mitchell said. "Then it stops tonight."

"*I told you not to lie to me!*"

"I'm telling you the truth."

"You just couldn't let go. Over a couple of babies like Bobby Ferraro and Drew Hudson. You had to keep coming. No matter what we did, *you* wouldn't do what I wanted you to do." He pointed again. "When you get to the tennis club, pull behind the main building," he said.

It had only taken about ten minutes, the way it did in South Fork, for the rain to start coming in hard sheets off the ocean, like waves that reached to the sky. Mitchell, even going about twenty miles an hour, was barely able to see more than fifty yards in front of them.

Mitchell had called Martha Cassidy, the hazing shrink, on the way back to South Fork, between calls to Sam. He'd apologized for calling her at home, even though she'd given him her home number the first time they'd spoken. Now he told her what he knew about Glenn Moore. She said it sounded to her like a classic grandiose personality. One that ultimately thinks it cannot allow itself to be harmed by lesser people. That it would be almost insulting for that to happen.

"From the way you described him, he's the perfect child," she said, "one who probably spent too much time alone growing up, so that his parents went overboard in praising his perfection, because that made him a wonderful boy and them wonderful parents. But his particular pathology, if it exists in this boy, would involve eliminating all threats to that perfection. If you're looking for a drive-through diagnosis, there it is."

"So it was never hazing," Mitchell said to her on the phone.

"Oh, it was hazing all right, but just as a manifestation of deeper problems. He apparently decided he couldn't eliminate this new problem, the other boy . . . "

"Show."

" . . . without killing him. So he started taking it out on other people."

Antoine the Cop had been right. Damn, he *was* good. Good as he said.

On the phone, Martha Cassidy had said, "You understand what the ultimate threat would be for him, don't you?"

"Tell me."

"Being found out."

In the truck now, Mitchell said to Glenn, "Why'd you have to grab Sam?"

"Oh, please." Sounding exasperated. "If he knew about poor Kenny Hudson, he'd find him eventually. Or you would. And Kenny would tell about the beating I gave him that night, after he would *not* shut his stupid *fucking* mouth. Even if Kenny the Jet opening his mouth now would mean no more money from good old Mom and Dad."

"Sam?" Mitchell said in a soft voice, bringing him back.

"Other side of the building," Glenn said. Then slid into a street voice suddenly and said, "Where my dog Dave got the chrome on him."

"Chrome?"

"Bobby didn't know, either," he said. "It's what the bad brothers call guns."

There were tennis courts to the right, a swimming pool directly in front of them, pool cabanas behind it and to the side. The front gate was open, held in place by a huge rock. Mitchell walked through the gate, Glenn following him. Mitchell remembered attending a wedding reception here about twenty years ago, for a sportswriter friend from the city. He knew that in the summer, they ran exercise classes in the big room where the dance floor had been.

There was a walking bridge off to their left that went down to the beach. Mitchell started toward it. Glenn said, "Uh-uh, that way, back around to the service entrance. Under that striped awning."

"Why the hell did you and Dave bring Sam to the beach club?" Mitchell said in a loud voice, as if wanting to make himself heard over the weather, not just the rain now, but the howl of the ocean wind.

"Why do you care?" Glenn said, just as loudly.

The cut of beach across from Fogg Pond, the place where Bobby Ferraro had washed up, was maybe five hundred yards west of them.

Dave Bender, in some kind of watch cap and army jacket, was standing underneath the striped awning that flapped now in the wind, Bobby's gun looking like a toy in his hand. Mitchell saw Sam sitting on the ground, his back to the wall of the main building, wearing the same blue blazer he had been wearing the first day Mitchell had met him at Hiram's. His hands were duct-taped together.

Glenn told Mitchell to go sit down next to Sam, then tightly taped his hands in front of him.

"I screwed up big-time," Sam said to Mitchell.

"Not nearly as bad as I did."

Sam said, "I thought I'd cracked the case."

"I'm the one who should have cracked it a long time ago," Mitchell said. He twisted himself around so he was facing Glenn. "I should have stopped pushing," he said. "I'll stop pushing now, and we all walk away. Bobby's gone. Drew's not coming back. I'll say it again: Just let us go and you've got my word, this ends right here."

"Your word, from the man with the words," Glenn said in a dreamy way. "No, no, no. You'll tell. Guys like you always tell."

"I don't have to tell anybody anything. You want me to leave town? I'll leave town."

Glenn said, "You believe that, David? That he won't run straight to your dad, or the closest newspaper?"

Dave Bender, Glenn's number one, said, "No fucking way."

"You always do what he tells you to, Dave?" Mitchell said.

"Shut up."

"Both of you listen to me," Mitchell said. "This isn't worth killing anybody over. Glenn, you told Mrs. Perry that night in the park you didn't kill Bobby, right?"

The park. Mitchell had been so sure it was Show who had done it to Kate, especially after Emmy Watkins talked about the grass stains on her boy's jeans when he came home that night. But when Mitchell asked about the dirty jeans at Macombs, Show laughed, saying that Two Mom had told him his whole life he was going to trip if he didn't tie his damn laces, and guess what? He finally did. . . .

"Bobby the snitch?" Glenn said now. "No, we didn't kill Bobby. Oh, we smacked him around that night, David and I did, after he called us over to his house and threatened to tell. Waving his little toy gun at us." Glenn laughed. "But kill him, after we'd bitch-tamed him all over again? What would've been the point?" Glenn shook his head. "I was surprised as anybody when he washed up that way. We just figured he must've done it to himself."

Mitchell said, "I'll tell Antoine to lay off you, that you're going to lay off Show now. Then you and Show finish the season. He goes to the pros next year, you go off to college, Sam goes off to college. And I'll be long gone."

"Oh, you'll be gone all right," Glenn said.

In the distance, through an opening in the dunes, through the hard rain, Mitchell could see the light of a distant boat. He wondered how rough the water was out there.

His only plan was to keep Glenn talking.

"Why'd you two do what you did at the camp?"

"Because it was *fun*," Glenn said. "The way it's been fun fooling these fools around here all my life. Because it was fucking fun, that's why." He smiled at Sam now, like he was posing for a team picture. "Mrs. Sam's Mom?" he said to Sam now, directing this at him, lapsing back into his street voice. "She do have a real nice ass on her, boy."

Sam started to get up, but Mitchell leaned in front of him, said, "Forget it."

Glenn wasn't even looking at him, he was staring off past the dunes. "I found out Bobby kept running to Coach with stuff I was saying about Show," he said. "The little hobbit team manager? Going behind *my back?* I don't *think* so."

Mitchell said, "What about Drew?"

"That disloyal little weasel? The minute Show showed up in the gym, he started sucking around him, like some kind of bitch. After I was the one who told Coach to give Little Drew more playing time this year." Glenn grinned, put his hands out, palms up. "And then there he was in the woods. All tied up.

"It was *fun,*" he said again, stepping out from under the awning. If he noticed he'd stepped out into the rain, he didn't show it.

"I never like to second-guess myself," Glenn said. "But my mistake was bringing Bobby into it. Then not letting up on him. If I had, he never would have threatened to tell on David and me."

Keep him talking.

"What about putting down Sam and his mom?" Mitchell said. "What was that all about?"

"I kept thinking *you'd* think it wasn't worth it if they were in danger, walk away. Only you never would."

"Enough talking," Dave said. "Let's do this."

"Antoine knows everything I know," Mitchell said.

"Who are they going to believe?" Glenn Moore said. "Some *criminal*? Or me?"

Mitchell said, "You actually think you can get away with killing us both?"

"Sam's going to wash up like Bobby did," Glenn said. "Another South Fork kid beaten half to death by persons unknown. And you, Mr. Mitchell, you're going to be so distraught about that, you're going to kill yourself. Or something like that."

The rain was steady now, not subsiding at all. It was the wind that came harder off the water. Mitchell thought: It feels like Land's End. End of the world.

Sam said, "You think you can get away with this."

Not even making it a question.

Glenn said, "C'mon, Sam. I've gotten away with everything my whole life. The two of you will finally be out of my life and nobody will be the wiser."

"Well, I will," Officer Carl Bowdoin said, from the top of the dune behind Dave Bender.

**A**s soon as Dave turned at the sound of Bowdoin's voice, Mitchell was moving fast. Glenn yelled, "David!" But it was too late, Mitchell put a shoulder on him like he was knocking him down in the open field, drove him back into the wet sand, stayed on top of him until he could put his taped hands on the gun, then roll away.

Dave Bender got himself up, started to charge at Mitchell until he saw that Mitchell was up, too, and had the gun pointed right at him.

"Got two hands on it, son," Mitchell said. "And I will fucking shoot you."

Dave Bender turned to Carl Bowdoin, as if suddenly Glenn Moore wasn't even here, or no longer mattered. "What are you going to tell my father?"

"*Shut up, David!*" Glenn yelled at him, trying to make himself heard now over the storm. "*You just shut your mouth right now.*"

As if he could still get his number one to do whatever he wanted.

Carl Bowdoin, his gun on Glenn Moore, said to Dave, "You're going to tell your father everything you did. It's the only chance you've got. We're going to drive to the station and you're going to make a statement."

Eyes wild now, Glenn Moore said, "You don't have to do anything, David. It's our word against theirs. They'll believe us. They'll believe *me*." He jerked his head at Mitchell. "Mitchell was right. They've got nothing that would ever stand up in court."

He was talking to all of them now. Or, Mitchell thought, talking to the ocean.

"This is *me* we're talking about here. They can't touch me. Whatever they *think* they've got, my parents will get me out of this. I'll be playing ball somewhere next year and nobody will remember this happened. *They can't touch me!* You understand that, right, David?"

"Yes," Dave Bender said, nodding, staring at him.

Hypnotized by him.

Glenn, pleading now, said, "So we're clear here?"

"Clear," Dave said.

"You got my back, then, like always?"

"No," Dave Bender said.

Glenn acted as if he'd somehow heard wrong. "What did you say?"

"I said no. You've been getting me to go along my whole stupid life. I'm not going along anymore. Even just now, all I heard about was you. *You'll* get out of this. *You'll* be playing ball someplace next year. Nobody can touch you. You're the man." Dave Bender shook his head. "Only you're not anymore. Because I am."

"I'm telling you to shut up!" Glenn said.

"You *told* me we'd never get caught," Dave said.

"We can talk about this, just the two of us, when we get away from here! But you've got to stop talking right now!"

"*No!*" Dave shouted at him.

It was all a crazy shout now. The rain. The wind. The ocean. The two of them.

Mitchell saw Sam, standing now, hands still tied in front of him, staring at Glenn Moore.

Carl Bowdoin kept his gun on Glenn, walked down off the dunes, removed the tape from Mitchell's hands, pulled a cell phone out of his uniform slacks, handed it to Mitchell. "Call 911," he said.

"For what?" Mitchell said, and Carl Bowdoin said, "For this," and turned and shot Glenn Moore in the right knee.

Moore screamed and went down in the sand at the base of the dune where Carl Bowdoin had been standing, hugging his knee to him. No one said anything. Bowdoin took Dave Bender's gun from Mitchell. Mitchell noticed he was wearing black driving gloves. Bowdoin rolled Glenn Moore over now, put Bobby's gun in his hand, fired two shots into the Atlantic.

"Are you *insane?*" Glenn Moore said. "What are you *doing?*"

Bowdoin ignored him, addressing Mitchell instead.

"You apparently confronted Mr. Moore about recent events surrounding the South Fork basketball team. He was about to shoot you when I showed up, people in the area having heard gunshots. I fired a warning shot." Bowdoin fired a shot of his own now, toward Portugal. "Then I had to shoot the boy to save your life."

"Thank you," Mitchell said.

"Isn't that what happened here, Dave?" Bowdoin said.

Dave Bender mumbled something.

"I said, isn't that what happened?" Bowdoin said.

"Yes," Dave Bender said.

Mitchell called 911 then. When he finished explaining what was happening at the South Fork Beach and Tennis Club to Officer Halsey, he handed the phone back to Carl Bowdoin, who nodded at Glenn Moore, still rolling in the sand, arms still hugging his knee, blood all over him.

Bowdoin said, "How'd you manage to dial up my number when you got here?"

Mitchell said, "I had about ten seconds when I came around the back of the truck. My phone book. Bowdoin's the first name in it. Select. Then hit send." He grinned. "I've always been a one-finger typist."

"First thing I hear after I say 'Hello' is you asking the boy why him and old Dave brought Sam to the beach club," Bowdoin said. "I was just hoping I guessed the right one."

Then he pointed his gun at Glenn Moore, as though he might shoot him again.

"I'm not sure what we've actually got on this asshole," Carl Bowdoin said. "And the fact of the matter is, his mommy and daddy might get him off, even with old Dave's statement." Bowdoin paused, looking down at Glenn Moore like some dead thing that had washed up here. "But somebody needed to put *him* down for once."

# 27

First Tuesday after New Year's.

Mitchell and Kate Perry sat in their usual seats in the South Fork gym and watched Show Watkins, Eric Daneko, and Christian Bowdoin lead their team past Center Island.

It was a close game until the middle of the third period, when Drew Hudson came off the bench to make three straight three-pointers and blow the game wide open.

Drew had come back to school the week before Christmas break. According to Sam, Coach Glass wasn't going to put him back on the team until Principal Norman Brodie ordered him not only to take Drew back but to start playing him again when he was ready.

"So is this what passes for a happy ending?" Kate had said when Drew got hot from the outside.

"Sometimes," Mitchell said, "you just have to be happy with the ending you get."

The ending they got:

Dave Bender, who was still giving his sworn testimony

at the South Fork Police Department when Mitchell and Carl Bowdoin finally arrived there from the beach that night—having waited for Glenn Moore's ambulance to show up—had been given immunity from prosecution in the state of Connecticut's case against Glenn.

He had also transferred to the Pennsylvania military school selected by the prosecutor in the Connecticut case.

Both he and his father had further been instructed that once Glenn Moore had gone through the system, the judge in the case would order ongoing probation for Dave Bender, for an undetermined length of time, in addition to community service. Under the terms of this agreement, Dave Bender was also forbidden from playing basketball at Carver Military.

His affidavit, which Mitchell had read and reread, was an amazing story of control and obsession, going all the way back to grade school. Dave Bender had always been mesmerized by Glenn Moore, by his looks and his money and his brains and his talent. He never came out and said it, not with his father sitting in the room with him while his words were recorded, but more than anything, he wanted to *be* Glenn Moore. Be with him. Be in his favor.

At one point, Hank Bender said to his son, "Did you ever consider what you were doing was wrong?"

And Dave Bender said, "I only considered that it was what he wanted."

There was no indication that it was physical love between the two of them. But Mitchell was sure it was love on Dave Bender's part. Or need.

Or both.

Even with Glenn Moore undergoing the first of two surgeries on his shattered kneecap, a felony complaint was drafted against him on the basis of Dave Bender's statement. There were additional sworn statements from Hank Bender, Carl Bowdoin—who had been working undercover for the Connecticut Special Victims Unit since Sam Perry's story about the assault against Drew Hudson had appeared in the *Long Island Press*—and Ben Mitchell himself about what had transpired on the beach that night, and what they all had heard. He even included the incidents with Sam and with his mother.

Martha Cassidy, the hazing shrink, was quoted this way in his story, after Mitchell hooked Sam up with her:

"It's as if Mr. Moore began to spin out of control the day Mr. Watkins showed up in South Fork," she said. "He began to act out, until he was all the way out of control."

Moore was officially placed under arrest while still recovering from the first surgery. When he was healthy enough to travel to Connecticut, he was arraigned in lower court on a series of charges, the most serious of which was involuntary deviate sexual intercourse against Drew, a first-degree felony. At the same time, a lower court on Long Island refused even to consider Glenn's charge of assault with a deadly weapon against Carl Bowdoin when presented with corroborating statements from Hank Bender, Dave Bender, Bowdoin, and Mitchell, all basically saying the same thing: that Glenn had made it all up, as an attempt to deflect attention from the serious charges against him in Connecticut.

Mr. and Mrs. Moore posted bail of $500,000 for their son, but not before their son had been officially indicted by what the prosecutor called a walk-in grand jury, convened immediately after his lower-court arraignment.

No trial date had been set in Connecticut.

No one in South Fork had seen Glenn Moore since his indictment. There was no way of knowing if he would get the chance to finish high school before his trial date was set.

Shelley Hudson had told the newspapers that she planned to file a civil suit against Glenn Moore in Long Island.

"Just in case," she told Sam Perry in an exclusive interview, "the state of Connecticut doesn't do enough to ruin his life."

That story was the last of a weeklong series Sam had written for the *Press* about Glenn Moore, beginning with the one he crashed into the final edition the night of Glenn's shooting, detailing what had happened on the beach and Dave Bender's subsequent confession.

Show Watkins had returned to South Fork High School the next Monday, a week before Drew Hudson did. Over the next two weeks, there were major pieces done on South Fork basketball for ESPN, *Dateline NBC, 60 Minutes,* and *Nightline.* Even though no one could prove that Glenn Moore or Dave Bender had had a direct hand in Bobby Ferraro's death, all of the stories had a similar theme:

People thought they knew Glenn Moore, high school basketball star, All-American boy, son of high-profile parents, the way people thought they knew other celebrity criminals from the world of sports. Or alleged criminals, as they were described on the television shows. But how, in the end, they didn't know them at all.

That's what the television psychiatrists said, anyway. And they knew everything.

The media circus came back to South Fork in full force, all the way through the holidays.

Now, with the holidays finally over, it had subsided again. Mitchell was still considering an offer from the *Press* to resume writing his column full-time, the paper promising him a syndication deal for the one sports column and one opinion piece it wanted him to write every week.

The South Fork basketball team, even without Glenn and Dave, was 7–1 since Show's return, tied for first place in the East End Conference, and was still considered, despite everything, a favorite to win the state championship.

When the South Fork–Center Island game was over, Mitchell and Kate made their way carefully across the icy parking lot to where she'd parked her car. His truck was all the way up on Farm Road; he'd arrived from the South Fork police station just five minutes before the opening tip, by which time all the lots were filled. He had spent most of the afternoon at the station with Carl Bowdoin, now an acting detective after Hank Bender's resignation.

"Do you think Glenn will get convicted?" Kate said. "Actually go to jail?"

"In cases like this, I always bet on the money to win," he said. "It doesn't always, of course. Tyson lost in that rape trial in Indiana with the beauty pageant girl. Martha Stewart lost. But both times, that was like Defense Attorneys "R" Us. Most of the time, guys like Glenn get off easy. Remember that Jayson Williams trial last year? The jurors actually said they thought he was too nice to convict of manslaughter, even though he was boozed up and waving a loaded shotgun around before he shot a hole through that limo driver."

"So you don't think Glenn'll be convicted," she said.

"Actually," Mitchell said, "I think he will."

"I don't understand."

"You will soon," he said.

He put his arm around her, leaned down and kissed her on the forehead. As usual, she smelled like some sweet corner of paradise.

"Is Dave's testimony enough to take him down?"

"No," he said.

"You're being mysterious again."

"Yes, I am."

"One last question: Do you still expect them to focus on what they did to Drew, as opposed to Bobby?"

Mitchell said, "Not anymore."

Then he opened the door for her and told her he'd see her at the house later.

"We always go to O'Rourke's after the games," she said.

"Not tonight, dear."

"Why not?"

He said there was one more ending.

**T**he door was being held open by a janitor's pushcart, mops and brooms and pails and huge garbage bags on it, as if the night man was waiting to clean this one last office before calling it a night. Mitchell stood in the open doorway, watched Glass scribble some notes at his desk, blue cards spread out in front of him. Same reading glasses as before.

Ken Glass looked up and said, "You know I have been instructed not to speak with the media, pending the school's independent review of what transpired in Connecticut. Quote unquote."

In the doorway, Mitchell held up the Nokia 3100 cell phone.

Glass said, "What, you're going to call the cops on me?"

Mitchell said, "I already did."

He stepped inside the office, shut the door behind him, and sat down in the same chair he'd sat in a month earlier, before he'd gone looking for Show in the Bronx.

"You had to know," Mitchell said.

"We did this already."

Mitchell said, "I told Carl Bowdoin about how much Bobby looked up to you. How much he wanted to be a coach. How he was going to be your eyes and ears. All that. I showed him the printouts of all the e-mails Bobby sent to you."

Glass sighed. Took off his reading glasses. Folded them. Put them in his shirt pocket. Every movement precise.

"We did this, too," he said.

Mitchell said, "I told Carl how I'd gone through Bobby's computer, the stuff from early in the season, stuff Glenn had left in there, probably because he thought it was harmless." Mitchell wagged a finger at Glass. "But I said that all along, I had this nagging feeling that I'd missed something. Carl said, 'So let's take another look at the stuff we took from his room.' So Carl goes into the evidence room, not much more than a storage closet down at the station, and came back with some floppies Hank Bender had taken. The clothes Bobby was wearing when he washed up."

Mitchell held up the Nokia.

"And this," he said.

"His cell phone," Glass said.

"And all of a sudden, I'm staring at the phone, and I'm remembering how his old man told me it was his favorite gadget. How he used to record goofy messages and then download them and e-mail them to the old man at his office. I asked Carl what Hank Bender had checked the phone for. Carl called Hank and asked him. Remember: small-town cops here. Hank said he'd only gone over the thing—himself—for incoming and outgoing calls, but there hadn't been any that weekend."

The only sound in the room was Glass's computer.

"I got on the phone then, asked if he'd checked it for any downloads, or whatever you call them. He said no. I said to Carl, 'What the hell,' and the two of us went to the AT&T mobile store over in Shore Haven, bought a charger for it, told the kid behind the counter to search the little sucker and see what he could find. So he goes to Applications, doing a play-by-play for us as he does, and then Extras, and then finally, aha, Voice Recordings."

It wasn't just the color disappearing from Glass's face now, it was like watching his face start to fall apart, like a wall starting to come down.

Mitchell said to Glass: "Check your e-mail, you cocksucker. I've got this gizmo that lets me get on the 'net from my truck."

Glass sat where he was.

"Go ahead, Coach," Mitchell said. "You probably deleted it the night Bobby sent it to you. His fucking hero. You know the download. His suicide note? He couldn't tell his father, but he could tell you, even with his hand shaking all over the place. Telling you what they made him do. What they did to him. Rambling all over the place when he started to cry. Telling you again how much he wanted to coach. And be like you." Mitchell felt his throat getting thick. "How he was going to just walk into the water then, how he wasn't even man enough to use his own gun on himself. Not him. Oh no, not the Broomstick Boy."

Mitchell said to Glass: "You worthless piece of shit."

Glass kept looking at Mitchell, but somehow his eyes were someplace else.

"I didn't do it," Glass said. "But they would have blamed me."

There was Glass's shallow breathing now, to go with the hum of the computer. Mitchell waited on his side of the desk.

"I was afraid they'd shut us down," he said.

Mitchell just looked at him.

"This season was my *shot*," Glass said, his voice raw suddenly, hoarse. "I *needed* it."

Mitchell's own voice wasn't much more than a whisper. "You were going to let them get away with it."

"Glenn said he knew they'd gone too far. That night. And they should have left Bobby alone, he never intended for anybody to die. . . ."

Mitchell was standing now. Glass looked up at him.

Pleading with him.

"I needed *him*," he said.

"You can go down with him," Mitchell said. "You can't imagine how hot dying declarations make prosecutors."

Mitchell turned to leave. Then he saw it right in front of him, and couldn't stop himself. He reached into the janitor's pushcart, pulled out the broom sticking out of it, and swung the stick part as hard as he could against the side of Glass's head, knocking the South Fork basketball coach over the back of his chair and sending him staggering back into the computer that contained what was effectively the last will and testament of Bobby Ferraro.

Mitchell stood over him and wound up and started to swing the broomstick again before Glass covered up and said, "No."

Mitchell stared down at him, blood coming out of the side of his head, beat-up, used-up little man.

"Please don't do this," Glass said. "I'm begging you."

The way Tom Robards had.

"That's what they all say," Mitchell said.

"If the kid puts this in the paper, it will ruin my life," Glass said.

Meaning Sam.

Mitchell said not to worry, the kid wasn't going to put it in the paper.

"I am," Mitchell said.

He left him there, walked up the stairs and down the long hallway to where the pressroom was, walking faster as he began to write the story inside his head, knowing exactly how he wanted to start it, already seeing it on the page. Then Mitchell was running.

FROM THE *NEW YORK TIMES*
BESTSELLING AUTHOR

# MIKE LUPICA

0-515-13364-7

"A hilarious satire of the NBA."
—*Orlando Sentinel*

**A THREE-RING CIRCUS ENSUES WHEN A WOMAN
PLAYS IN THE NBA FOR THE
FIRST TIME—AND FOR THE WORST
TEAM IN THE LEAGUE.**

"Sportswriter Mike Lupica takes you on a
wild, witty ride."
—*Lexington Herald Leader*

**Available wherever books are sold or at
penguin.com**